A Memory of Wings

A Memory of Wings, Volume 1

Emily Michel

Published by Emily Michel, 2021.

This is a work of fiction. Similarities to real people, places, or events are entirely coincidental.

A MEMORY OF WINGS

First edition. September 14, 2021

Copyright © 2021 Emily Michel

All Rights Reserved.

No part of this book may be reproduced in any form or by any electronic or mechanical means, including information storage and retrieval systems, without written permission from the author, except for the use of brief quotations in a book review.

Cover design by Emily's World of Design

ISBN: 9798461028787 (Print Edition)

For my cats

Asxdev hjm;

They tried to get their nonsense into the book often enough, so I obliged.

Chapter 1

Searing pain danced across Shax's shoulders as sleep attempted to pull him down into its blissful release. The old, familiar agony reminded him he could once soar.

"Shit," he said, his voice a ragged whisper in the darkness.

He sat up, half grateful the pain had roused him before he made an even bigger mistake. The sound of soft breaths from the naked man sleeping next to him broke the quiet. Shax hadn't set out to fuck anyone last night, and he sure as Hell hadn't planned on sleeping over. He hated falling asleep and avoided it whenever possible. It wasn't the sleep part. It was the falling part. He'd had enough falling for one demonic lifetime. The pain now rippling through his body emphasized the hazards of his new life.

But the man's kind, gray eyes, shining like liquid silver in the dimly lit room, reminded him of—he tore his thoughts away from the past. An itch had needed scratching, a wham-bam-thank-you-man liaison. It had nothing to do with the nearly identical eyes plaguing his dreams.

He slid out of bed, barely rustling the sheet half covering him, and stepped over the blankets puddled on the floor. Shax found his jeans where he'd dropped them, right next to what's-his-name's pants. Graceful as a cat, he put them on without a sound and stared at his bedfellow for a moment, watching the near-silent rise and fall of his chest. He gave in to temptation and rifled through the other's jeans.

Ah, there.

Shax thumbed through the man's wallet and pocketed the cash, leaving the credit cards and identification. Losing the cash was a minor nuisance compared to replacing a fucking driver's license, a pain in the ass he'd only wish on his worst enemy. Tucking the wallet back where he found it, Shax pushed aside a twinge of guilt and resumed the search for his own clothes.

He pulled on a soft, gray t-shirt and ran his hand through his hair. It was impossible to straighten the snowy white mess. He shoved his arms into his black leather jacket and picked up his boots. With a last glance at the sleeping form, he snuck from the room, closing the door with a soft snick behind him.

Shax plopped down on the chair next to the stairwell and sighed. Still trembling from his rude awakening, he dragged on his socks and crammed his feet into his boots. Tromping down the stairs, he kicked himself for not leaving before things got all snuggly. For the thousandth time in the last year, he reminded himself the best way to stay alive was to stick to the plan. And banging some hotel hottie was not part of the plan, no matter the color of his eyes.

He strode across the hotel lobby, his footsteps echoing on the tiled floor. The hair on his arms stood up. Just his luck to be discovered while sneaking away from an ill-conceived liaison. Shax slowed and glanced around.

Only the desk clerk.

The young woman watched his tall, whipcord-lean frame with an appreciative stare. He gave her his best smile. When she blushed, he finished with a jaunty wave. He stepped through the automatic doors and onto the streets of St. Louis. The Arch was a shining beacon reflecting the golden streetlights in the dark, wintry night.

His own shitty motel room, a mere two miles away, waited for him. Shax turned up the collar of his jacket and shoved his hands into the pockets. Even after a year, he was still getting used to the fragility of this body. The rules had changed, and he was no longer immune to the elements as he had been on prior visits to Earth when he had the full power of Hell coursing through his veins.

The denizens of the impoverished neighborhood he traversed scattered before him, some disappearing down dark alleys, others flattening themselves against the rough walls of buildings, silent and still. Some instinct gave those who paid attention an inkling evil incarnate walked among them. Lucky for them, tonight, Shax preferred to pretend they didn't exist.

A block from his destination, grungy, gnarled fingers reached out from an alley and grabbed his coat. Damn fool.

"Spare a dollar?" a creaky voice called out.

Shax faced his assailant. His amber eyes reflected the meager light, glowing like the otherworldly being he was. The old man with scraggly hair and dirty fingernails let go and backed off, terror gushing from him.

"Get thee behind me, Satan," the man muttered, crossing himself and fading into the darkness of the alley.

A grin stretched Shax's lips. Most people chose not to look too closely, but some just knew.

"Wrong demon, my friend."

He tossed a twenty to the shadow breathing in the alley. The old coot scrabbled for the money as Shax moved on.

His fingers numb from the bitter cold, Shax unlocked the door to his motel room and slipped in. He stripped and took a hot shower, chasing away the shivers. A year ago, Shax had enjoyed the best foods, the best beds, and the best lovers, both human and demon, that Hell had to offer. And now he washed off the night in a cheap motel shower. How the mighty had fallen.

Shax slid in between the sheets, the fabric rough on his skin, irritating the red wings indelibly inked on his back, the only remnant of what he'd once been. He tossed and turned as the compulsion took hold of him. A voice pulsed through his mind, hoarse from centuries of screaming curses at God, the Archangels, the Heavenly Host, and, most of all, God's most favored, humankind.

"Find her," Lucifer's voice said, prodding Shax to finish the task set for him a year ago. "Kill her."

He fought it every day. The voice had greeted him when he'd woken up in the Florida swamp a year ago, wings gone, sunburn turning his skin pink, urging Shax to find her. He suppressed it with the aid of copious amounts of tequila and vodka, some weed, and, occasionally, harder drugs. Sex helped, too, the pleasure driving away the residual pain of the first Fall, Lucifer's failed rebellion. Mornings were usually the worst. Any drugs were long metabolized, and lovers left asleep in their own beds, and nothing but the compulsion remained. Last night, he'd gone to bed too late and too sober. He braced for an entire day of fighting the impulse to find her.

Shax gave up trying to sleep when the sun peeked through the gap in his curtains, sending a beam right onto his face. He didn't know whether the hangover or the near-sleepless night was responsible for the pain shooting through his skull, but he knew just the fix. He rummaged through his bag, looking for the oxy he'd lifted off a dealer a few nights ago. Shax washed the pill down with the metallic water from the bathroom tap. God, he wished he had a bottle of vodka in his room, but he'd finished his last one yesterday.

Sitting on the bed, Shax bounced a foot up and down and flipped through the channels. He needed a distraction. There had to be a hundred channels, and he couldn't find a single show to divert his attention from, well, everything. Christ. He needed a good wallow in self-pity, and vodka would ease him into it nicely. Melancholy wasn't part of his customary state of being. In fact, he'd rather enjoyed the past twelve months of freedom, but the one-year anniversary of the destruction of the Gate to Hell seemed an appropriate time to grieve for what he'd lost. The list was short: a friend or two, a few special abilities, and his wings.

He shoved his arms into his jacket and stalked down the street to the liquor store, which should be open by now. Yanking open the barred door, he walked into the tiny space, making a beeline for the cheapest vodka he could find.

"Anything else?" the clerk asked, not quite meeting Shax's gaze.

"Nope." He paid with some of the cash he had, um, liberated.

"Have a nice day."

"It's about to be." Shax raised the bottle in a final salute and left.

Shax hurried down the street, the oxy finally kicking in. Pretty soon, he would drown the need to pull on the string tugging him inexorably toward his prey in various painkillers. He could get back to cramming as much debauchery as possible into his life before the dickbrained angels figured out how to rebuild the Gates.

So focused on drowning out the malevolent voice in his head, he missed the shadowy figure lurking at the bottom of the stairs to his room. A glimpse of fiery hair caught his attention as he placed a booted foot down on a patch of ice in the parking lot. His feet slid out from under him. Shax cradled the bottle of vodka next to his chest and stumbled into the pile of dirty snow behind him.

"Fuuuck," he cried to the heavens.

Low, gray clouds moved in to cover the cold blue of a late February sky. The icy slush threatened to sober him up, but he was in no mood to stand. If fate wanted him sober in a pile of snow, so be it.

A shadowed figure loomed over Shax and intruded upon his examination of the clouds.

"Shax? You okay?" Male and familiar, it took him a moment to place the voice. The last time he'd seen that bearded face topped with red hair had been at Hell's Gate. Shit, they'd found him after he'd worked so hard to get lost. He never wanted to deal with another demon for as long as the Gates remained blocked.

"A momentary existential crisis, Hinndal," Shax said, one corner of his lips twitching up.

"Hate those," the man said with a chuckle. He held out a hand.

Shax grasped it and used the leverage to remedy his prone state. He brushed off the snow.

"Thanks."

He plastered on what he hoped was a welcoming smile and turned to his old friend. The other demon's eyes were black ice, and the teeth showing in his answering grin sharp. It would surprise no one to discover Hinndal was a demon. In fact, he was an ass-licking toady to whatever Duke of Hell he could cozy up to, but Shax didn't hold it against him. One did whatever one had to in order to survive in Hell.

Hinndal pulled him down into an awkward bear hug. Shax patted him on the back, hoping to bring a quick end to the unwanted embrace.

"Where have you been, Shax? Aeshma thought you'd died. I told her you were too perverse to die in the Second Fall."

Thankfully, Hinndal let go.

"Sorry to disappoint Her Grace. Care to come in?" At Hinndal's nod, Shax led the way up to his room. He set the vodka down on the dresser with a loud thump.

Shax's mind fought off the lethargy of the opioid as adrenaline coursed through his system. Hinndal served Duke Aeshma. Getting caught up in her schemes was the last thing Shax needed.

"She's had to learn to live with disappointment." Hinndal settled his chunky butt on the only chair in the room, a hard, rickety thing next to the desk. "Things haven't been easy since we all ended up stuck here on Earth. I'm surprised to find you on your own. Couldn't find a Duke to offer protection? I always told you your attitude would get you in trouble someday."

"Can I pour you a drink?" Shax gestured with the vodka, ignoring the question.

Hinndal grimaced and shrugged. "Beggars can't be choosers, I suppose. Sure."

Shax grabbed the plastic cups the housekeeper left periodically and sloshed in a measure of the cheap stuff. He passed a cup to his guest and raised his own in a toast.

"Cheers, old friend," he said, fixing the vapid smile on his face. What if it was there for all eternity? God, what a horrific fate.

"Cheers!" Hinndal downed his drink in one gulp, wheezing as the rotgut hit his throat.

"Want another?"

"No, thanks. Think I've had all I can handle of that shit. Jesus H, how do you manage?"

Shax poured himself another and sipped. Although this body wasn't as easily intoxicated as the humans who surrounded him, it still wasn't good to mix too much alcohol with those pills. He'd found that out the hard way, passing out in an alley somewhere in Virginia, only to wake half-naked and shoeless. Or had he been half-naked and shoeless before passing out? Either way, it had been a killer trip.

"Well, I'm not in Hell, so I figure anything is better than that."

"That vodka may make you wish for the tender mercies of Lucifer's own torturers."

Shax snorted. There were many other things so much worse than cheap vodka, even here on Earth. "So, you found Aeshma?"

"Didn't have far to go. Came down about half a furlong apart in Montana in the middle of a Goddamn blizzard. We almost froze to death before we found a barn. You?"

"Fucking Florida, about ten feet from an alligator who thought I looked like a snack."

"Well, it wasn't entirely wrong." The hearty guffaw from his comrade drew an almost genuine smile from Shax. "Aeshma will be glad she still has the chance to finish what the gator was too stupid to do."

Mostly, Shax was grateful to whatever or whoever had set off the explosion, destroying the Gate. In a flash of light, the constant torment of Hell was a mere memory, as were his obligations to Lucifer. He'd spent the past year doing whatever he wanted, whenever he wanted, answering to no one. It had been the best year of his life since Lucifer's rebellion had failed.

If Aeshma found out Shax was alive, she would take his freedom quicker than he could curse his rotten luck. Joining her would mean giving up most of his autonomy. His only other choice was to run. It was one thing to keep off the Duke's radar, another thing entirely to avoid pursuit. In that moment, Shax knew Hinndal needed to die before he informed Aeshma of his survival. Another loss to grieve.

"What makes you think I'm coming with you to see Aeshma?" Shax sipped at the vodka again, keeping his voice steady. No need to tip off the other demon.

"She's the only Duke left. Haven't you heard? Michael is down here, and he is on a self-righteous mission to kill every last demon on Earth. He's got himself a small army, and they're hunting us down."

The Archangel Michael did nothing subtly. If the bastard had made that much progress, Shax was officially screwed. As if this day couldn't get any worse, he now had to deal with a ticking bomb, and the being holding the detonator was God's right hand.

"All the more reason for me to disappear. Joining up with Aeshma will only make the target bigger. You should come with me. Michael's smart. He won't worry about two insignificant demons when he has a Duke to go after. We'll stay out of his crosshairs."

"Nah. All the demons Michael's killed have been unaffiliated. Aeshma's kept her horde alive so far, and Michael hasn't figured out where we're headquartered. She extends her protection in exchange for loyalty. Your best bet is to jump on her bandwagon. I know you don't trust her, but you can trust me. We've known each other since Troy fell."

Poor fool. The duke certainly would protect her minions until the choice was between them or her. Then she'd choose herself and sacrifice her loyal demons to whatever would keep her alive for a little longer. Shax had garnered a reputation for being many things, but reckless wasn't one of them. He'd only join Aeshma if there was no other choice, and if Hinndal told her he was here, Shax would have no other choice. Experience told him his best chance against the other demon was surprise.

"Sure you don't want more?" Shax pointed at the vodka bottle, stalling.

"Nah. Aeshma would be pissed if I called her drunk. You wanna say hello?" Hinndal fumbled with a cell phone and tapped on it.

"Yeah, but I don't have to be sober, do I?"

The other demon snorted and shook his head.

"Cursed things never work right." He glared at the phone. "You any better at this? I liked the third century a whole lot better than this one."

"Let me pour myself another drink, and I'll help."

Hinndal's attention now on the phone, Shax got up as though moving to the bottle of vodka on the desk. He pulled a folding knife from his jacket pocket and lunged toward the demon, slicing through his throat before the call completed. Black blood sprayed over the room, covered his boots, and spattered his shirt. Shax snatched the phone out of Hinndal's grip and tossed it to the side as the other demon fell to the floor, choking on his own blood.

"I don't trust anyone," Shax said over the dying demon. "I can't have Her Grace know I'm alive. If it makes you feel any better, you won't be going to Hell. I have no idea where you *will* go, but it won't be there."

Hinndal tried to gasp, but Shax had done his job well. He had severed the artery and sliced through the demon's trachea, making breathing and speaking impossible. A horrible death rattle escaped from the gash on Hinndal's neck, and the bleeding ceased as his heart stopped.

Shax stumbled to the bathroom and wiped off the blood with a towel. Within an hour, it would disappear from the room and his clothes. At sunset, so would Hinndal's body. He searched the demon's pockets and found a wad of twenties. Satan's balls, there must be a thousand dollars here. He tucked the money into his jacket and waited.

Chapter 2

Kheone wiped away the sweat dripping in her eyes, smearing the black demon blood across her face. She clutched her short sword, stained dark with the same.

"How you doing, Serel?"

She spared a glance over her shoulder through the dim light of the smoke-filled warehouse, taking her attention off the demons for a split second. Serel knelt next to three humans, golden light coming from his hands as he attempted to heal the workers injured in the assault. The fools had been too afraid to take the escape she'd offered a few minutes ago. Kheone no longer had the strength to fight and keep the rift open at the same time. When the rift snapped shut, she left Serel to heal and protect them as best he could while she focused her efforts on the most immediate threat. Five demons. God help her.

"Don't worry about us, LT!"

Kheone shrugged off the nickname Serel had picked up from watching too many war movies and centered her attention on the threat in front of her. One body lay motionless at her feet while the four remaining demons fanned out in front of her, more cautious now than they'd been a minute ago.

The day started out bad and had only gotten worse. The shrill notes of the landline phone had interrupted her sleep in the dark hours of the morning. She'd prayed for a misdial, but, to no one's surprise, God hadn't seen fit to answer her prayer. Daleos' voice on the other end, pleading for help, galvanized her to action. She had gathered a small team and opened a rift. Before she could think through the consequences, they'd stepped through the red-ringed hole in space into a burning warehouse in Denver and confronted a horde of demons. The all-too-familiar situation had become rarer in recent weeks.

Daleos conscripted Emric and Maj immediately upon their arrival to flank the demons outside, leaving Serel behind to help the humans cowering in the corner. He was a healer and a scholar by training, the very definition of calm, but no amount of prodding and cajoling had overcome the workers' fear. He stood over them, brandishing an iron pipe and a plain but very functional dagger, ready to use his recently learned skills to protect those in his care. Although Serel's proficiency in practice was decent, he'd be lucky to bring down one demon, let alone four. Kheone was all that stood between them and agonizing death.

The roar of demon fire drowned out much of what was going on outside, but a few screams and curses drifted to her ears. There was nothing she could do for those on the outside, and the odds were good that she wouldn't survive this. She wasn't an archangel, but she hadn't spent the last ten thousand years fighting demons to give up now.

Her lungs heaved, pulling in smoke, which now filled the warehouse. She fought the urge to cough.

"Hello," a grating voice snarled. "I haven't seen you around before, angel."

Kheone's wild, wicked grin snapped the demon's mouth shut and caused its dagger to tremble. She loved when they tried to taunt her. It meant she scared them. If they knew who she was, all four would probably run out the way they'd come in, and where was the fun in that?

She scanned the demons' faces, looking for the sharp features and golden eyes of the punk who had scarred her neck. Kheone wanted to return the favor, someday, with interest. He was not present in this raggedy horde. Kheone pushed aside her disappointment and met the issue at hand.

The demons shoved out the smallest of their lot, a sword digging into the middle of its back. It gulped and ran forward, shrieking, waving a bejeweled, leaf-bladed dagger wildly, no discipline to the attack. She danced out of the demon's path, sliced its arm with her curved blade, and smiled when its scream pierced the crackling of the flames. The demon fell to the ground, twitching uncontrollably from the holy water she'd applied to her sword. The screams ceased as she ran it through the demon's heart. Her remaining enemies spread out.

Kheone held her body and sword in a ready position. Angel fire would be very useful right about now, but she must make do with her blade and thousands of years of combat experience. It should be enough. If not, she would take as many of these fiends with her as she could. Guardian Angels didn't run from fights, even the ones that might kill them.

These last three demons showed more cunning than the first two, attacking in a coordinated effort. She never knew what she'd get when she battled one of Hell's own. Some were little more than beasts, capable of great brutality but no thought. Some were clever. And then there was the demon who had lodged himself firmly in her nightmares, ruthless and sly, whose fierce gaze battered at the shield she raised over her heart, her head, and her soul.

Kheone buried the memory deep. She did not have the capacity to deal with her past while dancing with these devils. Her complicated defense was only going to hold them off for a moment or two. She spun and thrust and dodged, praying for reinforcements. Time was her enemy.

Her blade glowed red from the fire creeping up the walls, reflecting her own fury as she whirled around to face an opponent. Spotting an opening, she drove the sword into the demon's belly. It fell to the floor, clutching at its guts spilling from the gaping hole. The demon's scream faded, leaving only an eerie silence punctuated by the crackling flames.

She had no chance to savor the victory. The last two demons fought with renewed vigor, kicking, punching, and biting at her; their daggers were forgotten in their desperation, clinging to the hope for even one more minute of their cursed lives. She turned her sword, the gentle curve of it drenched in the black demon blood, to the next opponent. Knowing what its fate would be, this demon evaded its deadly edge, only for a pipe to knock it senseless. Serel stood behind it as the demon collapsed onto Kheone's blade.

"Thanks, Serel!" Kheone turned to the last demon, tugging her sword free.

"Anytime!" He gave her a tremulous grin and saluted her with the pipe as he returned to the humans, brandishing his weapon like he knew what he was doing.

The last demon standing, its hateful stare matching the evil within, took advantage of her momentary distraction. It grabbed her sword hand and broke her wrist with a sharp twist. Kheone held in her scream and dropped her sword, pushing the pain to the back of her mind. It sat there, a pulsing ball ready to explode later if she survived.

The demon pushed her away and picked up a length of chain, swinging it around and around in figure eights. The fiend stood over her sword. She could get to the blade, but it was going to hurt. Probably like Hell, but as she had yet to go there, Kheone couldn't be certain. She had a job to do, humans to rescue.

Kheone dove for her sword and knocked over the demon, dodging the chain by some sort of miracle. She grabbed her weapon with the unbroken hand. A presence loomed above her. Kheone hunched over the sword, preparing for her journey to the afterlife. It wouldn't be the glorious return to Heaven she'd always had before, but it would be a good death, befitting a Guardian Angel's purpose. Protect humanity from demons and from itself.

Demon blood dripped down onto the floor next to her, and a gurgling gasp drew her focus upward. The imposing form of the Archangel Michael, in all of his warrior glory, stood above her, the last demon impaled upon his golden-handled great sword. In the corner, Serel ushered the humans through the rift Michael held open. The archangel held his body ready for more grisly violence, and cold fury sparked in his brown eyes.

When the body stopped moving, Michael shoved it off the great sword. The corpse hit the floor with a wet thud. Kheone scrambled up, holding her broken wrist close to her chest, her sword in her left hand. He inspected her from head to foot. Apparently satisfied she'd suffered no life-threatening injury, he turned and strode to the rift.

A fierce smile slashed across her face, and she took a step to follow the archangel. Too late, she heard the soft scuff of shoes behind her. Agony ripped through her, tearing her breath away. A sixth demon no one had seen laughed, a low rumble she barely heard over her own gasping. It pulled the knife from her lower back. She tumbled to the floor as her opalescent blood mingled with the demon ichor, a rainbow glaze over a tar pit. Blessed Heaven, she'd almost made it.

Michael turned and stalked over to her attacker, menace rolling off the lethal predator ready to slay its prey. One look at the archangel and the fight drained from the demon. Michael said nothing as he leaped the final few feet and impaled the demon through the heart. The body collapsed at his feet, oozing blood all over the archangel's tan boots. Kheone's vision grayed at the edges, and her gasps grew more desperate. Michael turned from the demon and knelt at her side.

"I shall take you to safety, Lieutenant."

He lifted her into his powerful arms and walked through a new rift, carrying her into her own room in Kansas City. Six hundred miles in a single step.

"One small step for an archangel," she said. The loss of blood had made her light-headed.

Michael raised an eyebrow.

"Sorry." *So tired.* The world darkened.

"Open your eyes, Kheone."

Her body wanted to disobey him, but thousands of years of training made that impossible. Kheone complied. Worry creased his brow. Huh, odd. She'd seen many others hurt worse since the Gates disintegrated in an incomprehensible explosion of sound and light, but never once had Michael seemed even uneasy, let alone worried.

"I'll be okay. You're here."

Her words came out muffled and mumbled, and the crease deepened.

He placed her face down on the bed, so gently it was as if she'd floated there on her own accord. Michael tugged the kopis sword out of her grasp and set it on the nightstand. Without a word, he nudged her shirt up and pulled her cargo pants down enough to expose the wound in her back. Kheone hissed at the pain as he placed his hand over it. Warmth flowed through her body, and the walls of her room reflected the golden glow radiating from where Michael touched her. The sharp pain dulled to an ache, and the gray fog of unconsciousness receded.

Michael slumped into the small chair next to her bed. It creaked under his weight. She held her breath, waiting for the chair to fall to pieces. It didn't. Michael's expression relaxed into cool neutrality now that the danger was over.

"Thank you, Archangel," she whispered.

"How do you feel, Lieutenant?" Michael asked in his deep voice.

She chuckled, causing the ache in her back to twinge, reminding her she was still healing. Once, her angelic powers would have easily repaired these injuries. Since the Second Fall, all angels' abilities had faded, except for Michael's.

"Considering the demon stabbed me in the back, pretty darn good, but my wrist is broken, too."

He shook his head at her flippant tone, but she thought she caught a twinkle of amusement in his serious eyes as he enclosed her wrist in his large hand, ever so gently. Michael's expression remained carefully neutral, and Kheone gave him a tentative smile. Once again, golden light filled the room as he healed her. She sat up, wincing as her muscles protested, too newly regrown to appreciate the movement.

"Did everyone make it out?" she asked.

"Yes, everyone except the demons." As it should be. His muscles tensed, and his eyes glittered, the returning rage spitting off him like sparks from a fire. "Now, would you care to explain what in God's name you were doing, facing down a horde of demons on your own?"

Gone was the kind Michael with the gentle touch, rescuer of wayward souls and healer of injured angels, replaced by the Archangel Michael, Commander of the Heavenly Host. His voice rang out, cold as the winter snow, and it was all Kheone could do to bring herself to answer.

"You weren't here, and Daleos was desperate." Unable to keep the tremor out of her voice, she knew she'd made the right call. She needed to convince Michael. "I followed my training, Archangel. I gathered the few angels still here and rendered assistance to a fellow gathering. As far as I can tell, the mission was a success. Three humans saved, a demon horde crushed, and no angels lost to their schemes."

"Have your angelic gifts returned?"

Kheone shook her head. Michael's frown deepened.

"Then, you are not as invulnerable as you once were. Even a small wound has the potential to kill you by infection, and you cannot hold open a rift and fight. I do not wish to replace you as leader of the Kansas City gathering, but if you continue to disregard your own safety, I may have no choice."

Kheone jumped out of bed and almost pitched into Michael, her body still healing from the ordeal. She straightened up and confronted her commander, her nervousness gone in the shock of his threat.

"I will not put my safety over that of an entire gathering, Archangel. You taught me better. If I had to do it over again, I wouldn't change a thing. Even if it costs me my position."

"You are weak, Kheone. I cannot risk losing any more angels. There are too few of us."

Heat flooded her face, and fiery anger crawled over her at his words. She grabbed her sword from where Michael had placed it on the nightstand and brandished the blade at her commander.

"I may not have all the gifts I once had that *you* still have, but I am not weak. If you feel I am no longer capable of leading this gathering, you may as well drive this through my heart and put us all out of our misery."

She flipped the blade and proffered the hilt to Michael, who glowered at it. In a flash, he rose, grabbed the sword, and threw it against the wall. The sword clattered to the floor in the now silent room.

"Enough!" he roared.

Kheone withdrew, cold dread replacing the sizzling anger of a moment ago.

"Enough," he said again, quieter, running a hand down his face. Michael breathed deep, and his expression slid into the more familiar look of stoic detachment. Good. His rage and worry set her teeth on edge. "I did not mean for this to become a discussion on your leadership abilities. You did as I trained you and defeated four demons. That is...impressive."

High praise indeed from the archangel. Pride bloomed in her chest, driving away the dread of a moment ago.

"Serel brained one with a pipe first."

"Still impressive. However, I would have thrown the humans through the rift." A hint of a smile turned up the corners of his mouth. "I shall leave you to rest. You have done enough for today."

Kheone kicked off her boots and pulled back the covers. She dropped onto the bed, her vision graying once again as fatigue and injury caught up to her. Michael walked to the door and paused with his hand on the knob. He turned, his usually serious face inscrutable.

"I do not doubt your ability to lead the gathering, Kheone. In fact, I believe appointing you was the best decision I have made since the Second Fall. I was concerned you were more injured than it appeared and allowed my concern to override my judgment for a moment. I am glad you are recovering."

He walked out. Kheone stared at the spot, mouth open in shock. There were two things Kheone knew about her life. A good soldier obeyed orders. And the Archangel Michael cared about no one. Apparently, the second was wrong.

Chapter 3

Everything Shax owned fit into a single duffle bag with room left over. It took him all of fifteen minutes to pack up his life. The vodka ran out around noon, and he had spent the last several hours watching Hinndal's body while sobering up. The compulsion to find *her* returned with the force of a tidal wave.

The last sliver of sun disappeared, and a cool breeze blew through the stuffy motel room, though all the windows and doors were closed. Hinndal's body faded to gray dust, carried on the breeze into the world. It was done.

Shax stood and slung his bag over his shoulder. The bedside lamp glinted off something on the floor. Dread filled his guts as he took a step closer. A tarnished silver coin with worn edges had replaced Hinndal's body. The portrait of a Roman emperor—he could not remember which one—was barely discernible.

Son of a bitch. He'd last seen the coin when he had dropped it into a busker's open guitar case in Nashville about a month ago. A month before that, he had tossed it into a fountain in Philadelphia. Shax had rid himself of the coin many times since bouncing it off the head of an alligator and watching it sink beneath the waters of the Everglades on the day of the Second Fall.

The coin had graced many palms in its day, passed along from mint to merchant to farmer and back again until ending up in the hand of an apostle, along with twenty-nine of its fellows. On Lucifer's orders, Shax had posed as a priest and took the silver pieces from Judas moments before the man had hung himself in shame.

He picked up the coin from the floor of his cheap motel room, and his skin crawled. After two thousand years, the coin bore the stain of the Prince of Hell's rage and envy. Whispering the name of the victim to a coin, Lucifer would give it to Shax. Each name became a murmur in his mind until the target was dead. Only once he'd completed the mission was Shax able to enjoy a measure of peace. At least until Lucifer needed his services again, and the Devil always had need of his services.

Trying to get rid of the coin was a fool's task. It would merely return to him, over and over again, until she was dead. He had wanted nothing more than to be forgotten by angels, demons, and fate after failing to kill her once. The compulsion to find her since had nearly driven him insane. His duty awaited, and chances were she would kill him.

Shax clutched the coin tightly, closed his eyes, and whispered her name. "Kheone."

Between one breath and the next, the world spun around him, and cold enveloped him. Shax opened his eyes and stared at a two-story building across a quiet street. Its tan bricks glowed golden in the fading light, the porch in deep shadow. Lamps flicked on. The coin never dropped him where his target could detect him, but she was somewhere in that building.

Sliding the coin into his pocket, Shax dropped his mental shield for an instant. A golden thread of awareness drifted through the frigid twilight and to a window on the first floor. There was Kheone. But he sensed something else, too, a larger presence. On the second floor, a pulsating ball of red-orange hostility roiled. His guard snapped up, and he hurried off. He would know that feeling anywhere. An archangel waited in the building, and there was only one on the face of the Earth. Fuck.

He didn't even possess an appropriate weapon to confront an angel, let alone the Archangel Michael. Attempting his mission would be dangerous enough as it was, and dealing with the archangel only complicated things. If he wanted to live, he needed to come up with a plan.

He also needed a place to stay out of winter's cold, a place he could drink himself into indifference. Finding her, being so close, set his teeth on edge. Picking up his pace, Shax passed a sign that read *Hurst University* and crossed a busy street, putting distance between himself and the angels.

The drugs and alcohol he had taken earlier were long metabolized, and the voice in his head was at full volume. Its orders echoed through his mind, urging him back the way he'd come. Twitching and swearing at no one in particular, he drew suspicious frowns from others on the street. If he wasn't careful, somebody was going to call the cops, a pain in the ass he did not need. Another reason to find a place to stay.

Shax had taken what precautions he could, wiping Hinndal's cell phone and tossing it into the Mississippi River, but he couldn't do the same for his own. He would be lost without it. Aeshma wasn't one to allow a minion to wander off unsupervised for long. With any luck, the duke would assume Hinndal had run. With even more luck, when someone came looking for Hinndal, there would be no trace of him.

He rubbed his face, wishing for a cup of tequila or a shot of coffee. Or something. Instead, he pulled out his phone and looked up the closest, cheapest motel. He turned up the collar of his jacket and strode through the darkening city. The stars shimmered in the heavens. Only a year ago, thousands of winged bodies, angels and demons alike, had filled the sky. They tumbled through the upper reaches of the atmosphere, streaked through the stars, and plummeted to their doom. Some fell faster, some slower, and some winked out of existence.

Shax scraped his hair out of his face, tugging hard at it, hoping the pain would dull the memory. It didn't work. Up ahead was a liquor store. Tequila was perfect for forgetting, and he needed to forget tonight. She was so very close. He ducked in.

The memories would not leave him alone. A jumbled mess of light and sound and panic allowed the few solid sensations to stand out. The warm, vibrating handle of his dagger as it slipped from his fingers. The piercing sound of a horn. The Gate to Hell crumbling to dust with a roar, and Heaven's Gate following suit an instant later, the flash of it dazzling him. Terror ripping through his guts.

He hurried to the first motel on the list. He put half his cash down to reserve a room for the week. The room he'd rented was as run-down as the lobby, but the sheets and towels were clean. He chucked his duffle bag into the closet and hid the rest of the money under the mattress.

Shax unscrewed the lid of the tequila bottle and took a swig, rushing to forget her lithe body pressed into his as the force of the explosion pushed them through the barrier between the celestial realms and the mortal one. He had lost his grip on the angel, her wings on fire as she drifted away. His own leathery wings blazed, the agony of it forcing him into unconsciousness, but not before a scream ripped from him. He had never been certain whether it was due to the pain or the despair.

Another gulp burned down his throat. Certainly not the best tequila he'd ever had, but all it needed to do was dull his memories of the Second Fall. At the very least, the tequila made him care less. The biting edge of the liquor distracted him from all the problems in front of him.

When he finally confronted the angel, she would likely kill him on the spot, never giving him a chance to explain himself. Only in his dreams did she forgive him. In his nightmares, she turned him over to Lucifer.

Another few shots and he could forget for a little while. The night was long, and the bottle was full.

Chapter 4

A thunderous pounding pulled Kheone from her dreams, away from the chaos of the falling Gates. A dagger as black as Satan's soul fell away from her throat, leaving a trickle of iridescent blood. A blazing light flashed, and she tumbled through the ether, her wings smoldering as she plunged to Earth beside her kin. Meteorologists had called it an unexpected meteor shower. The angels and demons named it the Second Fall.

Damn Shax for almost besting her. And damn him for disappearing, too. How was she supposed to even the score if she never saw him again?

Pushing aside the fiery whorls of pain surging across her back, she reached over to her nightstand as the knocking continued, fruitlessly fumbling for her sword. Blazes, it was on the other side of the room, exactly where Michael had thrown the blade last night before she collapsed into bed. Had she really challenged him to kill her for her supposed incompetence?

"Kheone! You're late." Serel opened the door and rushed to her window, throwing open the curtains.

Light streamed in. Oh, Hell. In winter, training started in the dark. What kind of example did she set for her gathering by being late to her own training sessions? She needed to get over to the adjoining gym immediately. Kheone jumped out of bed and instantly regretted it. Her legs collapsed like limp pasta, and she tumbled to the floor.

For pity's sake, if slowly losing her angelic abilities was not enough, now she had shown weakness in front of members of her gathering. Michael set a high standard and didn't tolerate vulnerability.

Serel rushed over and helped her up. "Oh, dear, I was kidding. The Archangel gave us the day off."

Giggles from the hall caught her attention. Emric and Maj hovered in the doorway, their presence unnoticed in her panic.

"Ha, ha." She glowered at Serel.

"Sorry, LT. Guess I'm still getting a handle on this human stuff," he said, wearing a sheepish smile.

"Forget about it. I'm sure I'll laugh someday."

Kheone gave him a half-grin. His rugged face brightened, and Serel joined her on the bed. Emric and Maj slid into the room and leaned against the wall. Emric, slight with whipcord muscles and light brown hair, stared at her with thunder in their emerald green eyes. Maj, with skin and hair almost black, leaned against the wall, her left brow cocked up over midnight, eyes sparkling like stars in the sky in her usual bemused fashion.

"Care to join us for an Angels' Day Out?" Serel asked.

Ah, that explained Emric's annoyed countenance. Never her biggest fan, Emric seemed to have developed a big ole chip on their shoulder whenever Kheone became involved since the Second Fall. She had tried to address their attitude on multiple occasions in the past few weeks, but all she got in return were more disdainful looks.

"Is that the best idea, Serel?" Kheone pointedly met Emric's stare. The other angel had the grace to blush and refocused their attention out the window.

"Of course it is. You deserve a day off just as much as we do," he said.

Days off were a rarity for angels, though more necessary now they were stuck on Earth. Only God knew what happened to their souls when their physical bodies died now. Until they found a way home, it was best to keep them functioning at peak performance.

Maj snuck a glance at Emric. She straightened up and said, "You should come, Kheone. From how Serel tells the story, you deserve it more. He said you were a sight to behold yesterday."

Kheone and Maj had history together. Their first assignment together at an early Viking raid had given rise to the legend of the Valkyrie. Every once in a while, they still hoisted ale in honor of the Viking dead. Something had changed in the last few months, though, and Maj had stopped coming by for impromptu drinks, leaving Kheone more alone than she'd ever been before.

Rigid with fury, Emric turned to Maj. They seemed ready to yell at her but clamped their lips together.

Kheone waved away the compliment. "Just doing my job."

"There's doing your job, and there's killing four demons single-handedly," Serel said.

"It wasn't single-handedly. You helped, and Michael saved our butts."

"Stop being so humble, LT. Maj and Emric don't believe me. Come with us, if only to convince the whippersnappers."

Emric snorted. "You're stuck in the wrong century, Serel. No one uses 'whippersnapper' anymore."

"That is patently false." His voice was deadpan, but his eyes sparkled at the joke. "I just did. Therefore, *someone* uses 'whippersnapper.'"

The other angel rolled their eyes, but the smile stayed. If only Emric would remain that way. Kheone knew as soon as she opened her mouth, Emric the Annoyed would return. She needed to deal with this soon, or else the two of them would continue to circle each other until whatever grudge they held onto exploded into some disruptive spectacle.

"I really need to catch up on my reading," Kheone said.

"Don't be such a stick in the mud, Kheone. You're not an archangel," Emric said, scorn dripping from the final word.

As predicted. Kheone turned the full force of her glare on the subordinate angel, all amusement gone. Michael would have never put up with half the drivel they'd displayed in the past five minutes. Then again, Emric respected him. Somehow, Kheone had lost their respect in the Second Fall.

She stood and stalked over to Emric, her six-foot form towering over the petite angel.

"I understand you've only rarely been to Earth, and this is all new to you. I also know you're a prickly pain in the neck, but I'm sick and tired of this nonsense. What did I do to deserve your contempt in the past twelve months?"

Emric squirmed and looked everywhere around the room except at Kheone. Maj and Serel stiffened, waiting for the fireworks to explode. Emric mumbled something.

"I can't hear you." Kheone used her most commanding tone, a voice she reserved for moments when it counted, the one she'd picked up from the Archangel Michael.

"I said, 'You act like you're better than the rest of us.'"

Kheone sucked in a breath and let the sting of the words wash through her. She'd tried hard to balance friendship and leadership since she'd landed in the alley behind the Crown Center last year. Apparently, she'd failed. Did everyone think like Emric?

"That's because she is, you dumbass." Serel rose from the bed, and his eyes narrowed in exasperation. "How would you have fared against six demons?"

"Run like a child," Maj said with a chuckle. Emric crossed their arms and shot her another anger-filled look. "Oh, come on, it's true. Don't get pissy. You know your limits, Em, and running from that many demons is smart unless you're an archangel. Or Kheone, I guess."

"Thanks for the invitation, Serel," Kheone said, turning from Emric. "But it's obvious my presence isn't wanted. Another time. Enjoy your day off."

She waved in a shooing gesture, and Emric and Maj trudged out. Maj glanced over her shoulder and gave her a shrug as they walked away.

Serel rested a hand on her shoulder, the light touch easing her anger and frustration.

"Seriously, LT, join us," he said. "Emric is being a jerk, not an uncommon event, and they'll both lighten up once they realize you aren't the killjoy they think you are."

"How do you know I'm not a killjoy?"

He smiled. "I've seen you in the speakeasies a hundred years ago, the dance halls during the Second World War, the feast halls of the Anglo-Saxons. Emric hasn't, and Maj has forgotten."

"That was before, Serel. I'm in charge of this gathering. I have a reputation and an image to maintain."

"Fine. Do whatever you have planned but join us for drinks and dinner. You gotta eat, right?"

"I don't—"

"We'll be at The Cheesecake Factory about six-thirty. Who doesn't like cheesecake? Stop by and have a drink or some dessert. What can it hurt?"

Maj's voice carried down the hall. "Hurry up, Ser. The movie starts in thirty minutes."

"Gotta run. See you at six-thirty!"

The door banged closed behind him before she could protest, leaving Kheone alone with her thoughts. Serel wasn't wrong. She'd been merely one of Michael's many trusted lieutenants before the day he'd rescued her from the slush in the dirty alleyway. Kheone was the only lieutenant who had survived the Second Fall. He had given her command of the Kansas City gathering as soon as she recovered. Apparently, there was some bitterness in the ranks about this. She should talk to Serel, see how deep the animosity went. Maybe she'd get lucky, and it was only Emric.

Kheone had learned most of what she knew about being a leader from Michael. He was never just one of the team and kept himself apart from the others. But she wasn't an archangel and didn't merit the angels' instinctual, automatic obedience to authority. If she wanted to lead this gathering, if she wanted the other gatherings to respect her, Kheone needed to build relationships and earn their trust. Meeting them for a drink or a meal was a small step in the right direction.

Good, that was settled. Now she had to decide what to do with a whole day to herself. Kheone grabbed her shower caddy and headed to the shared bathroom down the hall. A nice, warm shower would ease the lingering ache she felt from the fight yesterday and let her weigh her options.

She did, in fact, have reading to catch up on. After all, the library here was the reason Michael had chosen Hurst University for their refuge. When they weren't training or hunting down demons, many angels spent what spare time they had searching its extensive collection of mythological and religious texts, some incredibly rare, all of them useful. It was the best chance to find a means to rebuild the Gates and return both angels and demons where they belonged.

She should spend her day off reading, but just this once, her special place tempted her to abandon obligation. With an entire day to herself, not merely an hour or two before bed, she needed to remember why she was a guardian angel and why humans were worth saving.

Her soul needed feeding, and only one way would bring her any peace.

From their first steps into the wide world, humans created art. Drawings on cave walls and etchings on rocks, telling the stories of ordinary days. Incorporating decorative elements into everyday tools evolved into an explosion of things of beauty for beauty's sake. Whenever Kheone found herself annoyed by human failings, of weak souls tempted by easy paths, greed, and power, she remembered all the beauty they created, often out of the pain those failings caused. Paintings, sculpture, architecture, film, books, photographs. Art fed her soul, and she knew exactly where to find the banquet.

Thrilled with her decision, Kheone rushed through the rest of her morning routine, pulling on her usual uniform of black t-shirt and cargo pants. She charged out of the bathroom, eager to get on with her day, and ran smack into a broad chest. Strong arms steadied her as she rebounded from the rock-hard muscle.

"Good morning, Lieutenant," Michael said in his rumbling voice.

She blinked at him in surprise. The archangel rarely stayed in town after a mission. Some other gathering always had need of him. He trekked around the world to ensure the other leaders had the resources necessary to ensure the safety of all the angels trapped on Earth. He hunted down the demons who now plagued humanity. With no master to answer to, they caused much chaos and destruction.

"Apologies, Archangel."

He nodded gravely. Michael did everything gravely.

"Do you have a moment?"

"Of course."

They headed to her room. Michael strode in, taking up most of the space with his bulk. Built as anyone would expect God's general to be, the archangel was tall with thick muscles outlined by his long-sleeved black t-shirt and golden hair shorn almost to the scalp. He was the most beautiful being she'd seen in ten thousand years.

His stony gaze roved over her as though he was a medical scanner from a sci-fi TV show, looking for any evidence of her injury from yesterday.

"How are you?"

Irritation crept over her. She'd answered him last night, and the shower had washed away any lingering discomfort.

"Honestly, Archangel, I'm fine. It's almost as though I was never stabbed in the first place."

His brows drew down into a scowl. Michael expected everyone else to do everything gravely too. Kheone looked down at her feet as the heat rushed to her cheeks. Despite her best efforts, she'd picked up some bad habits from the humans.

"I apologize. I'm well."

"No apology necessary." Cool indifference replaced the scowl. "I came to inform you I would be here today since you will not. Is there anything we have not discussed recently that I need to know?"

Kheone shook her head. Her reports on the gatherings' progress in training were thorough, and no new information had been discovered on what had destroyed the Gates, nor what could fix them.

"How goes the search through the library?"

"As well as can be expected. Serel is there most days. He's very efficient in weeding out the duds and finding some promising texts."

She gestured at the thick book on early Egyptian mystics sitting on her nightstand. The tome she was ditching in order to visit the art museum.

Michael nodded, face set in stone, unreadable. He said nothing, however, and as the silence stretched, Kheone found her fingers and toes twitching as her unease grew. Had she said something wrong?

"Is there anything else?" she asked when she couldn't take any more.

His gaze found her, and a shiver crawled down her spine. Kheone never understood how his brown eyes could be so cold.

"How were you able to defeat those demons alone? Six would be bothersome for me, but no other angel on Earth could survive such an attack."

"They were rash, and I got lucky." At his glare, she clarified. "I'm not being glib. They misjudged my abilities and had no strategy. Serel helped. And let's not forget who swooped in at the last minute to save my ass."

Michael blinked at her use of the coarse language, a reminder of how much the past year had changed her. Had changed all of them, except for Michael. He clung to the old ways like lichen to a boulder. Kheone tried, but the people, the language, the art, they infected her, affected her, in ways she was only beginning to realize and still did not understand. The occasional swear word was the tip of the iceberg.

His stare unnerved her, and the shiver down her spine was hard to suppress. What was he thinking? She'd only followed her training, training from this very archangel. Had she done something wrong without meaning to?

Michael tore his eyes away and breathed out a loud sigh. His shoulders slumped, and he ran a hand over the stubble on his head.

"I owe you an apology. I allowed my concern for your wellbeing, as well as that of your companions, to get the better of me. I am sorry I took my failure to anticipate your situation out on you."

Her body almost went boneless, and she avoided crumpling at his feet only because her back hit the wall behind her. The Archangel Michael never apologized or admitted fault. Perhaps his time on Earth had changed him, after all.

"You have exceeded my expectations, Kheone. As your gifts fade, your skills expand more than any of the others. It is a testament to your dedication."

"And my training."

Michael gave a nonchalant shrug, but the corners of his mouth twitched up.

"Yes, and your training. Your day off is a well-earned reward."

"Thank you, Archangel."

"Call me Michael when we are alone, please. You have earned that, as well."

She nodded, once again at a loss for words. A year into the Second Fall, and the arch—Michael *had* changed.

"Thank you, Michael." Kheone savored his name on her tongue.

Without another word, he turned and left. Reeling from the emotional wringer the archangel put her through, Kheone flopped on her bed and stared at the ceiling while she waited for the world to stop spinning.

Chapter 5

Jesus Fucking Christ, he needed to drink better tequila.

The damned buzzing in his head was worse than ever. Combined with the hangover, it had Shax cursing his faded regenerative abilities. When the Gate had exploded, his link to the powers Lucifer bestowed had vanished along with it.

Gone were the days when most wounds healed in minutes, travel was via rifts in space, and he could wield demon fire. If you didn't count the coin's ability to transport him to wherever Kheone was, Shax had only one major trick up his sleeve. Unfortunately, healing was not it. These monumental hangovers made thinking hard. Sometimes he envied those who had burned up in the Second Fall.

He kicked off the scratchy sheets of the too-firm bed and searched out some ibuprofen. Downing three with a large glass of water, he contemplated the oddly shaped stains on the ceiling while waiting for the pills to kick in. An hour later, he felt up to washing off the tequila sweat from last night.

Finally feeling capable of planning out his day, Shax pulled out the silver coin and stared at it. Memory flooded his senses, sight, sound, smell, all conjuring up the last time he had seen Kheone. Circumstances beyond his control had left her alive. At least, that was what he told himself.

The silver shining from under centuries' worth of tarnish was nearly the same color as her irises. The bright intensity of her gaze reflected the animosity and rage of all their past confrontations, both on the battlefield and in smaller, more private moments. Shax could deal with hatred and anger. He was a demon, after all, and had trafficked in those emotions, day in and day out, for millennia. It was the pity in her gaze he truly avoided, almost as if Kheone realized the depths of his own self-hatred.

He had held his obsidian blade to her throat on Lucifer's orders. Once he looked into her eyes, he knew. He couldn't do it. He could not end her very existence. Just as Shax never questioned the Prince of Hell, he did not question this instinct. The blade dropped from his unwilling fingers, the edge leaving a thin line of pearlescent blood on her throat. And then all Hell broke loose.

Shax closed his hand around the coin. Whether or not he was ready, he needed to face facts. Standing in the middle of a swamp a year ago, Shax had thrown the cursed thing, hoping to never see it again, hoping to live his own life, free from the pain of his sins and released from the hold Lucifer had over him. He had deceived himself. One never escaped Hell, not really.

First things first, though. Shax needed to replenish his supply of cash on the off chance his untraceable credit cards were not, in fact, untraceable. It was amazing how little a thousand dollars bought him in this century. Half was gone with this crappy room, and he had become accustomed to eating regular meals and drinking decent liquor.

Hinndal had found him too easily, and Aeshma could be on his heels. He enjoyed the anonymity cash offered at the moment. It might very well keep him alive long enough to do something about his angel problem.

Decision made, Shax pocketed the coin and walked down to the front desk with a fixed smile, radiating friendliness. He would try the easy way first. Most humans responded in kind to politeness. It built trust, all too often giving him a toehold in their psyche for later manipulation, both ordinary and magical. His demonic gift for psychological manipulation had gone with the others, leaving his keen sense of human nature as his only tool to exploit these weak-minded beings. It would be more than enough.

"Good morning," he said to the clerk, a middle-aged, bored-looking man.

"It's afternoon."

"Then, good afternoon. Could you tell me where the nearest mall is?"

"Google it."

Shax fought off the part of him that wanted to bring out the scary demon and put the lowly human in his place. Damned shame he needed to keep off Aeshma's radar. He narrowed his eyes at the man, and ice infused his voice.

"Perhaps you should practice your manners, sir."

His tone garnered the clerk's attention. The fear rolling off the man as his instincts kicked in was sweet perfume. He gulped and pulled out a pen and paper, hand trembling.

"Here." The clerk's voice cracked at the end. He tore off the paper and gave it to Shax.

"Thank you." The ice had melted from Shax's voice, though his words were still clipped.

Shax turned on his heels and left before he gave the man a reason to give in to his fight-or-flight response. He pulled out his phone and looked up Crown Center. It was the opposite direction of where he had come from last night. He wished to stay closer to the university, if at all possible.

Zooming out on the map, Shax familiarized himself with the area. He ruled out the Power and Light District, a hub of entertainment, clubs, and bars. It was a long walk, and it would be much better to hit such a place after dark when people were drunk and distracted. For now, he was torn between the Country Club Plaza, which sounded full of trinkets awaiting liberation from rich douchebags, and an art museum that stood between him and the Plaza. The latter was an even better target for petty theft, especially since this museum was free. With the patrons' attention on the art, they rarely noticed missing wallets and jewelry until much later. The only potential downside was the security. If that was the case, he would simply move on.

Shax turned up his collar against the cool breeze and started walking. Much to his surprise, he enjoyed the brisk walk. The sun was almost warm, the neighborhoods picturesque, and early flowers sprouted out of the ground wherever there was a yard or park. He still would have traded it in a heartbeat for the ability to create a rift. Or fly. Satan below, he wished he could stretch his wings and fly.

As nice as the day was, the chill in the air still got to him. His fingers took a few minutes to warm up after he entered the building. Once they did, Shax inspected the crowd, looking for likely marks in the galleries. The distracted parent. The young man in fervent discussion with a young woman over a painting, sexual tension screaming at him. The art student was so focused on her work she failed to notice the stranger standing much too close. Before long, he acquired a few wallets, two watches, and some promising-looking pills.

Shax turned the corner in the museum and stopped breathing, stopped thinking, stopped everything. His gaze locked on the tall, slender figure standing in front of a painting halfway down the gallery. Her skin glowed in the spotlights illuminating the display, and the blue highlights in her short, black hair stood out in stark contrast. She was beautiful, like a bird of prey was beautiful: fierce, powerful, deadly.

He didn't have to see her face to know exactly who this was. It was inked onto whatever was left of his soul. If he'd had any doubts, the heat coming from the coin in his jacket pocket would have told him.

Kheone.

His brain kicked in, screaming at him to run. Instead, he ducked around the corner, heart beating an irregular rhythm in his chest.

Shit, shit, shit.

Shax's fingers twitched, and he reached for the dagger that was no longer at his hip. He had not missed his blade since that day. With a hilt made from Cain's bone and its obsidian blade forged in the destruction of the Garden of Eden, his blade sent souls to oblivion. No afterlife, no resurrection, no Heaven, no Hell, not even Purgatory. And Lucifer had ordered him to kill her with it.

He had no idea why. Once someone rebuilt the Gates, he would answer to Lucifer for allowing the angel to live. The destruction of the Gates was only part of the answer. He had no desire to explore any further reasons.

Fate was a twisted bitch. With no weapon to truly kill her, he could not challenge her. He had run from his contract, papering over his feelings with drugs, alcohol, and sex. And on his first day in this city, he had crossed paths with the very angel he'd been unable to kill.

The people milling around him threw scowls at him as he hugged the wall as if his life depended upon it. Shax took a deep breath and straightened up. Today's haul would have to be enough. He could not fulfill his duty yet, but since Kheone was so tantalizingly close, he would not let this chance go to waste. Patting his pockets, he assured himself the prizes he had lifted were present and accounted for. Shax stepped around the corner.

Kheone was gone.

He expected the lightness of relief, but a heaviness filled his chest.

Where did she go?

The flash of daylight on a glass door caught his attention. A hundred feet away, a tall figure with dark hair strode outside. He followed but stopped five steps later. Kheone sat down on a bench next to the grassy lawn surrounding the museum, lifting her face to soak in the meager sun.

Shax ducked around a corner to empty the wallets of their cash and a single diamond earring before tossing them over a low wall into an empty flower bed. If they were picked up, his fingerprints would fade in the same way as his demon blood. If they weren't, well, not his problem. Tucking the cash in his pocket, he checked on Kheone.

His timing was impeccable. She stood and walked down the sidewalk bordering the wide, green expanse. He watched and waited. It hit him in the silence of the trees, the calm of a decision made. Something was missing. The buzz in his brain, his constant companion since he awoke on the banks of a Florida swamp 366 days ago, dampened only by debauchery, was gone. Oh, he was so completely screwed.

Shax made a valiant last-ditch attempt to review his options rationally. He could leave, run for the hills and never look back. Give up on this absurd crusade. That would be the smart thing to do. The likelihood of the Gates being rebuilt was minuscule. Entwining his fortunes with an angel was mad at best, suicide at worst. Or...he could follow her. God alone knew why. There was nothing to be gained.

His body decided before his brain caught up. Tapping into his remaining gift, he transformed in a blink. Where once stood a tall, young man with white hair now sat a small, black cat, ears pricked forward, tail swishing restlessly. The cat sighed and trotted out to where he had last spotted Kheone. Their fortunes were already entwined, thanks to the cursed coin and Lucifer's orders. Shax didn't yet know of a method to free them both, but he would not find one without her help. Catching her scent, he followed it through the crowd, trying to stay in the bushes to avoid notice. Every once in a while, he got close enough to pick her out of the crowd, her six-foot height making her taller than most. He hung back and grew the distance between them before following again at a slower pace.

About thirty minutes later, the sun painting the sky pink as it sunk toward the western horizon, she arrived at a restaurant, a large, dry fountain in the courtyard. Shax slunk under a bush and watched her walk into an ostentatious building with *The Cheesecake Factory* in bright red neon over the entrance. He darted across the courtyard, dodging feet, tables, and chairs, looking for a place to hide until she came out.

An angel walks into The Cheesecake Factory sounded like the beginning of a bad joke. The only thing worse would be, *An angel and a demon walk into The Cheesecake Factory.*

Chapter 6

Kheone fiddled with the straw in her water, feeling like a spotlight pointed at her, saying she didn't belong. When would the others be here? It was already past six-thirty. If they stood her up on this rare foray into socializing, it didn't bode well for future endeavors. And she really wanted to change her relationship to the gathering. Reading in her room and going to the museum alone were getting old fast.

At first, keeping her professional distance had seemed necessary. Honored Michael had chosen her to lead the Kansas City gathering, Kheone needed to live up to his high expectations. A year into this new normal, though, the angels were well-trained, and the demon hordes were much diminished. Peace fell upon most of the gatherings, with occasional exceptions like last night.

"There she is. Pay up, losers!"

Serel's voice rang out behind her, good humor lending golden tones to his words. Kheone turned, brows drawn down in disapproval. Emric and Maj followed behind. Her arm was wrapped around their waist, their arm around her shoulders like...lovers.

She was negligent for not seeing it earlier. Every angel had their own manner of dealing with the Second Fall. Some drank, some cried, some pulled so far in on themselves she was afraid for their souls. Some took lovers. Kheone went to museums.

Catching her gaze, Emric dropped their arm and took a step away. Maj looked like she was going to say something but thought better of it and merely glowered at her lover.

"You bet on whether I would be here?" Kheone asked coolly, choosing to ignore their behavior.

Serel took a seat on the bar stool next to her, slinging an arm around her shoulders. Stiffening beneath the limb, she attempted to shrug it off, but his strength prevented her from doing so without drawing any more attention.

She was tempted to do so anyway, but she had accepted the invitation and all it entailed.

"Of course we did, LT. How often have you been a no-show at a party?"

The smell of alcohol on his breath told a tale of their earlier activities. Kheone reminded herself they deserved a day off after surviving yesterday. She only wished they did not command so much attention from the rest of the crowd. Michael preferred they all went unnoticed.

"Too many," muttered Emric, sending Kheone a sour look.

"Come on, Em," said Serel. "Give the poor lieutenant a break. She has to answer to a higher authority."

"I'm sure Em wouldn't mind answering to *that* higher authority," Maj said with a sly grin, nudging the other angel.

Emric punched Maj's shoulder.

"Ow, no need to hit so hard."

"There is if you won't shut up."

"Children, knock it off!"

Serel smiled widely, but there was an icy edge to it. One could push him, but only so far before the hammer fell. His easygoing personality and gentle humor made him better at managing the angels' often contentious personalities than she. The angels respected Kheone, but they liked Serel and followed his subtle cues, the ones she always had to make explicit. It didn't hurt that he had a soft touch when healing, endearing him further to his patients. And they had all been his patients at some point. She sometimes wondered why Michael had chosen her as leader over Serel. When next it came up for discussion, she'd recommend him should something happen to her.

Emric and Maj settled onto bar stools on the other side of Serel and got the attention of the bartender. Maj ordered a round of beer and turned from Kheone and Serel. She and Emric engaged in soft conversation, oblivious to all else.

"What have you been up to today, Kheone?" Serel asked. "Please tell me you didn't stay at the dorm and read all day."

Tempted to stick her tongue out at him, the dignity of her position caused Kheone to refrain from tactics better suited to a five-year-old child. Though, to be honest, she probably would have stayed at the dorm all day to read had she not chosen to go to the museum and join the others here.

"I can have interests outside the mission, you know."

"Sure, you *can*. You just haven't showed us you *do*."

"Well, I went to Nelson-Atkins."

"The place with the shuttle-cocks?"

Serel snickered. Kheone sighed. Sometimes, the rest of the gathering was no more mature than twelve-year-olds, but she refused to roll her eyes.

"That's the one. It's a wonderful collection, and I see something new every visit."

Kheone grieved for all the angels had lost. But when she stood in front of a wondrous work of human ingenuity, hope filled her. Even if the angels never found a way home, this place had beauty despite the pain, maybe even because of it. There was a chance the angels could learn something from these divinely limited beings.

"Wait, you've been there more than once?"

"As I said, I can have interests outside of the mission." She smiled at him sweetly, as though she did not want to take his arm and bash him over the head with it.

"You surprise me, Kheone."

"Then you're too easy to surprise."

He burst out laughing, finally earning the attention of the other two angels. She liked Serel, always had. Out of all the angels in the gathering, he invariably had a kind word or a joke to lighten the mood. He was a better healer than a fighter, but yesterday had proven he was more than capable of having her back.

"Maybe you're right," he said, sipping at the beer the bartender had placed in front of him. "But wouldn't that be better than the opposite?"

"What is Kheone right about?" Maj asked.

Serel merely shook his head. Kheone lifted her glass in salute. He was right. It was remarkable, given the many years they had been alive, to know you have not seen everything, to still be surprised by the world.

Emric glanced between Serel and Kheone. Whispering something to Maj, they took a small sip of their beer before excusing themself. There wouldn't be a better time to figure out what had Emric's hackles up. Kheone turned to Maj.

"Spill the beans, Maj. Emric's hostility isn't going to get them any points from me, and the Archangel doesn't put up with this kind of crap. What did I do?"

Her battle buddy sighed. "I don't want to speak out of turn..."

"I'm asking as your friend, not your leader. What you say at The Cheesecake Factory stays at The Cheesecake Factory, okay?"

Maj smiled a little then. Kheone had wanted this excursion to open up new avenues of communication, build new bonds. What she said next put that in jeopardy. Hopefully, The Cheesecake Factory clause would soften the blow.

"I like Emric," Kheone said. "I really do, and I know it's been a hard adjustment for them, spending so much time on Earth surrounded by humans who don't understand our ways. But I can't tolerate insubordination. If they don't shape up, I'll have to bring the matter to the archangel, and you know what will happen then."

Maj's face grayed. The punishment for insubordination was a brutal beating followed by exile. The only worse ritual had been the Rite of Revelation, but none had invoked that since Lucifer's insurrection.

"Fine." Maj set her expression into resigned determination. "Em's upset because they feel we have to hide our relationship. Everyone knows the archangel frowns on fraternization, and yet here you are schtupping the boss."

The beer shot out of her nose, and she choked on what remained. Kheone hadn't known the human body could even accomplish these things simultaneously, for crying out loud. Serel patted her on the back and handed her some napkins to clean up. Maj pressed her lips together to keep from laughing, but her eyes twinkled merrily at Kheone's reaction.

"Schtupping?" Kheone choked out when her coughing fit subsided.

"Yeah. Or boinking, screwing, banging, knocking boots—"

Kheone held up a hand, and Maj stopped spouting euphemisms for sex. How did this rumor get started? She was rarely alone with Michael, and, until the past twenty-four hours, their relationship had only been coolly professional.

"Where on earth did Emric get the idea I was 'schtupping' the archangel? And who calls it schtupping?"

Serel wisely kept his mouth shut, but he patted her shoulder, offering condescending comfort.

"And they called me old-fashioned," he muttered.

"Well, aren't you? Why else would the archangel come swooping in to save you and then tear us new ones when you got hurt?" Maj asked.

"He did?" Kheone looked to Serel for confirmation. Her friend nodded. *Oh.*

If Michael had acted like an overprotective jerk, then she understood Emric's attitude. In fact, Emric had been a close confidant of the archangel in Heaven. Since being trapped on Earth, Michael seemed to rely more and more on Kheone's counsel. Sidelined from their established role and worried about being busted for fraternization because of their relationship with Maj, and the picture became clear.

Kheone turned to Maj but clamped her mouth shut when Emric reappeared from the bathrooms and returned to the bar, still glowering. One look at Maj and Emric paled.

"You told them, didn't you?"

"I had to, Em," Maj whispered.

"I'm only going to say this once, so both of you, pay attention. I have never had sex with our commander," Kheone said.

"Yeah, right," Emric grumbled.

She grabbed their face in her steel-strong fingers and forced their gaze to meet hers.

"I don't lie. And I don't care you and Maj are together."

Color flooded back into their face as Emric tried to sputter out a denial.

"Don't bother. I saw you when you entered, and I'm fine with it. We're stuck on Earth for now. If you bring each other some joy, I'm happy for you. I won't tell the archangel, but you should and soon. I'll go to bat for you when you're ready."

Emric slumped. She had taken away the anger fueling them. Maj slipped under Emric's arm and pressed a quick peck on their cheek.

"See, Em, I told you we'd be fine."

"Can we not talk about it anymore?"

"Of course, love."

"Thank you, Kheone," Emric said. "And I'm sorry. I've been a fool."

"Yes, you have. And I accept your apology." Kheone held out her hand, and Emric took it.

"Take me home, Maj. I've had enough fun," they said.

"Your wish is my command."

"What about dinner?" Serel asked.

"We'll grab something," Maj said.

They walked out together, still wrapped in each other's arms. Kheone tamped down the flare of longing. She'd never had that kind of bond with anyone. Sure, she had found occasional one-night stands and short flings, but never someone worth risking everything for.

"You won't tell Michael, will you?" Serel said in a low voice.

"I said I wouldn't." She signaled the bartender for another beer. If everyone doubted her today, then she needed it.

"Thank you. They're good together. Maj softens Emric's edges, and they give her a bit more confidence. How about you? Anyone special out there for you?"

She shook her head again and chuckled. "No. Managing you miscreants doesn't exactly give me time to develop a relationship. Last time I schtupped someone, the leaves were still green on the trees."

"I believe the term is sublimating."

Kheone nudged him with her shoulder but couldn't wipe the smile from her face. She really needed to go out with her friend more often.

"Thanks, Doctor Freud."

"Vat are friends for?" Serel said in an outlandish, pseudo-German accent. He ordered another round and checked his watch.

"Someplace to be?" Kheone asked.

"Yeah, but I wanted to talk to you."

"Oh? What about?"

He looked over his shoulder, the smile vanishing as he surveilled the room for eavesdroppers.

"I think I found something useful to our little predicament."

Her brow crinkled in concern, but she remained silent.

"There's this book in the library. I've skimmed it, and I think it has part of the answer to what happened in..." He glanced around again and lowered his voice. "The Second Fall."

"Really?" Kheone's heart picked up its pace, and her limbs went cold.

"Yeah. You're the next best linguist in our gathering. Can you meet me tomorrow before training?"

"Sure. Where?"

"Far side of the library. Then you can rift us in."

"You didn't take the book?"

"I thought it would be safer there. Don't worry. I hid it."

"Safer than a building full of angels?"

Serel shrugged. "You'll see."

"All right." Kheone couldn't keep the skepticism out of her voice, but she trusted Serel. She'd have all the answers in the morning.

"I hate to eat and run, but I try not to make a habit of breaking promises to a beautiful woman." He waggled his eyebrows suggestively.

"Go." She waved him away. "I'll see you in the morning."

Serel stood and saluted her before leaning down and planting a wet kiss on her cheek. "Goodnight, Kheone. May tomorrow bring more surprises."

Kheone watched him leave, a jaunty spring in his step.

"No luck, hon?"

The bartender returned and cleared the beer glasses. Kheone hadn't paid the woman much attention before. Now that she was alone, Kheone took a closer look. The bartender was pretty, round, and soft, with shining, dark brown eyes and hair as black as Kheone's was blue.

"Just meeting friends for a drink. Besides, he's not my type."

All angels were beautiful, blessed with God's grace, but Serel stood out. His chiseled features would have looked cruel if not for the faint laugh lines around his mouth giving away his good humor. His luscious auburn hair was thick and wavy, and his brown eyes sparkled with wit and intelligence.

And yet, Kheone had never thought of Serel as a potential bedfellow. No angel from her gathering was. She was their leader. Besides, Kheone had a very specific type, one with a name she rarely even dreamed about, let alone allowed to flit through her conscious mind. If only she could banish the tall, golden archangel from her dreams.

"His loss, but I hate to see someone as lovely as you go home alone."

Realization dawned on her. The bartender was flirting. It had been a while. Michael kept her busy the past year. Her sexual adventures were few and far between since the archangel had figured out they would be stuck on Earth for the indeterminate future. Most of them she'd picked up in bars and clubs. And every time, it had come as a pleasant shock anyone would want her. Kheone was used to thinking of her body as a tool to accomplish a mission, not as something to bring her pleasure. She often missed the early signals of the courting dance. Tonight, however, she'd found someone more forthcoming than most.

Kheone smiled at the compliment, and the bartender laughed, a warm, rich melody that rolled through her.

"My name's Faye. I get off in thirty minutes. If you meet me out front, you'll be getting off within the hour."

The laugh, the curves, Faye's beautiful, shining eyes should all be fuel for the fires of desire. Instead, the warmth of human connection and appreciation for a lovely woman filled her thoughts. Besides, Michael's recent behavior had her full attention. Kheone shoved aside any temptation.

"Best offer I've had in a long time," she said, placing her hand on the bartender's, "but not tonight."

The woman shrugged and gave her another smile.

"Should I bring the check?" she asked.

Kheone nodded and nursed her last beer. She settled the tab with a generous tip and headed out.

The stars twinkled in the night, joining the airplanes high above. An owl burst from a nearby tree and soared noiselessly into the sky as she crossed the courtyard. The hum of car engines filled the air from the streets surrounding the restaurant. Icy needles of wind punched through her jacket, and she shivered. When she'd been a full-fledged angel, the heat, the cold, the wind, the rain, none of it had bothered her. Now Kheone had to worry about sunstroke and hypothermia. Everyone did, except Michael. Being an archangel had more perks than she had realized.

A small shadow separated from the darkness under the bushes and approached, amber orbs reflecting the meager light from the lamp in the courtyard. Kheone tensed, reaching for her boot and the blade tucked within.

"Meow," said the shadow. Its form became more distinct as it came closer.

A cat, small and black, wound itself around the legs of the unoccupied tables and chairs.

"Here, kitty, kitty." She clicked her tongue, hoping the cat would respond. "Here, machka."

Cat in a language she had not used in centuries. The feline came running up to her. Kheone crouched on the pavement and stroked its sleek fur, making soothing noises.

"Hello there, cat." She scratched behind its ears. "Where did you come from?"

"Prrr."

It was all the answer she was going to get. Another shiver passed through her. She needed to head home, the warmth of the blankets on her bed calling for her.

"Good kitty," she said and took a few steps away.

Kheone opened a rift and walked through. The little cat chased after her, barely making it through before the opening snapped shut, singeing off the hairs on its tail. Yelping, it darted off before she could ensure the creature had suffered no further damage.

Chapter 7

The smell of snow hung ripe in the frigid night. Low-hanging clouds blocked the moon and stars, leaving only the lamps surrounding the campus buildings and lining the walkways to light Shax's path. Of course, his cat's eyes did not need the light. Shapes which would be dim and blurred to humans were clear and vivid.

Shax sheltered under a bush and examined his tail. The smell of burnt fur filled his sensitive nose without the coppery odor of blood. He gave the tip of his tail a tentative lick with his tongue and immediately regretted it. Burnt fur tasted worse than it smelled.

He crawled out from under the bush and trotted down the block. Finding a shadowed corner, he transformed back into his human form. The frigid night seeped under his jacket, licking at his skin, and a quarter-sized spot on his ass stung like a bitch. He pulled out his phone and found a twenty-four-hour diner nearby. Thank God for college students.

Staying in the shadows, his long strides ate up the distance to the diner. He slid into a booth and ordered coffee, the tips of his fingers numb from the few minutes' walk. When the server returned with the mug, he cupped it in his hands to warm them.

Shax flexed his warmed hand at his waist, once again reaching for the missing obsidian blade. Most days, he was glad it was gone. Damned thing sang with death and despair. But without his blade, he had no chance to complete the contract. There had to be some other way.

Anything he did to her right now would mean her eventual resurrection after the angels fixed the Gates. Lucifer would be more forgiving if he tried something, anything, to rid him of the angel, even though Shax would have to do it all over again at a later date. Pleading a lack of means would go over like a punk rock band at a country music festival. He needed to figure out how to fulfill Lucifer's bidding if he wanted to avoid spending the next century or two or ten in agony over one trivial angel. He'd already experienced enough misery at the Prince's hands.

The server filled his cup once more. He savored the bitter warmth as another option wriggled through his brain. Shax could run, put as much distance as possible between him and this city, and stay the fuck away. If he never saw Kheone again, he would have—what was the term those shady politicians used on TV shows? Plausible deniability. Should it take eons to repair the Gates, he might forget he had ever seen her.

Yeah, right.

Maybe the compulsion would release him someday, but Kheone's face stayed with him, haunting his dreams and calming his nightmares. Lucifer had whispered her name to a coin and ordered her death. Once, Shax had every intention of fulfilling the order. But as he'd pressed his obsidian blade to her throat, Shax had looked into her silver eyes. Eyes that never held a trace of fear in them, only anger and, sometimes, pity. Eyes that would meet death with the same courage she met life. And he'd been unable to kill her.

Oh, sure, the Gates had exploded in a torrent of fire, providing a reasonable excuse for her continued survival. But he'd already loosened his grip on the dagger. In his heart, Shax knew something deep inside him had decided in the moments before the Gates fell to spare Kheone. He could try to fool Lucifer, but he'd never fool himself.

Rising, he pulled out a twenty and dropped it on the table. The voice telling him to find the angel and kill her may have vanished, but the compulsion to do so was a mere thought away. He allowed his defenses to drop and tapped into the knot of awareness in his brain. A shining filament tugged him back to Kheone.

The best he could do for the moment was to keep watch. Kheone and her ilk were at least predictable. For example, he could predict with one hundred percent certainty if they discovered him, he'd be dead. It would probably happen instantaneously, which was a far better fate than if Aeshma should find him. Looked like his cat form was going to get a workout. As soon as he found a dark shadow, he changed.

The first tiny snowflakes fell as he wandered through the neighborhood, catching on his fur and muting the noises of the night. Shax followed the draw of his connection with Kheone to what he assumed was a dorm. A clock tower in the middle of campus rang out twice. With a resigned sigh, he found an evergreen bush with a clear view of the entrance and huddled under it. He would wait her out.

Tik-tok, tik-tok. His tail measured time, and his eerie amber eyes glowed as they caught the light coming from the lamps dotting the campus. Grateful for his fur coat in this cold, his eyelids became heavier, and he slept.

A grumbling engine and an annoying mechanical scraping woke him. The snowplow continued its work down the road. The gray light of the early morning lit the snow which had accumulated while he slept, lending a ghostly blue tint to the crisp air. A glaring rectangle appeared in the middle of the porch, and Kheone stepped outside, glancing around as if worried someone would jump out at her. She walked off. Shax waited a moment and followed her footprints through campus.

He turned a corner. Kheone stood by a blocky, four-story building, rough-hewn stones framed by concrete supports. The tall, narrow windows were dark in the early morning. A nearby lamp cast its golden glow upon her shining hair and threw her face into shadow. A portrait of light and dark, hope and despair, love and hate. Shax took a few steps toward her, his own loneliness drawn to hers.

Shax missed company. Sure, he could entice nearly anyone he wanted into bed. It was great for a night or an afternoon or, occasionally, a morning. But he did not have any companions, let alone friends. A few days ago, he had killed one of the few demons he counted as something resembling a friend. Hinndal had not deserved his fate, but Shax had no choice, not if he wanted to enjoy his freedom while it lasted.

Before he could catch Kheone's attention, a low, ominous note reverberated through the air, echoing off the buildings around him. A shiver of dread started at the top of his spine and traveled down, stealing his breath and stopping him dead in his tracks. What the—

He had heard that sound before. He still heard it in his nightmares. Shax swept his gaze around, trying to find the source. Shit, this could not be happening again.

The musical tinkling of falling glass drew his attention skyward. A large object fell from the top floor right above where Kheone sat. His paws moved before he could think, and they changed into human feet mid-stride. Shax launched himself at Kheone, knocking her into the snow just before the sickening thud of a body dropped three feet from them, spewing angelic blood. The snow gleamed with the shimmery and opaline substance, and so did they.

Kheone stared at him with eyes wide and mouth agape. She shoved the heel of her hand into his chin, rattling his teeth. Pain shot through his skull, and his vision grayed at the edges. He rolled, used his legs to push her off him, and scrambled away.

She barreled toward him, teeth gritted, a bull chasing a matador's cape. A second note sounded, louder and expanding. He covered his ears, and Kheone's momentum carried her into him, knocking him off his feet. A bright light bloomed above them, brighter than the sun, removing all shadows for an eternity of an instant.

Pressure forced them to stay on the ground, and blackness followed, so complete it rivaled the depths of the abyss itself. The icy ground against his back, the warm, heavy weight of the angel, and a body full of pain told him he wasn't dead. Shax blinked, clearing the red afterimage of the explosion, and looked up. At least, he thought it was up.

Kheone filled his vision, silver eyes snapping with rage and contempt, her proud features contorted into something out of the worst nightmares of Hell. And he should know; he was one. She wrapped her hands around his neck and squeezed. On her throat was a small, dark scar, a reminder he'd almost killed her, had spared her life. He could not hurt her any more than he could grow his wings back and fly away. Shax reached up and grasped her wrists but offered no further resistance. Sparkles flooded his vision as he fought unconsciousness.

Chapter 8

Kheone would recognize those haughty features anywhere, painted in her memory, as permanent as the blue-tipped, black wings tattooed across her back. The harsh lines of his chiseled jaw and amber eyes, darkened in despair, fueled her nightmares. Some mornings she awoke with the cold edge of obsidian on her throat and the smell of leathery wings wrapped around her. There had been no sign of Shax since. Her hopes of punching him in the nose faded, appeased only by the fact he must have burned up in the Second Fall. But then the dirtbag had tackled her to the ground, intent on finishing the job the explosion a year ago interrupted.

She wrapped her hands around the demon's throat, triumph coursing through her body. The tables had finally turned. Fueled by their last encounter, their first encounter, and every encounter in between, wrath rose in Kheone's breast, a fiery rush urging her to end him, clouding her vision and her judgment. Serel's sightless eyes accused them both as she wrestled with the demon who had caused his demise. Shax deserved death for his role in this. He deserved death merely for existing. All demons deserved death.

He wheezed and choked as she strangled the life out of him. His powerful hands gripped hers, but Shax did not fight back. He did not claw at her, kick at her, or try to buck her off.

He pulled in a last, desperate breath when she adjusted her hands to speed the process.

"I didn't do it," he croaked, all the usual spitefulness gone. "I swear."

"What? Swear to God?" Cruel coldness in her words, Kheone tightened her grip, and Shax's hands fell away.

"Remember. Sound."

Sad that those would be his last words. What sound—oh. That sound. Twice in her memory, she'd heard this specific doom-filled note, now and...

Her hesitation was all Shax needed. Before she could place the note, he pushed her over with his legs, holding her hands above her head, his entire weight keeping her flat on the ground. But unlike him, she fought, bucking and wriggling, trying to dislodge him.

He coughed. "We have a bigger problem, Blue."

"Don't. Call. Me. That," she spat.

"For Christ's sake, stop!" he said, voice hoarse from her not-so-tender ministrations.

"You have no right to invoke God's name."

"Kheone, listen to me. I didn't kill your friend. You saw. I was down here when the explosion went off. He was up there. How would I have done this?"

"You set the bomb and ran. And Serel—" Her voice caught on a sob. "Why him? He was a healer, a scholar. He never hurt anyone."

"I didn't do it!" His voice echoed off the buildings.

"Bull!"

Anger flared in his eyes, their amber color now resembling the orange glow of the inferno. He adjusted his grip, holding both her hands in one of his. She only needed a second, and she'd be able to break free. Kheone suppressed the smile that fought to escape as she tasted her upcoming victory. Shax reached over with his free hand and grabbed a shard of glass from the sidewalk.

She hissed as he shoved the shard into her open palm, drawing it down. Blood dripped off her wrist. He tossed the piece of glass to the side, a streak of black blood on his own palm, and grasped her hand in his, intermingling their blood.

"I swear to you, Kheone, I had nothing to do with the explosion that expelled us from the celestial realm, nor with the death of Serel. I swear on Lucifer's throne and the remains of my soul."

A blood pact. If he lied, he died a true death and disappeared into oblivion. She stilled. Golden light radiated from where their hands met, and warmth flowed through her, stealing her breath. She blinked, and the wound and the light vanished.

"Good. Promise not to kill me yet?" he asked.

Kheone nodded, and he let go. She examined where the wound should be. Nothing but a faint sense of loss where he had touched her. A remnant of their new bond? Shax stood and offered her a hand. She glared at him and rose on her own.

"The same magic destroyed the Gates." Shax's voice was oddly calm, considering she had been a hair's breadth from slaying him. Perhaps he was used to it. "I was otherwise occupied then, too, if you recall. I don't have the mojo to work that kind of magic."

Recognition dawned. She'd heard the sound the instant before the Gates toppled. Heaven above, Shax was right. No single demon would have the strength to set off such a devastating explosion.

"Well?"

"Just waiting for you to drop dead or lightning to strike. Whatever," she said.

"You still don't trust me?"

Kheone rubbed at the scar on her throat, her reminder of the last time she let Shax get close. She stared him down, keeping her gaze cold and steady and refusing to answer his inane question. He shrugged and turned to walk away.

It hit her. She had a rare opportunity to interrogate a demon. None ever seemed to survive the raids Michael planned. Perhaps Shax would have some answers not only to what happened tonight but also the day a year ago when they fell from the celestial realm in a blazing storm. Or perhaps she could tease out some clue as to what the demons were doing. Because her gut told her they were up to something.

"Wait!"

He glanced at her over his shoulder, brows raised in question.

Voices floated toward them from around the corner, and footsteps pounded. Her gathering would kill a demon without hesitation, and Michael would know immediately Shax was no human. She had to get him away from the scene or risk losing whatever information he carried.

Kheone opened a rift behind him, the red light glinting off the glass strewn across the sidewalk and making the snow glow like a hellscape. She shoved Shax through and into a locked utility room in the basement of their gym, protecting him from the oncoming storm of angels. The rift closed with the sizzling snap of a static discharge. Shax glared at her, anger and shock warring for control of his expression. She would deal with him later if she could get the others off his scent.

She had closed the rift not a second too soon. The gathering of angels came charging around the opposite corner, Michael in the lead, golden and furious. Wordlessly, he sent pairs off in every direction before approaching Kheone at a run.

"Lieutenant, are you injured?" His arms grasped her shoulders as he raked his gaze over her, looking for any injury with an intensity she had not seen before.

Kheone looked down and finally noticed the glimmer of Serel's blood streaked her from head to foot.

"The blood isn't mine, Archangel. It's Serel's." Once again, her voice caught on the name of her friend.

"Have you swept the area?" He let go and withdrew a step. She shivered as the cool air replaced his warm touch.

"Not yet."

Michael looked down upon her with disappointment chiseled into his brow. She cringed away. Hopefully, he would give her a chance to explain once she interrogated Shax. The archangel knelt over Serel's body, ignoring the blood spread over the sidewalk. He moved the body around, pulling clothes out of the way to get a better look at the wounds. Finally, Michael closed his eyes, hands on Serel's body.

"Tell me what happened, Kheone." His voice was soft, almost sad. But Michael did not get sad.

"I was supposed to meet Serel. There was an explosion, and his body fell from the library."

If she left out the rest, was it technically lying?

"That is all?"

Shoot, he was calling her bluff. She had one more piece of information to grant him and hoped he didn't ask too many questions.

"The explosion might be connected to the Second Fall."

Michael's eyes shot open, and he frowned at her. "What evidence do you have?"

"I heard a sound just before the explosion, same one I heard then."

"Are you certain?"

Her intel came from two unreliable sources: her memory of the day the Gates fell and a demon. Kheone shook her head.

Michael stood, brushing snow and dirt off his knees. He peered at her, doubtful.

"I find it unlikely Serel's death is related to the Second Fall."

Good, the doubt was over her conclusion, not her word. Guilt washed over her. When he found out she had held something back, Michael would be pissed.

"Until we have proof of their connection, we will proceed as though this is an isolated incident," the archangel continued. "I have everything I need for now. Take Serel's body to the dormitory while the others finish their sweep. I will clean up this debris and call off the authorities. Join me on the fourth floor of the library once your duty is complete."

"Yes, Archangel."

Michael turned his attention to the glass on the ground, a small frown turning down his lips and creasing his forehead. With a wave of his hands, the shards floated up to the broken window and reassembled themselves. She missed being able to do things like that.

Kheone hoisted Serel's limp body over her shoulder and performed the only talent still available to her. She walked through the rift to Serel's room and placed the angel, much lighter in death than in life, on his bed. At sundown, the angels would gather to sing as his body faded into dust.

"I'm so sorry, Serel. I wish this hadn't happened to you."

Kheone smoothed his hair from his brow and covered him with the blanket she found at the foot of his bed. She hadn't lost an angel from her gathering since the Second Fall, whether from pure luck or her excellent training regimen. Kheone had lost compatriots in battle too many times to count, but this one hurt more than the others.

Serel was her friend. They'd laughed together last night. And now he was dead.

With no time to deal with her grief, she shoved it down deep and opened another rift, joining Michael in the library. The eerie red light from emergency exit signs greeted her as she stepped onto the fourth floor, as did an odd tingling on her skin from the leftover angel magic. Serel must have fought back, somehow. Kheone followed the sound of feet scuffling in the far corner and discovered Michael flicking a flashlight over empty shelves. Books of all kinds lay strewn across the floor as though an earthquake had knocked them off the shelves.

"Will we be able to clean this mess before the librarians show up for work?" Kheone asked, her soft voice only getting a grunt of acknowledgment from the archangel. It wasn't important right now. She sighed. "What have you found?"

"The wounds upon Serel's body were likely the result of the explosion and the subsequent fall, except for two penetrating wounds in his abdomen. I cannot tell if these were the cause of death, if he died upon impact, or if the explosion killed him."

There were too many questions. But why, for all that was holy, did today's explosion mirror the one condemning all the angels and demons caught in the wasteland to walk the Earth as near-mortals? And what did Shax have to do with it, if anything at all?

"None of this makes sense," she said, drawing Michael's sharp gaze.

"We shall see, Lieutenant. Do you have your flashlight?"

Kheone pulled out a penlight. Michael looked high. She looked low. They came to a section where there were no books for a five-foot radius, a perfect circle of calm in the midst of destruction. This was the epicenter of the explosion.

"Why was he here before the library opened?" Michael asked.

"We were supposed to meet outside. He said he'd found something he wanted to show me."

"What?"

"I don't know. A book, obviously, but he never mentioned the title."

"Hmm." He glanced out the window. Red and blue lights flashed outside. "It seems the authorities have taken an interest. I shall take care of them. The search is yours, Kheone. Others will join you shortly to assist. Report to me when you have finished."

Piercing sirens filled the air when Michael opened a rift and stepped through. They cut off abruptly as the rift disappeared.

Kheone continued up and down the aisles, looking for clues. A flash of gold caught her attention. There was a bit of something reflecting the beam of her flashlight under a bookshelf. She got down on her hands and knees and reached under the shelf. Her fingers closed gingerly on a cool, hard object with jagged edges. She sat on her heels and examined her find. A bit of brown pottery with symbols inscribed in gold leaf rested neatly in her palm, taking up most of the area. The edges curled up, telling her it was part of a cylinder or cup. She didn't recognize the symbols off the top of her head, but she would bet her immortal life they were part of a spell.

Kheone flattened to the floor, the industrial carpet failing to cushion the press of it into her hips, and swept her flashlight around, looking for any other pieces. Another glint caught her eye, one bookshelf over. Crawling a few feet, she reached under the shelf and felt around. She hissed as her fingers touched the sharp, hard fragment. It was almost too hot to hold.

This piece was much smaller, an irregular shape about the size of a quarter. A symbol inscribed on the fragment glowed red. Messenger was the direct translation. Angel was the meaning. And it reacted to her presence.

Tucking the pieces into her pocket, she spent a few more minutes searching. Either whoever had killed Serel cleaned up the evidence, or the explosion destroyed it. Another rift opened, and Maj stepped through with a few others. Her face wet with tears, she walked up to Kheone and pulled her into an embrace.

Kheone fought her own tears. Now wasn't the time, not for her. She still had a demon to interrogate, pieces of a puzzle to decode, and a report to make. Maj looked at her with a question on her lips.

"I will mourn later," Kheone said before she could ask.

Maj nodded and dashed away the tears leaking from her eyes. "Okay, let's prove just how divine we are and get these books back on the shelf. Kheone, go get some rest. You look like death warmed over."

Her friend walked off, directing the others to various piles of books. Kheone opened a rift to her room. She couldn't rest yet. Kheone had a caged demon to question.

Chapter 9

He wasn't dead. Yet. He would have bet good money on this encounter leading to his immediate demise.

Shax slumped down to the smooth concrete floor, his back to a wall. He stared at the dreary, industrial beige wall where a few minutes ago, a rift had closed on Kheone's smug face. Surrounded by cleaning supplies and stacked tables and chairs, his own breathing sounded unnaturally loud in the stuffy confines of the room. The musty air held a tang of bleach, adding a strange note to the metallic taste of fear in his mouth.

Kill her or run. Those were his choices. And his sorry ass had gone with Door Number Three: save her life.

What was wrong with him? Shax cradled the hand he had cut to make the blood pact, his other thumb stroking where the gash had been. His body still tingled where they had touched, and a lightness of being he hadn't felt since he called Heaven home suffused him.

Heaving a great sigh, he stood up and tried the door handle. Locked. Shax put his shoulder to the door, trying to force it. Still no luck. He transformed into his cat form, to no avail. There were no windows and only a small drain in the middle of the floor, too small for a cat to squeeze through. The only way in or out was the locked steel door.

The cheap fluorescent light flickered. Shax leaned his head against the wall and looked up at the struggling fixture. He was not ready to die, but she deserved to kill him. After all, the last thing she remembered about him was *he* tried to kill *her*. That took the fucking cake, killed by the very angel Lucifer had sent him to eliminate. Irony was a bitch, and Shax suspected God was, too.

Why did he even care what she thought of him? He had needled her from the first moment he'd seen her, looking down her nose as their masters had exchanged prisoners. The look on her face when he'd slit the condemned demon's throat was something he would carry with him to the end of days.

Mostly horror and disgust, he had also seen disappointment. They had been enemies ever since. Shax had tempted souls from under her nose, damning them to the nonexistent mercies of Lucifer, and picked more than his fair share of fights with Kheone. Her opinion of him mattered not one bit.

The tiny voice in the back of his mind chimed in. *Keep telling yourself that, dickhead.*

Lost in his thoughts, he almost missed the subtle hint of ozone in the air warning of an imminent rift. He grabbed the end of a broken broom, the first thing he touched. Rising, he prepared as best he could for what came next.

Kheone stepped through, purple rings of exhaustion under her reddened eyes, her silver irises dulled by grief.

"Hello, blackguard."

"You need to work on your insults, Blue."

He'd expected to get some sort of response out of her. Anger, annoyance, anything to chase away the fatigue rolling off her in waves. But she only leaned against the wall across from him, stiff-shouldered and wary.

"Not in the mood. Let's get this over with. You tried to kill me. Give me one reason not to return the favor."

Just because he had stayed his hand a year ago didn't mean shit to the angel. She should be grateful. Without him, she could have died in the blast or been smashed by the other angel's body today. Without him, she wouldn't have realized the connection between this murder and their exile.

"I didn't try to kill you. I saved your life."

A derisive snort brought the barest twinkle to her eyes.

"I did. If I hadn't been there, that body would've fallen right on you, and you'd have two dead angels on your hands." He smirked at her. "Well, not *your* hands."

"Not now. Before."

He wondered if she would remember. His own memories had been fuzzy at first, only Kheone coming through loud and clear.

Shax gave her his best roguish grin and tried to lighten the mood. "The Devil made me do it?"

"Ugh." Her sharp tone was an improvement over the dull one of a moment ago.

"I had my orders." No use explaining he could not carry those orders out. She would never believe him. "Circumstances have changed. With the Gate gone, I am no longer bound by Lucifer's command. You can trust me."

"Not likely."

"How about because I'm the only other witness and the only one who knew your friend's death and the destruction of the Gates are related."

She straightened from the wall, never taking her eyes off him.

"If you didn't have anything to do with Serel's death—"

"I didn't. Blood oath, remember?"

"—then you're of no use to me. Give me a better reason to keep you alive. Demons are too cowardly to work alone. Tell me who you're working with, and maybe I'll let you go."

"Satan's balls, Blue, I've been trying to stay off the radar. I'm not working with anyone."

"So, what I'm hearing is you'd rather die now than later?" Her words took on a menacing tone, and she reached for something in her boot. If memory served, she kept her favorite knife there.

He had to give her something. "I'll help you."

Kheone raised her eyebrows, disbelief replacing distaste, but she did not draw her blade.

"Liar," she said.

"Off the top of my head, there are only about a dozen beings capable of that kind of magic on their own," Shax said. He ticked them off on his fingers. "Lucifer. The Dukes of Hell. Archangels. A few sorcerers."

She scoffed.

Shax continued, ignoring her incredulity. "Lucifer is still chained. Rumor has it that there's only one Duke left on Earth. If an Archangel is involved, I'll eat my coat. So we're looking at a powerful sorcerer, some other entity we're not tracking, or a weird alliance between these beings. Believe what you want, but you need my help."

"I still don't trust you."

"I know you don't, but you have nothing to fear from me."

"We have been enemies since the beginning of civilization, Shax. I have everything to fear from you."

"I never wanted to be your enemy, but no demon can deny Lucifer. When he ordered me to cross my sword with yours, to steal the souls you'd redeemed, to kill you, I had to. With the Gates gone, he can't control me. I am here of my own free will." Shax looked around the small room and grinned his roguish grin at her again. "Well, mostly."

Kheone peered at him, judging his words. After a moment, she nodded, and for a fleeting second, he thought he detected the faintest upturn to her lips.

"Help me find the bastard who killed Serel, and not only won't I kill you now, I'll make sure no one else will, either. Not even Michael."

Shax rubbed at his face. He had slept little, waiting under the bush for Kheone to do something. And then fought for his life. There was nothing he could do about it now but accept his new fate and come up with some way to get out of this mess alive.

"Fine," Shax said through gritted teeth. "You keep Michael, or any other angel, from killing me, and I promise to help you find who killed your friend."

She nodded.

"You first. Tell me what you found out," he said.

Kheone dropped her gaze, addressing her feet.

"We're not sure what killed Serel. Could be the fall or the explosion or something else."

Kheone reached into a pocket and pulled out two fragments of pottery with symbols inscribed in gold leaf.

"Found these. The only symbol I know is *angel*."

When Shax reached for them, she curled her fingers around the pieces. He dropped his hand and examined them. Something about them was familiar, but he couldn't put his finger on it.

"Have you shown these to anyone?" he asked.

"Not yet. Michael left before I found them."

"Would you mind transcribing the symbols on them for me?"

"Okay."

A long, awkward silence descended into the storeroom. Kheone looked everywhere but at Shax. He could not keep his eyes off her.

"How are we going to do this?" he asked when the quiet was too much to bear. "Are you going to let me go?"

Kheone bit her lip in thought. Something about the simple gesture made her vulnerable. She had been his nemesis since forever, projecting only strength with the occasional burst of anger whenever he wormed his way under her skin. He never imagined her vulnerable. Two beasts fought in head. One wanted to take advantage of her exposure, strike at her, kill her, even. The other wanted to curl around her and protect her.

"I know a place where we can meet in private. I'll take you there now."

Kheone straightened and offered a hand to help him up, the same one he had stabbed to form the pact. Shax took it and found himself mere inches from her. He tamped down the twist of longing that snaked through him at her simple touch. Grief and fear and doubt all vied for control on her stately face. Mostly, she looked tired. He wanted to pull her into his arms and offer what comfort he could. His better judgment quashed the impulse. It would only earn him a knife in the belly.

Wordlessly, Kheone opened a rift. Shax walked through, his steps muffled by grass. They stood in a small stand of trees. People hurried by, no one lingering on this cold, cloudy morning. A large Neoclassical building dominated his view, a gigantic badminton birdie on the vast lawn. He pushed aside the other name for the object, knowing he would start giggling like a teenage boy. He recognized it as the museum where he had found Kheone.

The angel walked over to a tree and patted the rough bark.

"Meet here every evening at seven, but not tonight."

Right, angel funeral. Held the sunset after death. If he was sober enough, his furry alter-ego might make an appearance. The plan was to be anything but sober, but his plans had not turned out well lately.

"If I'm not here, I'll leave a message in the branches. If you can't make it, leave a message for me. Michael doesn't come here."

"Got it." Shax turned to go, but something in her posture caused him to hesitate. He looked behind him. "It will be okay, Kheone. We'll figure out who killed your friend."

"I know we will. I'm just not sure I'm going to like the answer."

"Perhaps not, but the Valkyrie bitch I know won't let that stop her."

"Regretting your promise yet, Shax?" This time a wry smile graced her mouth.

"As soon as the words were out of my mouth."

"Goodbye, turd goblin."

"That was almost a good insult."

Kheone stepped through the red rift and disappeared from view.

Shax gazed at his hand, still tingling from her brief touch. Christ, he needed a drink. Judging from the position of the sun, it was mid-morning. Should be somewhere open for service by now. He found a seedy-looking bar halfway to the motel and claimed a spot in the establishment, as far from the other patrons as he could get. There was plenty of space at the ill-kept bar. He signaled to the bartender and placed one hand down on the bar. It came away sticky. Sometimes he hated people.

"A burger and the cheapest bottle you've got," he said when the man finally answered the summons.

"Bottle of what?"

"Vodka, whiskey, whatever's cheap. All I want to do is get drunk and stay drunk."

Drinking alone in his crappy motel room was less appealing than drinking in this crappy bar. At least he had some company here.

"You driving?" asked the bartender.

"Don't even own a car."

"Fine. A burger and a bottle of corn whiskey coming up. Pay first."

Shax gave the bartender most of his cash and poured a glass when the man finally delivered the bottle. He drank down the contents, the cheap alcohol scorching his throat. Repeating the process twice more before his burger arrived, his nerves settled. The voice in his head telling him this whole deal with Kheone was a horrible idea mellowed into a soothing whisper.

Chapter 10

The silence of her room weighed on Kheone, alone at last with her thoughts and her grief. She still had so much to do before she could rest, but the urge to abandon her duties and crawl into bed washed over her. She compromised with herself and dropped into the desk chair, staring at the print of Georgia O'Keefe's *Apple Blossoms* hanging on the wall.

The Shax she found today was not the same demon she had first met ten thousand years ago in the blackened wasteland of the Garden of Eden. That Shax was smug, callous, and merciless.

Tall and slender, the demon standing off to the side had caught her attention on the day they had met. His shock of white hair over a sharply sculpted face highlighted eyes glinting with bitterness in the sunlight of the blasted plain. A paradise no longer, Eden was merely a battlefield where the forces of good and evil duked it out, over and over, the result always a stalemate.

Midway between the Gate to Heaven and the Gate to Hell, a gathering of angels and a horde of demons had convened to exchange prisoners. Some Duke, who had long since disappeared, led a horde of demons surrounding three angels captured in the latest skirmish. Michael led the gathering of angels with one captive. Fear radiated from the duke as he kept glancing at the white-haired demon leaning against a large boulder.

This demon with leathery wings folded against his back seemed uninterested in the ceremony occurring a few paces away. He tossed a long dagger between his hands. Its dark blade absorbed the bright light permeating the entire area, throwing a shadow across his body. He caught her looking at him, and a seductive smile graced his full, pink lips.

"Like what you see, Blue?"

She pulled her gaze away and focused back on the task at hand. They had to be prepared for anything. Demons were untrustworthy.

He didn't seem to appreciate her easy dismissal of him.

"Name's Shax. You are?"

She ignored him some more.

He sighed, a big heavy release of breath meant to draw her attention. Kheone kept it right where it belonged. At least she did not have to worry about this halfwit while he jabbered at her.

"Bet you this nice, shiny dagger you can't guess what it's made of."

She did not care.

"You know what this dagger is missing?"

Kheone turned to look, unable to suppress her curiosity. Nothing seemed to be missing.

"Your blood, that's what's missing." Shax grinned triumphantly at her, knowing he had won this round.

Disgusted with herself for falling for his taunt, Kheone turned away again. She just needed to stand there, watching Michael's back, without letting these infuriating demons get under her skin. This punk seemed particularly good at pushing her buttons.

Her inattention merely egged him on.

"First mission, little angel?"

She clenched the pommel of her sword and fought the impulse to use it. Breaking the uneasy peace of this moment would ruin the chances of retrieving her fellow angels. His rude mouth needed a fist in it, and she would be happy to put hers there the next time they met. And she was not a little angel. She was as tall as he was.

When she did not respond, he continued, "Generous of the big guy to let you tag along."

Kheone kept her focus on Michael, a much more pleasant sight than the bedraggled demon. She watched as he sealed the bargain with the Duke, a blood oath which meant death for the one who broke it. The horde parted, allowing the three angels to walk into the waiting arms of the healers Michael had brought. In a flash of red-rimmed rifts, their compatriots whisked the freed captives away to Heaven's Gate, to safety.

The angels shoved their lone prisoner forward. Shax saluted Kheone with his blade when the Duke looked to him and swaggered to the front of the horde. The demon waited on their knees, face pale, still in chains. Shax pressed his black dagger to the demon's neck and locked his dead gaze on Kheone.

"No, please, I was—" the demon pleaded.

Without a word, Shax drew the dagger across the demon's throat and black blood spurt everywhere. In disgust, she turned to follow her gathering to their Gate.

"I never got your name, Blue. Did the archangels forget to give you one?" he called to her.

Try as she might, Kheone could not let this last, desperate jab at her pride stand. Her blue-black wings unfurled as she launched herself at him, drawing her sword. Forged in the heart of the sun from cosmic dust and quenched in the long-dry springs of Eden, the blade was light and heavy all at once, a contradiction in space and time. It gleamed like silver and was as thin as an atom. Unnamed angels did not receive such gifts. In fact, only one archangel gave out this gift, the hallmark of a Guardian Angel—Michael himself.

Amidst the catcalls and blood-curdling screams of the demon horde, Kheone shoved Shax up against the rock he had so casually leaned against a few moments before.

She held her blade against his neck. A wrong move on his part would cover her in black demon blood.

"My name is Kheone, you piece of filth. Never forget it."

Kheone pushed away from him and flew back to her own post.

He shouted after her. "You need to work on your insults."

His laughter had followed her all the way to Heaven's Gate.

The Shax she had seen today was…softer wasn't the right word, but something had tempered the base qualities in the demon she had known, leaving a being she might be able to work with. It was certainly easier to think about Shax than of the upcoming requiem.

With a groan, Kheone pulled out some paper and a pen from the desk. She reached into her pocket for the two pieces of pottery she had found in the library. The feeling she should know what they meant grew as she transcribed the markings. Maybe it was the lack of sleep over the past few days, or maybe it had something to do with her fading powers. She finished and folded the piece of paper. Frustrated at her lack of progress, she returned it to her desk drawer.

Perhaps Michael would have better luck making heads or tails out of the markings. If she kept to the bare facts and didn't mention the deal she had struck with a devil, everything would be fine.

Kheone dragged her leaden weight up the stairs and knocked on Michael's door. The archangel answered, only a towel wrapped around his lower body. His broad, muscular chest took up much of the doorway, and the towel barely covered what it needed to. He was easily the most handsome being she had ever seen, rippling muscles well-defined, and everything perfectly proportional. Before she could stop the errant thought, she wondered if even the parts she could not see were, too. Heat rose in her cheeks, and she tried to cover her surprise and embarrassment with an apology.

"I'm sorry, Archangel. I will return when you are ready."

Kheone turned to go, but Michael reached out and grasped her shoulder.

"No need, Lieutenant. I was not expecting you until later. Please come in and sit while I dress."

He stepped into the room, and she followed him, pulling the door shut behind her. Kheone walked over to the table, which doubled as a desk, and sat with her back to Michael. This embarrassment at near nudity was a new feeling, perhaps a condition of being corporeal for so long. Instead of viewing a physical form as merely a tool to allow her to move through this world and interact with the humans, she felt certain urges on a more regular basis than she had before. The bartender wouldn't have tempted her so last night, otherwise.

To distract herself, Kheone examined the papers on the table. In an attempt to help her after her injury and Serel's death, Michael had sketched out a patrol schedule. The archangel was a fierce warrior, but some of the skills required to operate a near-mortal army, with the logistics needed for rest, food, and travel, were difficult for him to grasp. Kheone often had better luck wrapping her head around the minutiae of management, which was one reason he placed her in charge of the Kansas City gathering. The other was her skill on the battlefield.

She picked up a pencil to fill in some blanks. Trying not to think too hard of a fully naked Michael behind her proved impossible, and all she achieved before he joined her was a seven-day calendar.

"I am not so incompetent at scheduling I was not able to write the days of the week." Michael even smiled as he said this.

A joke? The Archangel Michael knew how to make a joke?

Kheone had never heard him make a joke before. She had never seen him care about an underling the way he had when the demon knifed her in the kidney. Dizzy with all the new sides of him she'd met lately, as well as the new sides of herself she'd discovered, Kheone managed a weak smile in return.

"You have to start somewhere."

"Indeed." His eyes twinkled with a warmth she rarely saw. He reached out with a roughened finger and lifted her chin, forcing her to meet his gaze. "You look tired, Kheone."

She held her breath at this intimate touch, another oddity in the past few already strange days. Before today, Michael had only touched her during training, combat, or healing. His finger was cool on her skin, the opposite of how warm his hands had been when he had healed her.

"Serel was a talented healer and a reliable soldier. And my friend. I'll miss him."

"You cannot let the loss of one warrior weigh too heavily on you. Until we discover how to rebuild the Gate, we will lose many more." He removed the finger from under her chin, slowly, almost reluctantly.

Kheone put a little more distance between them, both physical and emotional.

"I haven't lost someone duty-bound to me in a while."

"It is our fate as leaders." Michael sat up tall in his chair, his voice all business now. "I thought you would be asleep. What brings you here?"

Kheone pulled the fragments out of her pocket once more. "I found these in my search of the library."

She handed them over. The piece which had burned her earlier lay inert, its magic apparently used up. Michael turned the fragments over in his palm and peered at the inscriptions.

"The symbol on the smaller one glowed, and it was hot to the touch," Kheone said. "They both look like part of a spell meant for angels."

He studied them for a moment more before looking at her. "I concur."

"Do you recognize the writing?"

Michael shook his head. "I led the Heavenly Host and rarely visited the realm of humankind. Written languages are not my forte."

"Is it what killed Serel?"

"I cannot tell with only two pieces."

A thought hit her. "What if there are more still inside his body?"

Michael rose and placed the pieces in the center drawer of his desk. Kheone's hands itched to hold them again. The rational part of her brain said they would be safest with Michael, but some instinct did not want them out of her sight.

"There are not. I would have found them when I examined him earlier. Do you have anything else for me?"

Only the word of a demon and a deal she knew would come back and bite her. "No."

"I will see you at sunset, then?"

"Of course." She rose and left.

Too little sleep and too many emotions left Kheone exhausted. Grief at Serel's loss, anger at Shax's return. Worry over Michael's recent behavior and shame at her bargain with the demon. There was something else, too, nameless and thrilling, which hummed through her blood. She was too tired to figure it out.

Kheone kicked off her shoes and slipped under the covers of her bed, but her roiling thoughts allowed no peace. Tears dropped from her eyes as she realized she would never hear Serel's kind voice, never feel his healing touch, never call for his aid for a member of the gathering, ever again. They had been lucky and had not lost a single member of their gathering despite their unrelenting hunt for demons until Serel.

And there was no guarantee she'd ever see her friend again. In the eons before the destruction of the Gates, the physical bodies of angels and demons were extremely resistant to death. Those destroyed in battle or the occasional accident merely regenerated in a painful but relatively quick process. Only a rare magical weapon could obliterate a soul. Lucifer and his Dukes wielded weapons like these, as did each archangel and a few of their chosen lieutenants.

Time would tell what happened now when an angel or demon died. Serel had a theory or two. Her favorite, the one she clung to, was their souls waited in Purgatory, lost until the Gates were rebuilt. For now, she would grieve Serel and hold on to the hope they would meet again in Heaven someday, knowing it was likely wishful thinking. That explosion reeked of power she did not understand, and she feared the nature of his death meant oblivion.

Eventually, tears wrung out of her, Kheone succumbed to exhaustion. She woke to a rumbling belly and a cool breeze blowing in from the still-open window. The clock by her bedside told her she did not have long to prepare for the requiem. Kheone took what few moments she had to run her fingers through her hair, brush her teeth, and wipe her face with a cool washcloth. She slipped into Serel's room with not a moment to spare and joined the circle of angels bathed in the pink light of the fading sunset.

The instant the sun sank below the horizon, all the angels' voices rose in a keening wail, and they beat their breasts in an ancient ritual of grief. The wail faded, and Michael's bass voice began the song, a single note, pure and clear. One by one, each angel joined in. Kheone added her sweet alto, weaving her voice in and out of the deeper voices before the sopranos added theirs. Once the last voice joined the choir, what had been a simple melody blossomed into a full-fledged harmony.

Kheone lost herself in the song, pouring her anguish into the music. Notes echoed off the bare walls in Serel's room and down the hall, creating a cyclone of sound around them. The song ended the way it began, and voices dropped out one by one, starting with Michael's. For a shining moment, a single, clear soprano lifted Serel's name up to Heaven. As the last note faded, so did Serel's body, leaving only silvery dust to vanish with the light.

Complete silence wrapped around the gathering until Michael's calm voice broke it.

"God be with you."

"God be with you," the angels replied and filed out.

Kheone hung back, Michael's stare burning into her. When the last angel's footsteps faded down the hall, he took a step toward Kheone before hesitating. Michael wasn't one to hesitate. He had thrown Lucifer into the Pit before word spread of the Morning Star's capture. Why had he paused now?

He reached out, slowly, as though afraid of startling her, and used his roughened thumb to wipe away the tears which had unknowingly coated her cheeks.

"Do not cry, Kheone."

"Why?" she asked.

Michael looked pained. "I do not like it."

He stepped closer, and Kheone held her breath, waiting, uncertain what she waited for. The immeasurable pain on his face ripped through her gut as though her own. Michael dropped his arm and blinked, tears shining in his eyes. He opened a rift behind him and retreated without another word.

Chapter 11

Shax's whiskey-addled brain had decided lingering in the bushes outside the angels' dorm was a great idea. He was pretty sure he pressed his luck being so close to the gathering, but he couldn't stop himself. The lure of angels singing had proven too great, at least to his drunk-ass self. Shax hadn't heard angels sing since his banishment to Hell.

A deep voice dismissed the angels after the last note faded. Must be Michael's. Something about the voice struck a chord in the recesses of his mind. Shax dug deep into his memories without luck. Michael was Lucifer's brother. Perhaps he merely sensed a familial resemblance.

The only sounds remaining in the courtyard outside the dorm were the whistling breeze in the leafless trees, the hooting of an owl, and the scratching of some small beast sensing his feline presence. He lifted himself onto his four paws, ready to leave, and stuck his nose out of the bushes. Caution had always been his friend, and it did not let him down this time, either.

Kheone rushed out of the building. Her face was slack with grief, and glistening tracks of her tears caught the meager light from the lamp in the middle of the courtyard. She collapsed onto the bench and hugged her knees to her chest, heaving with silent sobs.

The angel looked up into the crystal-clear night sky, staring at the stars, a vignette of anguish painted in muted grays, blues, and browns. Her pain called out to him. Before he could stop himself, he squeezed out from under the bush and padded over to her.

Shax sat at the edge of the sidewalk and stared at her. "Meow."

She started and grabbed for her boot knife. As her gaze locked on him, her shoulders relaxed. Her hand came away empty.

"Well, hello there, machka."

He blinked at her. She had called him that last night, too. When he did not immediately approach, she uncurled from her huddled position and slowly put her legs down. She held out her hand and clicked her tongue, making the summoning noise people had been using for thousands of years on the domestic feline.

Shax strutted over to her in his best cat fashion and twined himself around her ankles.

She scratched behind his ears. "Aren't you a brave kitty?"

"Prrr," was his only answer.

Kheone scratched under his chin and ran her hand down his back. He purred and occasionally meowed when she stopped giving him attention for a moment, mimicking actual cats. It was important his disguise held up to inspection, after all. Certainly, it wasn't because he enjoyed the affection she was lavishing upon him.

The door to the building opened again, and Shax dashed under the nearest bush. Kheone sighed and turned to deal with the interloper.

A slight angel stumbled outside, their hair mussed and eyes red.

"Yes, Emric?" Kheone asked.

They sniffed. "I, um, I just... Never mind. It can wait."

"I'm heading inside. The bench is all yours."

She smiled at them, a thin, tired line.

"Thanks, Kheone."

Kheone reached out and grasped the smaller angel's hand. She gave it a squeeze and headed inside. The other angel took her place on the bench, allowing the sobs to escape, unlike Kheone. Shax left before this growing knot of bothersome compassion led him to comfort another Goddamned angel.

Using the bushes as cover, he slunk away, only daring to walk in the open once the building was between him and the angel. Keeping his cat form, Shax made haste for the edge of campus. Knowing Michael, he likely spelled the boundary of the university to detect demons after the events of this morning.

He needed to get the taste of compassion, of grief, out of his mouth and out of his mind. Neither should occupy any of his attention, and the fact they did so now was beyond annoying. After all, his heart was notorious for leading him into trouble.

Shax summoned a cab to take him to the Power and Light District. The pulsing beat of dance music escaped into the bitter night, and even this early, drunk people staggered around. He hated dance music, but the need to quash the bee in his bonnet, which would not shut up, was more urgent. This place seemed perfect for leaving troubles behind. Strolling into a club, Shax sidled up to the bar and ordered a shot of tequila as the opening salvo against the urge to return to Kheone.

The first drink burned on the way down. The second settled the buzzing in his brain.

"Another," he shouted at the bartender.

He finally relaxed and took stock of his surroundings.

Sex perfumed the air, as intoxicating as the tequila. Young couples ground their bodies together on the dance floor, hands roving over curves and muscles. Lips met, and pairs would sneak off to darkened corners to fool around in the shadows. A couple exited to the alley behind the club and returned disheveled a short while later.

Grinning, Shax slouched on the bar stool. Lust, seduction, indulgence, and excess were familiar territory, the closest feeling he had to a home. He wasn't the only one trying to silence a bee in his bonnet tonight.

A curvaceous brunette wedged herself next to him, her shoulder grazing his arm. Her liberally applied flowery perfume overwhelmed the earthy undertones of desire. She turned her pretty face up to him, a shrewd smile on her full, pink lips. Shax returned the smile with his best dead-eyed stare, hoping to scare her off. She simply widened the smile and signaled the bartender.

"I'll have what he's having," she said.

The man poured her the same well-brand tequila Shax was drinking. She slapped a credit card on the bar.

"Let's start a tab. I'll pay for his next drink."

She downed the tequila like an old pro, although she looked twenty-two, tops.

"That's not necessary." Shax kept his voice bland, not wanting to encourage her any further.

"Not a problem. It's my soon-to-be ex's credit card. Found out today he cheated on me. Came here to blow his money, blow off some steam, maybe blow something else, too, while I'm at it."

Shax couldn't keep himself from laughing, his steely facade crumbling at this epitome of Midwestern womanhood trying to get a pity-fuck out of him. She was fearless, and he understood exactly where she was coming from. When his ex had cheated on him thousands of years ago, he'd led an entire village to ruin after weeks of wine-fueled debauchery, leaving only ashes and broken things in his wake. He was pretty sure he'd been the basis of the Greek god Dionysus. It was the last time he had cared about anything until—

He pushed away the thought. Shax hadn't planned on company, but who was he to refuse a gift when one fell into his lap? He gave in to the swirling sensuality of the club.

"Another round, then, to toast your imminent freedom." He waved the bartender over. "Limes and salt, too, please."

The woman tossed her long, brown locks over her shoulder and gave him a seductive smile, and she stuck out her hand.

"I'm Daisy."

He matched her smile and took the outstretched hand, stroking her knuckles with his thumb. She shivered, and her smile broadened.

"Shax."

"Like the basketball player?"

"Sure." Shax shrugged. It didn't really matter. He would likely never see the woman again after tonight. She could call him Jesus for all he cared.

The bartender slid a saltshaker down the bar and brought two more shots of tequila with lime wedges on the rims. Shax licked the back of his left hand between his thumb and forefinger, his eyes telling her there were other things he would rather be licking. Her gaze followed his tongue, her own darting out to lick her lips. He had her if he wanted her; she had made that clear from the beginning.

Shax dusted the wet spot with salt from the shaker and passed it to the woman.

"Cheers!"

"Cheers!"

She clinked her shot glass against his. They licked off the salt and downed the tequila. Biting into the sour-bitter lime, the woman shook off the burn. Her smile faded as a blonde woman approached, a disapproving glare on her otherwise lovely face.

"What are you doing?"

"Making new friends. Making Wade pay." She giggled at her play on words, the tequila working its magic.

A sigh escaped the blonde's red lips as she focused on Shax, judging him and finding him wanting. She leaned in to whisper to the brunette. Dammit, he had already forgotten the woman's name. His keen ears caught every word.

"You don't know this man. He could be—"

She cut off her friend and turned to him. "My friend wants to know if you're an ax murderer."

Shax laughed. The blonde was cautious and distrustful, listening to the little voice in her head saying he was bad news. She was smart.

"I have never murdered anyone with an ax." He kept his voice serious but let his amusement show as a small twist upward on his lips.

It was not a lie. He had never killed anyone with an ax. Shax preferred to use his dagger or his bare hands in a pinch. And most of those he had killed had been much less human than these young women. Lucifer didn't waste his most talented assassin on humans. He much preferred tempting them to killing them, proving humanity's unworthiness.

"Then I'll buy you another round."

"This is a bad idea," the blonde hissed to her friend when she thought Shax wasn't listening.

"If you don't like it, go find somewhere else to be."

She dismissed her friend by waving the bartender over and turning to Shax.

"Fine. Come find me when you're ready to go."

The blonde huffed off.

"Another round," the brunette announced loudly. The bartender studied her, then turned his attention to Shax.

"Last one for a bit," he said conspiratorially. The other man nodded and poured.

Her pretty pout disappeared when he took her hand. His long experience suggested she would be a much more effective distraction than an entire bottle of tequila. Staring into her eyes, he stroked the delicate skin with his tongue and smiled as she shivered from the intimate contact. After dusting the area with salt, they downed the shots quickly. Shax took the lime from his glass and pressed it to her lips. She bit down and swallowed, leaning in and grabbing his hand.

"Dance with me," she said.

Tugging with more strength than he expected, she led him out to the dance floor, where they added their own notes to the lust permeating the room. Shax lost himself in the rhythm, in her touch, in the scents all around, and the buzzing in his brain fell blissfully silent.

The brunette inched closer with every song, taking advantage of any opportunity to touch him. He let her, barely admitting to himself he liked the touch of another being. She pressed her entire body against his, pupils dilated and nearly breathless with desire. Resting her lips close to his ear, her breath tickled his skin.

"I know someplace a little more private."

Got her. Not like it had been difficult. The woman was primed for his seduction, looking to pay back her boyfriend. Revenge sex was one of his favorite kinds, the raw emotion adding a certain spice to the experience. And with the horrible buzzing gone, Shax was in the mood to indulge his carnal impulses.

His smile told her all the things he'd like to do to her in private. Blushing, she clutched his arm and led him past the restrooms. After a quick check over her shoulder, she opened a door marked *Employees Only*. A set of stairs led down into a basement hallway, and she hurried into the last room on the right.

"I used to work here. This room isn't used for much, and it locks. We won't be disturbed," she said, pulling the door shut behind her.

In answer to her unasked question, Shax took her in his arms, pressing their lips together. Soft and pliable in his hands, he breathed in deeply. Her scent of flowers and sex chased away the fingernails on a blackboard memory of Lucifer's compulsion.

Her fingers untucked his red t-shirt and slid underneath, playing lightly over the tight muscles and sparse hair. They danced around to his back and up, clinging to his shoulders. He shivered when they crossed all that remained of his glorious wings. The elaborate tattoo of cardinal-red angel wings was a reminder of when he had served God. Upon his Fall and bondage to the Prince of Darkness, they had become bat-like and leathery, the shame of it a curse. When those wings had burned off in his Second Fall, this tattoo had replaced them. God only knew why.

Shax trailed hard kisses down her neck as he worked the zipper of her lacy, electric blue minidress. Brushing first one strap off her shoulder, then the other, he tugged the dress down, letting the slight garment drop to the floor. She stood before him in a lacy bra which showed off her considerable cleavage nicely, the sparkly pendant she wore nestled between her breasts, and a thong to match. He ran his fingertips along the edges of the bra, and she shivered in anticipation.

"Oh, God," she moaned.

"God has nothing to do with it."

He slipped off his jacket and tossed it off to the side. A loud clink drew his attention to a silver coin spinning on the floor next to him. Shax blinked, and the hunger he had experienced a moment ago vanished like fog in the sunlight. Kheone. His stomach sank as his crap life flooded back, the haze of lust lifting, leaving him with only the angel on his mind.

The brunette—he tried once more to remember her name, but it was long gone—took a step toward him, a slight frown dampening the desire present a moment before. He held up a hand.

"I'm sorry," he breathed. "I can't. I—"

She reached out to him, cupped his cheek.

"Oh, come on, now. I very much think you can."

Shax spent a long second considering her offer. He could, he realized. He just didn't want to.

Retreating a step, he shook his head. "Sorry, sweetheart, not going to happen."

Her face reddened at the rejection, and she snatched her dress up from the floor. She yanked it on.

"Creep," she said under her breath as she stormed out of the room.

Shax picked up his jacket and the one-inch coin with a resigned sigh. The coin had done its job, reminding him why he was here and who was calling to him. He had a mission to complete and a promise to keep. How in the Nine Circles of Hell was he going to find who had killed Serel? He was no detective, and luck rarely favored him. He was a git for making that bargain.

Instead of heading into the club, he found a side exit and staggered back to his motel. The cold air of a Midwestern winter soon sobered him up. Goddammit. The whole point of this excursion had been to get drunk enough to forget these wretched feelings. A demon with feelings was a dead demon.

He passed through a quiet, darkened business district, the workers gone for the night. The echoey tap-tap of high heels on concrete drew his attention, and a rich tinkling laugh drifted through the black night, sending shivers up Shax's spine. In a blink, he transformed into his cat form and climbed the nearest tree, freezing in place. Two figures walked down the sidewalk arm-in-arm, one petite and curvy, wrapped in a silvery fur coat. The other was a middle-aged man with gray at his temples and a slight paunch. They stopped under a streetlamp, and Shax got a good look at the woman. He fought the urge to vomit as his stomach turned.

Aeshma.

Looked like his luck, what little of it there was, had run out.

"This is me," she said, stopping at the black sedan near Shax's tree. "Thank you."

"Always happy to provide a safe escort for a lady," the man said.

He stepped closer, leering down at the beautiful demon. She ran her fingers up his arm, gazing at him with a faint smile on her perfectly pink lips. With inhuman speed and strength, Aeshma grabbed the man by the throat and pinned him to the tree with a single hand. A sneer replaced the siren's smile.

"Make a sound, and I'll rip out your throat." Ice coated the words, colder than the surrounding February night. "Nod if you understand."

The man nodded.

A large figure emerged from the car, holding the rear passenger door open. The interior light illuminated another massive form in the back seat and a smaller one at the wheel, though Shax could not make out their faces.

"Good," Aeshma said. She pulled out a small knife and held it to the man's pinky. The steel blade glinted maliciously under the streetlamp. "Now, you can get into the car, or we can see how fast you can type with only nine fingers."

"Jesus, lady, I'll come with," he rasped.

Disappointment flitted across her face. "Ugh, now it's too easy."

She moved her hand from his throat to his cheek, caressing it with her palm. The man sagged against the tree until, with a quick flick of her wrist, she severed his pinky. Aeshma slammed his head against the tree, silencing him before he could scream. He crumpled into a heap at her black stilettos.

Aeshma motioned to the bodyguard, who waited by the car.

"Put him in the car."

The bruiser lifted the man from the ground and shoved him into the back seat. The door slammed behind them, leaving the Duke of Lust alone on the street. She bent down and picked up the severed finger. Aeshma lifted her head, her stony stare sweeping the street, and her eyes met Shax's. She held the knife to those perfect lips and licked the blood from the blade. She slipped into the front seat, and the car drove off.

His bad luck drew Hinndal to him in St. Louis, put Kheone directly in his path at the museum, and, now, Aeshma. He didn't need this bullshit in his life. He had spent the past year keeping well away from any angels or demons, and it was for nothing. Just fucking great.

Shax dropped out of the tree, human once more, and headed toward his motel.

Could he still run? A wry chuckle escaped his lips. If a Duke of Hell and the Archangel Michael were inhabiting this city at the same time, there was nowhere he could go to escape the consequences of their eventual showdown. If he stayed, he might be able to guide the outcome in his favor. Somehow.

And he had a promise to keep.

Chapter 12

A soft cough brought Kheone out of her much-needed, dreamless sleep. She grabbed her sword on the nightstand before she had even opened her eyes.

"That will not be necessary, Kheone." Michael's wry voice was soft.

She let go of her sword and showed him her empty hand. The archangel stood a few feet from the end of her bed, an open rift behind him. Fully dressed, including snow boots and a thick winter coat, a packed duffle bag hung over one shoulder. The cold was getting to him, too.

Kheone sat up and stretched. "What's going on?"

"I apologize for the intrusion." Another apology. How odd. "I wanted to allow you as much rest as possible, but I must leave shortly."

Leave? In the middle of a murder investigation? That didn't seem at all like the archangel she knew. Her question must have written itself on her face because before she could ask it, he continued.

"You no longer have an experienced healer. The gathering in Boston has a healer to spare. I must assess their ability to part with one."

She nodded her understanding. Some angels retained their full ability to heal themselves, but many had lost the ability in part or in whole. They had been relying on those who could heal others since the Second Fall, but it was a rare talent. Most gatherings had only one healer. Serel had been theirs. With him gone and the demons planning something, this put their gathering at risk for high casualties.

"Anything else I need to know?"

"I also contacted an expert in ancient languages," he said. "I will take the fragments of the device to her. This may take a few days. I have made certain you are more than capable of leading the gathering during this difficult time."

It only took a few thousand years of training and mentorship. Michael used Hurst University as his headquarters but rarely stayed longer than a few days. He traveled between all the gatherings around the world, ensuring they had the training and resources to battle any demons which might show up in their regions. She had half-expected him to stick around this time, though. Unexplained deaths did not happen every day. Kheone was both flattered by Michael's trust and worried he had left so much in her hands.

"Safe journey, Michael," she said.

With a curt nod, the archangel reached into his coat and pulled out a piece of paper, placing it on her desk. He turned on his toes and strode through the open rift, not sparing her a glance.

Caught between pleasure at the effect she apparently had on him and troubled by it, Kheone put the incident out of her mind. As much as she would like to consider Michael's recent behavioral changes and what they might mean, more important things needed her attention right now.

Kheone picked up the paper he had left on her desk. The patrol schedule she had glimpsed yesterday. She looked it over. Considering the administration part of leading wasn't his strong suit, this schedule was well done. The only thing she would change is the pairing of Emric and Maj, only because she knew the two were—what had Maj said?—knocking boots. She doubted Michael did.

Kheone quickly changed into workout clothes. Crossing the courtyard to the gym, she looked for the little black cat she had started calling Machka in her head. She even called out in a small voice that did not carry. No luck. A stab of disappointment struck her heart. Perhaps her recent loss caused a bond to form so quickly.

The large, silent gym echoed her footsteps as Kheone turned on the lights and took her place at the front of the room. A few moments later, the rest of the gathering trickled in. Some still had grief etched into puffy faces. Others looked grim. None smiled.

"Good morning, angels," she said, the bell tower ringing out seven chimes. "You know what to do."

The angels paired off and sparred. Kheone monitored the sessions, offering suggestions to the losers and encouragement to the winners. When the clock struck eight, she dismissed them. Maj stayed behind, leaning on the wall next to the entrance.

"What's up?" Kheone asked.

The other angel grinned, a fleeting thing evaporating almost as soon as it began. "Funny, I was just going to ask the same thing."

"Michael's gone to recruit a new healer." She left out the part about the fragments. The fewer angels who knew about them, the safer they were at the moment.

"Not that." Maj waved dismissively. "Where did you go after the library? I came to check on you once we replaced the books on the shelves, but you weren't there."

Crap. What could she say which was true but wouldn't reveal her devil's bargain with Shax? The fewer angels who knew about that, too, the better. Kheone licked her lips.

"I needed a moment. Or a hundred." She shrugged. Truth, but she neglected to mention she had spent them in the presence of a demon.

Maj pressed her lips together. "Okay. You know you have friends, right? We're supposed to help each other through something like this."

Kheone walked over to her friend and hugged her.

"I know," she whispered into Maj's soft, black curls. "But sometimes you have to grieve in private."

"Don't let it become a habit."

"Promise." Kheone let her go and took a deep breath, steeling herself for the next words out of her mouth. "I'm going through Serel's room later. I could use some help. You up for joining me?"

Tears pooled in Maj's eyes, but she nodded.

"I'll be there after I shower. Join me when you're ready," Kheone said.

She gave her friend's arm a quick squeeze, and Maj left. Kheone turned off the lights and secured the room. Strolling out into the courtyard, she stopped still. Almost like magic, the little cat sat on the bench.

"Good morning, Machka." The old word for cat had become his name.

"Meow."

She scratched under his chin—she didn't know how she knew, but Machka was definitely a boy.

"Sorry, I can't stay for more. Too many things on my plate."

Kheone walked toward the dorm, intent on getting on with her day. The cat followed and darted into the hall when she opened the door. The small creature stuck to her heels as she walked to her room and scurried in. Apparently, she had a cat now.

The halls of the dorm were nearly silent; only the faint drone from the TV in the common room made any discernible sound. Post-training was usually a boisterous affair, with most of the gathering eating in the kitchen. Serel was often in the middle, making and passing out breakfast to the hungry angels. Without him, there was no reason to flock to the kitchen. Something to bring up with Michael when he returned.

The cat meowed plaintively, parking himself by the cupboard where Kheone kept a few snacks. Was he hungry? She racked her brain to come up with something she had in her room a cat might eat. She found a can of tuna salad. Cats liked fish, didn't they? One way to find out. She put the contents of the can on a paper plate and placed it in front of her new friend.

The little cat scarfed half of his snack right down, then returned to her for more attention, twining himself between her ankles. She rubbed his head and stroked along his back, the purrs growing louder by the minute. The cat looked up at her and meowed some more. He leaped onto the bed and curled up at the foot. Yawning, Machka gave a little chirp before his tail covered his nose and his eyes closed. Kheone opened the window enough for him to leave when he wanted and went to take her shower.

With damp hair, she gathered some boxes from a storeroom and walked up the stairs, dreading what she might find in Serel's room. Her footfalls felt loud and heavy but drew no attention. She tried the handle and met resistance. Someone had locked the door, an unusual move in a building full of angels. None of them had valuables to protect, and privacy was rarely a concern. Kheone used her master key and slipped inside. Sadness lingered in the air of the now empty room, though it looked much the same as the night before.

She began with the small closet, folding the items neatly. Like all the angels, most of Serel's wardrobe consisted of black t-shirts and cargo pants. Perhaps someone could use an extra change of clothes. As Kheone dumped a bin filled with socks into one of the boxes, an envelope fluttered to the ground. An elegant hand had written *Father Arturo Fauci, Dept. of History*, on the front.

Her fingers itched to open it, but the better portion of her nature stopped her. The letter wasn't for her. It was for Father Fauci. Serel had left her one last task.

Footsteps stomped up the stairs, encouraging Kheone to shove the letter into a pocket. Maj stepped in the room, her expression deliberately blank.

"Hi," she said.

"Thanks, Maj. I know this isn't easy for you."

The two angels worked in silence and quickly finished packing Serel's possessions. Sad, really, how little he had to show for his long life. She had first worked with Serel three thousand years ago, when she had guarded the soul of a mystic in China, and he healed the devout. Although they had worked together several times since then, Kheone had only come to know him in the past year. Her friend's entire existence fit into three boxes, most of those clothes which would be shared by the rest of the gathering.

If she died, what would she leave behind? Nothing more than Serel had. Her possessions weren't really hers. She had lost the only thing she ever felt was truly hers in the Second Fall. Another would wield the Guardian's blade when she perished if it was ever found.

Kheone and Maj left the boxes stacked at the foot of the bed.

"I have patrol in a few minutes," Maj said, voice quiet, reluctant to leave.

"I know," Kheone said. "Go. We can leave this here for now."

In a few days, when emotions were less raw, she would see if anyone could use the spare clothes. The rest would go into storage. All they would have left were their memories and the hope to one day reunite behind the Heavenly Gate and bask in God's glory.

Maj left, and Kheone went to check on her cat. There was no trace of him. Damn. After packing her dead friend's things, she could have used some feline company. With a sigh, she pulled out the university directory and looked up the name on Serel's letter. The Chair of the History Department was, indeed, Father Fauci. She hurried to the kitchen where the community phone hung on the wall, an old-fashioned model chosen because most of the angels knew how to operate it. Kheone made the call.

"History. Fauci speaking."

She had not expected him to answer his own phone. "Hi, Father. My name is Kheone. I'm a friend of Serel's."

A lingering pause, followed by the faint sound of a door clicking shut over the phone line.

"Yes, Serel mentioned you. I am sorry for your loss."

"Thank you. I wasn't aware he had any friends outside our gathering. He left a note for you. Will you be in your office later?"

"My schedule is pretty full today. Can you come by around six?"

"Certainly. Thank you, Father."

In a few hours, she might have another clue in Serel's death. A frisson of dread shook her from head to foot.

Chapter 13

His ears twitched, listening for any sign someone knew a demon lurked in their midst. Shax heard nothing of import. A few muted voices floated through the halls, and clanking sounds came from what he assumed was a kitchen. He looked at the window. He could just leave.

With Kheone out of the room and off on some errand, Shax would never have a better chance to poke his nose where it did not belong. He padded over to the closed door. It would, of course, be easiest for him to transform into his human form, open the door, and return to his cat form. And then he would die when some angel saw him. See, easy. Shax needed a solution that did not require opposable thumbs.

He stretched up on his hind legs, attempting to reach the lever-style handle, but his paw only brushed it. Christ's balls, not enough leverage. Okay, time for a different tactic. Shax sat on his haunches and leaped. Gravity did the rest. The handle turned, and the door cracked open. He slunk out.

Inordinately pleased with himself, he trotted down the hall, ears twitching, alert for any sign of movement from the angels. He poked his head into a room with a TV on the far wall. The only occupant was a large angel lounging in a recliner. Two computers sat on a long table, the chairs in front of them vacant, and shelves filled with both board games and books stood at the other end of the room. Nothing here of interest.

A noise at the other end of the hall sent Shax scurrying back into Kheone's room. He hid behind the door. An angel stuck her head in and called, "Kheone?"

Shax made himself small and thought invisible thoughts. He blended into the shadows. As long as she didn't look too closely, he should escape detection. After examining the small room and determining Kheone was not present, the angel left.

He counted to one hundred before continuing his exploration. As he passed the now quiet kitchen, many scents greeted his nose. Bitter coffee, warm tea, burnt toast, spicy cinnamon. Kheone's soft rain and earth, and another ten or so scents which were definitely angels, though he didn't know whose. Under the muddle of extraneous odors, stronger than the rest, was the sharp smell of burning pine, like a campfire.

Shax crept into the kitchen, his nose and whiskers twitching. He wound around the room, trying to catch the faint trail, unsure why it drew him. This scent was difficult to separate from all the other smells permeating the air of the kitchen. Spilled milk, something rotting in the trash, grease. Step by step, he followed the scent trail to the pantry. It was in there, whatever it was. He performed his door-opening trick again.

The scent flowed out, released from its confinement like water from a dam. He couldn't tell where, exactly, it came from. Shax walked away from the pantry and took a few breaths, clearing the residual odors from his nose.

He approached again with more caution, taking shallow breaths. He jumped up on the second shelf. The smell of campfire was weak here. Jumping down, Shax took a deep breath. Yes, the scent was concentrated at the bottom of the pantry.

Shax threaded through several twelve-packs of soda stashed there without rhyme or reason. The scent seemed to come from the far left corner, but he couldn't fit behind the cases. What could be there?

He should leave it alone, make his exit out Kheone's window and find some way to tell her to look here. Of course, how would he explain it to her? And why would she believe him?

Sorry, Kheone, I've been pretending to be your cat?

That would go over well. No, the only way to solve this was to risk being found. Shit.

Heart pounding, Shax transformed. All archangels could sense demons, but Michael had left. Right? His only hope was no other angel had the same ability.

Shax moved the cases of soda to the side and laid down on his belly, peering into the dim recesses of the pantry. Nothing. Fuck. He reached his arm in and felt around on the floor in case there was some sort of invisibility spell on it. Still nothing. Double fuck.

Boots thudded down the hall. Shax shoved the soda into the pantry and returned to his cat form in the blink of an eye. He crouched low to the floor, ready to dart out should anyone discover him. The booted feet continued past the kitchen and down the hall. The outside door opened, the crash bar making a jarring sound.

After a moment's silence, Shax made a mad dash to Kheone's room. He pushed the door closed as best he could. Cowering under her bed, Shax waited and listened. He stopped breathing and would have sworn on a bible his heart stopped, too.

Nada, nothing, diddly with a side of squat.

Shax released the breath he held, and his heart resumed its normal rhythm. Luck was not something he was used to. He had pressed it enough for one day. Shax loped over to the window and leaped out, landing on the other side of the bushes surrounding the building. Creeping close to the ground, he reached the end of the dorm.

Now what?

Every instinct he had told him whatever was in the pantry was important, but he could not tell Kheone about it. She would ask how he knew, and he would have to lie. Or, worse, tell the truth.

They would meet tonight. He had time to think of something.

Chapter 14

Kheone glanced up from her desk at the clock. Cripes. She had barely enough time to visit this Father Fauci before she made her first rendezvous—God, no, that made it sound like something else entirely—meeting with Shax. She pulled out the little scrap of paper with the symbols from those pottery shards written on it along with Serel's letter and rushed out the door.

She'd had a day. Although Kheone kept telling herself she was in charge, it felt more like directing traffic from the middle of a busy street. At night. While dressed in black.

The angels were understandably upset. Serel had been an integral part of the gathering, in ways she had not realized until he died. The patrol schedule was the only thing holding her grand plans together, but she had to cover a few too many shifts. Michael had kept her off the original schedule, but with only eleven other angels, Kheone could not avoid a patrol herself. Her first began at midnight, leaving little opportunity to do the things necessary for a leader, like eat and sleep, let alone conduct a clandestine investigation with a demon.

Once she settled the angels into their new routine, things would be better. Her conscience reminded her that perhaps Michael would allow her more leeway if she told him the truth. Of course, he could take the easy road: run Shax through the heart and lock her up until the end of time or the Gates were rebuilt, whichever came first. She had tried to loop him in on their theory, and her anger at the unfairness of his dismissal burbled up. Until she had proof, she would not bring it up to him again.

Kheone swallowed her emotions, something she used to be good at, like any good soldier. It became harder to do every day. Being mortal, or near enough, sucked.

Kheone reached the history building as the bell tower struck the quarter-hour. Taking a deep breath and sending up a quick prayer the priest would still be in, she climbed the stairs to Father Fauci's office.

The door stood open. She knocked anyway.

"Come in." A man's low voice called out, muffled by the floor-to-ceiling books and two comfortable-looking, overstuffed armchairs.

Kheone poked her head in, her body following reluctantly.

"Hello, Father. I'm sorry for being late."

Father Fauci stood up from behind the desk. He was a short, stocky man with salt and pepper hair.

"Kheone, right?" He peered at her from behind the reading glasses perched on his nose. The smile he wore seemed genuine, if sad, and his dark eyes glinted with intelligence. He gestured at the chairs. "Serel spoke of you. Please, have a seat."

"Thank you," she said. She pulled out the letter addressed to him. "I found this in his room. It's for you."

She handed him the envelope before making herself comfortable. He gave it a thoughtful look as he took a seat behind his desk.

"Have you read it?"

Kheone suppressed a gasp and shook her head. "No."

"Of course you didn't." He chuckled. "Angels. You do always play by the rules. Well, almost always."

Father Fauci took a silver letter opener out of his desk and slit open the envelope. He pulled out a piece of paper. The ink had bled through in a few places, but not enough for her to read it. All the priest's attention focused on the letter. When he finished, he tucked the page back into the envelope and placed it down on his desk.

"What does it say?"

His smile was kindly, but there was steel in his gaze. "Tell me, Kheone, how well did you know Serel?"

"Not as well as I should have." Had she known him better, perhaps he would have clued her in on whatever got him killed sooner. "Serel was a healer and a scholar. I am a guardian, a courier of souls. We worked together several times before last winter, and I respected him. He was a reliable teammate, and I considered him a friend."

Nodding as though she's confirmed something Serel had told him, Father Fauci's gaze bored into her as the priest considered what to say next. He tapped his fingers on the desk, merely an inch from the letter. The tapping ceased, and the priest cleared his throat. He had made up his mind.

"What if I told you Serel's death had something to do with the destruction of the Gates?" His voice was hushed, as though he was afraid someone might be listening. He tented his fingers, and his gaze softened a smidge.

Kheone pressed her lips together and tried to slow her racing heart. She and Shax must be on the right track if they weren't the only ones who suspected this. But what did the priest know, and what did he merely guess? Only one way to find out.

She took a deep breath. "I've already come to that conclusion, Father. It's why I'm here. I need to know what Serel knew."

Father Fauci picked up the letter and held it out to her. "Go ahead."

Kheone nearly tore the envelope in her rush to pull out the page. Serel's neat handwriting covered the top half. The bottom half, the part where the ink had bled through, had a unique illustration. She saved it for later.

Arturo,

If you are reading this, I am likely dead. The book is safe, and my notes are secure. You can trust Kheone to follow through. She is the most honorable being I've ever known and has rescued more souls from damnation than any other angel. Although she may lack patience for scholarly work, she is intelligent and diligent. I have no doubt Kheone will use her knowledge to rebuild the Gates and return both the celestial and physical planes to normal.

I have enjoyed our friendship and scholarship. I hope my fate is not oblivion, and I will see you again in Heaven.

Serel

At the bottom, Serel had drawn a careful picture of a cylinder and wrote the symbol for angel on it. The same symbol she had recognized on the piece of pottery from the library. Empty squares dotted the rest of the cylinder as though he had known something needed to go there but had no idea what. Or he had been afraid to write it down.

"Serel and I discussed the fate of human and angelic souls," the priest said, interrupting her perusal. "Demons, too, to be honest. With the Gates gone, what happened to the souls? I feared oblivion for all of them, but Serel felt there was room for hope. He'd seen the Gate to Purgatory still stood before falling and believed it could act as a holding area until he found a way to rebuild. He mentioned he'd found a book which might help."

Kheone nodded. If only she had been early to meet Serel, perhaps she would not be sitting here now, hoping for answers from the priest.

"Do you know what's in it?" she asked.

Father Fauci shook his head. "He wouldn't tell me. Whatever he'd translated had him very worried. Serel seemed the type to take notes, yes?"

Kheone nodded slowly. But he must have hidden them somewhere. Not in his room, but somewhere she could find them.

"Any idea where they might be?"

"Sorry, Father, I didn't even know about the book until the night before he died."

She now knew her next task. Locate those notes. Serel's room was out. The only thing there of relevance was now in Father Fauci's hands. She didn't know where else to look.

"Be careful, Kheone. Trust no one you don't have to, not even Michael."

She opened her mouth to protest. Why not Michael? He was an Archangel, their commander, the right hand of God. Father Fauci's cool stare stopped her.

"He has the well-being of every angel on Earth to consider. If push came to shove and he decided this book harmed their well-being, do you think he would hesitate in destroying it?" He asked.

"Even if it meant we'd never be able to go home again?"

The priest shrugged. "From what Serel told me, Michael isn't the same archangel he once was. He seems intent on ridding the world of demons. Perhaps his zeal to protect those angels who had the ill fortune to be outside Heaven when the Gate blew up skewed his priorities."

He clamped his mouth shut, biting back any further criticism of the great archangel. If he had said this a week ago, Kheone would have chided him for it, but she noticed some of those same changes. She had been happy to hunt and destroy the demon hordes now plaguing the Earth, but in the recesses of her mind, Kheone wondered whether they would ever see Heaven again. The Michael she knew now would do anything to protect the angels left on Earth, including destroying a chance to return to Heaven.

"It's possible we've been too caught up in surviving and have neglected our responsibility to find a way home. I'll do what I can to fix this. May I keep the bottom half of the note? Serel's drawing may prove useful."

"Of course."

Kheone carefully tore the note in two, giving Father Fauci the top half. "Thank you. I'll try to keep you out of this, but I may have questions. My wheelhouse leans more to combat tactics and blades than books."

"My door is always open. God be with you, Kheone."

"God be with you, too, Father."

The hall was empty, and a glance at her watch told her she was late for her meeting with Shax, too. *Son of a motherless goat.* Once out of sight of the office, Kheone opened a rift and a quick, sharp pain stabbed through her temple as it closed behind her. Rubbing at the spot, her long strides ate up the short distance to the meeting place.

Chapter 15

Once again, Shax lurked up a tree in cat form. He had arrived early and watched the sun slip below the horizon a while ago. He waited, and the stars pierced the purple velvet sky. Then Shax waited some more. Damn the angel. He hadn't expected her to keep him waiting so long.

A reddish light in the trees flashed, and Kheone stepped out of a rift. He transformed into his human form. When she stood under the tree, he dropped, still silent as a cat. She whipped around, brandishing a knife, ready to defend herself. He hadn't been silent enough. Shax held up his hands.

"I'm unarmed," he said. A small grin crossed his lips.

"I'm not."

"I can see that."

He took a step closer, and she brandished her blade.

"Close enough, demon."

"Still don't trust me?"

Kheone snorted. Cute.

"I made a blood oath," he said.

"You made an oath you didn't kill Serel and knew nothing about the destruction of the Gates. Not that you wouldn't try to kill me at the first opportunity."

He shoved his hands in his pockets. "If it makes you feel any better, I don't trust you, either. What's stopping you from turning me over to Michael?"

"I gave you my word. Anyway, you're more useful to me alive than dead."

"Careful, Blue, you're starting to sound like one of us."

Shax gave her a cool smile as the blood drained from her face. *Gotcha.*

With a sigh, Kheone slid the knife into its sheath at her belt. She twitched as he took a step closer. Although safe for the moment, Shax didn't doubt for a second she would draw her blade and kill him if he pressed the issue.

"Here." She pulled a small scrap of paper from a pocket and took the last couple of steps toward him, holding it gingerly by the edge. He took the scrap from her, and she retreated, putting more distance between them.

He raised an eyebrow at her.

"The symbols from the fragments? You wanted me to write them down," she said.

"Ah, thanks. How is Michael taking it?" He suppressed a shudder as the archangel's name left his lips. Any who spoke that name in Hell soon met with the wrath of Lucifer. Only a few had lived to tell the tale, enough to send the message to the rest of the denizens of the inferno.

Kheone pressed her lips together, considering whether to answer him. She reached some conclusion.

"He dismissed my concerns."

Stubborn archangel, too confident in his own opinions to consider he might be wrong. Not unlike his brother, whom Shax had served all these years. He pinched the bridge of his nose, hoping it would relieve the headache brewing from lack of sleep and the increase in his stress levels. At least since he had been spending time with Kheone, the Godforsaken buzzing in his brain had vanished. That was a worry for another day.

"I still don't know why I agreed to this," Kheone said, almost as if to herself.

"Because who could deny this handsome face?" His grin widened.

She sniffed in derision, but he thought the corners of her mouth twitched.

Shax unfolded the piece of paper. Under a lamp lighting the stairs nearby, he tried to make heads or tails of it. Some ancient runes seemed familiar, but he couldn't quite remember what they meant.

"Are you sure this is correct, Kheone?"

"Yes. Do you doubt me? I transcribed them from the source."

"No, I just—They look familiar, but I don't know what they mean."

She approached cautiously as though he was a dog who would bite her at the slightest provocation. It wasn't far from the truth. All he had to do was let the compulsion take hold again, and she would have a one-way trip to wherever an angel went now the Gates were gone.

"This one is angel." She tapped the symbol. Her fingers, calloused from eons of wielding a sword, scratched on the paper. "I'm not sure of the rest."

"Why are you being so cooperative?" He grimaced at the suspicion in his voice.

"We're partners, right?" Kheone looked at him, blinking in confusion. "Partners share information. You have what I have."

Oh yeah, right. He had always worked alone, sharing only when absolutely necessary to keep his head firmly attached to his body. Shax swallowed the guilt sticking in his throat. He had two pieces of information she should know.

In order to tell her about the thing hidden in the kitchen, he would have to reveal his small, furry alter ego. That was definitely not going to happen. How else could he keep tabs on her and keep her safe?

He could tell her about Aeshma. That couldn't hurt anything, could it? She was the most likely suspect in Serel's death. There was no reason to withhold this piece of information from Kheone.

"Shax, hello? Do you recognize any of the symbols?"

Shax set aside the guilt and other inconvenient feelings and peered at the paper. He could always tell her later. He pointed at a symbol, both similar and different from the one meaning angel.

"This means demon."

"Okay. Why would the device have both angel and demon inscribed on it?"

"Got me. I tempt people to sin. I don't solve puzzles. This was a bad idea, Blue. You picked the wrong demon. I'm no Sherlock Holmes."

"You think I am?" She walked away.

He missed her warm presence at his shoulder. "That's not what I said."

"I've put my life on the line for you, Shax. Michael won't believe me until we can uncover some evidence linking Serel's murder to whatever happened to the Gates. Neither will any of the other angels. And any of them would kill me for working with you."

"You think this is easy for me, trusting an angel? Jesus Christ, Kheone, how many times have we crossed blades over the fate of some wretched soul? If you won't trust me, then let me be on my merry way. I swear you'll never see me again." He turned and walked two steps before she called out to stop him.

"Wait."

Shax turned around to see her arm outstretched, reaching for him.

"You're right, Shax. We're used to working against each other, not with each other. I'm sorry."

He nodded, accepting her apology, knowing what it likely cost her.

"Did you ever find out why Serel was in the library?"

Kheone shook her head. "He said he'd found something useful for our situation. We'd arranged to meet." She sighed. "Serel was a scholar and a healer. He spent a lot of time in the library, trying to catch up on modern medicine and looking for a way home."

"Really? How close was he?"

"Why?"

"It's called motivation, Blue. If he was close, someone may have wanted to stop him. The angels may want to return to Heaven, but the demons want nothing to do with Hell."

"I don't understand, Shax. Demons belong there, as angels belong in Heaven. Demon powers are fading without the connection. I thought all demons craved power."

"Hell is pain." Shax kept his voice flat, belying the incredible suffering every demon went through. How could he make her understand Lucifer wasn't some benevolent dictator?

"We live in anguish every minute of every day, severed from the presence of God and tortured by the memory of our state of grace in Heaven. Lucifer retained all his archangel gifts and bestowed them as rewards for loyalty and cruelty, and sometimes just because he could. He could free you from pain with a touch. The euphoria from that alone was enough to ensure his orders were carried out. But he caused pain, too, almost as capriciously as he ended it."

Kheone stepped closer, and the hand not hovering over the knife fluttered as though she wanted to reach out to him.

"With the connection to Hell gone, so is the pain. Most demons are so twisted by the eons of torment they continue carrying on the Devil's work even without his presence."

A soft touch cut him off. Kheone had given in to her impulse and threaded her fingers through his. Warmth spread from the point of contact, surging through him, chasing away the hurt those memories brought. He wondered, for a moment, what her touch would feel like on other parts of his body. Shax repressed the thought. It would never happen.

"But not you," she said gently.

"Not me." He wanted to live in a world without pain, without coercion. And yet, here he was, being manipulated by an angel. He almost laughed at the irony.

"So, if a demon found Serel investigating how to rebuild the Gates, he would be a prime target for extermination," Kheone said.

Shax nodded.

"When I went to the library," she continued, "I didn't feel any demonic magic. Angel magic everywhere, but nothing with the foul taint of demon."

"Gee, thanks."

"I—"

Shax held up a hand. "I was kidding." *Mostly.*

He thought for a minute. If a demon made the bomb, was it then filled with angelic magic? With the current relationship between himself and Kheone as an exception which proved the rule, angels and demons did not work together. Shax heaved a breath. He needed to see for himself, and a cat's nose could more readily pick up on the subtleties of scent than a human's.

"Can you get me into the library?" he asked.

Kheone narrowed her eyes in distrust. "Why?"

"Because if you want to find out who killed your friend, I need to go see the crime scene for myself."

"We cleaned up already. I don't know what you'll find."

"Maybe the taint of demon magic is too small for even an archangel to detect. Maybe only another demon will recognize it."

"Yes, fine, I can do that."

The words snapped from her mouth, her nose scrunched up in adorable irritation. Kheone opened the rift, and Shax stepped through. She took a step toward him.

"No, you stay. You'll just interfere with my ability to sense another demon."

"How will you get out?"

"Come back for me. Thirty minutes should be enough."

He grinned at her, letting his feral side show through. Shax knew she wondered what his special gift was. Let her think he could turn invisible or mess with human minds. He needed to keep her in the dark about his other form for the moment. It had proven useful thus far. Besides, Kheone would see his disguise as a betrayal.

"Maybe. If I remember, instrument of darkness."

The rift snapped closed behind him before he could shout back that her insults still sucked. Finding himself alone, Shax transformed into Machka.

The fallout from angel magic permeated the stacks, although the air had cleared. Every time he rubbed up against a book or a piece of furniture, his nerves jangled. He padded slowly up and down the stacks, taking deep breaths through his cat nose. Shax opened his mouth, tasting the air, using the special organ at the roof of his mouth—there.

The strongest scent was sharp pine with an acrid hint of smoke, the same as in the kitchen. It was most likely Serel's. Whoever it was had been here often, and although the angel's blood had vanished, the scent coated the books, shelves, and carpet below Shax's paws. Other angels had been here since, but their scents were faint smears on books and residuals of footsteps. Kheone's stood out, her pleasant scent of earth and rain a balm to his nose. The sharp sting of lemons and old wine wound around her scent. Michael, maybe? Intermingled with all the rest was the sweet smell of rot, the smell of a demon, and it wasn't his. One of his brethren had been here, all right, probably around the same time Serel died.

Shax sneezed to clear the scents from his nose and huffed another breath of air. He could only determine the demon had been in the library but wasn't able to get a clear picture of exactly where. Foregoing the temptation to linger on Kheone's scent, he picked up Serel's once again. It led him to a shelf in the middle of the aisle. He crawled up and continued following the scent until he was on the top shelf. Serel's scent covered the book on the end, along with a slight undertone of decay. Both the angel and a demon had touched this book in the last forty-eight hours.

Shax leaped down to the ground and changed into his human form. The title on the spine read *Ancient Rituals of Sumer*. He tried lifting the book from its place on the shelf, but pain shot up his arm at first contact.

Shit. What was he supposed to do now?

Chapter 16

A half-hour later and Kheone's fingers still tingled from where she had touched Shax. His warm spicy scent, like pepper, lingered on her skin, even from such a brief contact. Reaching out to him had not been a conscious decision. His attempt to hide his pain with a blank face and an expressionless voice failed utterly. Her tea sat, cold and untasted, on her desk. She'd spent most of the last thirty minutes pacing and worrying for a rotten demon.

Kheone opened a rift, and another spike of pain pierced her temple, gone almost before she could register it. More than ever, she wished she could talk to Serel.

"Shax?"

Keeping her voice barely above a whisper, she tiptoed through the fourth floor of the library, waving her flashlight around while keeping her senses alert for any movement.

"Christ!" A distinct thump followed Shax's voice.

She followed the invectives to the last row of bookshelves and found him there, leaning against the shelf with a smirk on his lips. He slung his coat over his shoulder, hair glowing like a halo from the light directly above him. Just like the angel he wasn't. A book sat in the middle of the floor.

"Miss me, Blue?"

Oddly, the nickname didn't bother her as much. Maybe it was the way he said it, a wistful tone replacing the venom he used to inject. She shook off her musings.

"Not in this lifetime," she lied, her first one.

"Mm-hmm, sure." He nodded, his lips twitching up a bit more, seeing right through her.

How was that possible? The blessed Archangel Michael could not tell she held something back when she had failed to give him a complete account of Serel's death. And she should feel worse about lying, even to a demon. Anger bloomed in her chest, covering her embarrassment at being found out.

"I was trying to offer you an easy out, but if you're going to give me a hard time, I'll go." Kheone turned on her heel to leave.

"No, wait—" A small growl of frustration came out of the demon. "Fine. No more teasing. I...I need your help."

She turned, keeping her composure though she fought the smirk which wanted to plant itself on her lips. She'd won, but she didn't need to rub his nose in it. He seemed reluctant now he had her attention.

"Yes?" Kheone prompted him as the silence between them grew to an uncomfortable level.

Shax pointed at the book on the floor without looking at it, his voice as sulky.

"Serel touched that book, but I can't. It burns."

Expressionless, Kheone bent over and picked up the book. A slight prickle ran from her fingertips and up her arms, then dissipated. Embossed in flaking silver leaf on the worn leather cover, more moss-toned than the brilliant green she could glimpse in the cracks, was the title, *Ancient Rituals of Sumer*. The ragged, yellow edges of the pages smelled faintly of must.

"This hurt you?"

"That's what I said. Why would I lie?" He showed her his palm covered in red blisters.

"Looks like you tried." She cautiously opened the book.

The reason he could not touch it became obvious. Runes decorated the front and back plates, written in angel blood, which usually evaporated within an hour. Someone had used magic to stabilize the blood. Kheone leafed through the pages of the book, hoping something would jump out at her. The language was Latin but made absolutely no sense, as though someone had just thrown a bunch of words in a book.

"Well?" Shax snapped at her, crossing his arms. He tapped his fingers impatiently as he waited for her verdict.

"It's a book, Shax."

"No shit." He reached out and took it from her, then dropped the book immediately, hissing in pain.

"Are you mad?"

Kheone grabbed his hands and turned them palm up for examination. More blisters formed, bright red and hot to the touch. As she watched, the redness faded. It was a lot like how her body had reacted to the small piece of pottery she had picked up here after Serel died. She ran a finger over the blisters. Shax pulled his hands away with a sharp intake of breath.

"I'm sorry," Kheone said. "That looks like it hurts."

He cradled his hands next to his body and gave a sharp nod.

"When we're done here, I can get you some bandages."

One side of Shax's mouth quirked into a half-smile. "Thanks, but that won't be necessary. It'll be fine in an hour."

She raised her eyebrows. "You can still heal?"

"Stuff like this, yeah. Not much more."

With nothing else she could do, Kheone picked up the book and opened it, discovering a familiar rune inside the front cover. She took a step toward Shax, holding the book in front of her. He backed away.

"Hold still, you big baby. I won't let it touch you."

Shax glared at her but did as she said. As she approached, the rune in question glowed. The rune last night had meant *angel*. This one meant *demon*. It matched the pottery fragments. The book had been spelled to protect it from demons, likely by Serel. But why?

"What does that mean?" Shax asked.

"It means I will have to handle this book. Serel didn't want a demon to touch it."

"Some demon did, though. Maybe before Serel enchanted it, or maybe after, and they got a painful shock to the system. But the amount of angel magic dwarfs the demon magic here."

"So..." Kheone tried to wrap her head around the puzzle. Serel had felt a need to protect the book from demons, a demon had been here, but there was more angel magic than demon.

"Whatever killed Serel was likely fueled by angel magic, Blue. Keep up, now."

She hated the smirk which kept popping up, suggesting he knew more than she did. Really, neither of them knew anything. They could only guess based on the limited evidence they had. She narrowed her gaze, trying to figure out his game.

"I can think of a better scenario. A demon killed Serel, releasing all of his innate magic into the air and skewing the sample." Kheone gave him a fierce smile. Take that, foul vassal of Satan.

To her surprise, Shax rocked his head back and forth, considering her remark.

"I suppose that's just as likely."

"More, demon. Angels don't kill other angels. A demon killing an angel is much more likely."

He sighed. "I have something I need to tell you. I saw Aeshma the other night."

Her hands closed into tight fists so she wouldn't take out her knife and stab him right here in the library. After her big speech about sharing information, he was going to keep that from her?

"You selfish son of a—" Kheone cut herself off.

"That was almost an insult."

She wanted desperately to slap the grin off his face. She resisted and took a few deep breaths. It was good information.

"She's a good suspect," Kheone said.

"She might be passing through."

Kheone snorted in derision. "That's a pretty weak straw to grasp."

He held up his hands. "Fine, this doesn't look good for Aeshma, but I've worked with her before. She's not usually this direct, and none of her demons would be foolish enough to take on an angel without her permission."

"Demons can be pretty thickheaded." Kheone was not going to give him credit for his logic. And she had a Duke of Hell on a shining platter, all ready for justice.

"True." He gave her a rueful smile this time as he looked down at the ground. His white hair flopped over his eyes. "At this point, we can't tell who is responsible, and we have no idea where Aeshma is to get her side of the story. The good news, though, is we've made some progress."

"What progress?" she yelled at him, frustration finally getting the better of her. The more she found out about Serel's death, the less any of it made sense. She needed answers now, and Shax stood there, waiting patiently. He had not made his promise because he cared about Serel, or her, or some abstract sense of justice. He had done so to save his own life.

Sweeping his hair back, Shax looked at her. Something about his striking amber eyes settled her. She brushed the feeling aside. He had met her gaze, that was all. Many humans and not a few angels wouldn't look her in the eyes. He kept his voice soft and calm, in stark contrast to her sharp, agitated tone.

"We know a demon was involved, probably Aeshma or one of her horde." He ticked them off on his fingers. "We know it's unlikely a human killed Serel. And we have to consider your gathering, Kheone. Angels have fallen before. It isn't beyond the realm of possibility it happened again, after ten thousand years."

"Well, damn." Her shoulders sagged in defeat. With inconclusive evidence, she had to consider every possibility. Even the impossible. It galled her to think Shax might be right. "All the angels in my gathering are suspects, then."

Even Michael. She could not utter the thought out loud. Michael, who had thrown Lucifer into the Pit before God had even ordered it. Michael, who had served faithfully as God's warrior all these millennia. Michael, whose golden glory stole her breath. Michael, who had changed. Maybe even him.

"Are you sure?" Shax asked. "Is there no one you trust?"

"If you'd asked me a week ago..." She shrugged. "But now I have to suspect them all. I hate this, Shax."

He came closer and touched her arm. Even through her layers of clothes, a feverish warmth flowed from where his hand rested. Shax jerked it away, and a thoughtful expression crossed his face.

"I know, Kheone, but we have to follow where the evidence leads us. Is there anyone else Serel was working with on rebuilding the Gates?"

"I'm not telling you that. You'd probably kill them if they existed."

He waved away her objection. "Consider it a rhetorical question. If any names come to mind, go find out what they know."

Kheone nodded. She'd done so with Father Fauci, but her instinct was to keep his name out of this for now.

"What will you do?"

He shrugged. "Go on a demon hunt, I guess. See if Aeshma or any of her minions are still in town. Maybe search for another unprotected copy of the book. Sorry, Blue. It seems every answer only seems to raise more questions."

Kheone gave him a wan smile. Shax was fulfilling his word as best he could. She never expected this kind of integrity from a demon and found it impressive.

"Questions are what we have, so let's go find some answers. Where to next, demon spawn?"

"The museum is fine. And I'm not demon spawn. Lucifer is not my father. If anything, I'm the spawner." He gave her another feral grin.

"Ugh."

Kheone couldn't quite suppress the smile. She hid it by turning away and opening a rift. Shax gave her a jaunty salute before he stepped through, his white hair picking up the red of the rift. A dull ache started at the crown of her head and flowed down, dissipating once it reached her neck.

She'd expected demons or maybe a powerful sorcerer. But one of her own angels? Possibly more, as that kind of magic was impossible for a single angel. What was the expression? It had come out of left field. She had to include her own gathering in the list of suspects, which meant keeping her suspicions to herself. She couldn't accuse Michael or any of her gathering without some sort of evidence.

With so many thoughts swirling in her mind, Kheone decided the short walk to the dorm would do her good. She would be long gone by the time security arrived to investigate. The headaches today after opening rifts concerned her. The last couple of days had been emotionally and physically draining. Hopefully, it was a coincidence, not a pattern.

Chapter 17

"If you came with excuses, Emric, I don't want to hear them," Kheone said to the sandy-haired head poking into her room shortly before lunch the next day.

She shoved the worn book under her pillow, hoping the angel thought she was only hiding porn. Kheone had barely cracked it before she had heard someone in the hall.

Emric shook their head, cheeks painted red. Good, a little shame was fitting. Showing up late for the morning workout was unacceptable. The looks on Emric and Maj's faces when she yelled at them after dismissing the others were two parts guilt to one part smug. She sent them off with a warning. Any further transgressions would result in Kheone notifying Michael. That had shut them right up and replaced smug with fear.

Kheone did not wish to lead with fear, but the sooner they both realized she had their best interests at heart, the better. Michael would not tolerate such behavior.

"Phone call for you, LT."

She ceased breathing for an instant, the inflection in Emric's voice a near copy of Serel's. Kheone blinked away the tears and shoved the grief down, far down. It hurt, a pain as deep as the one she had glimpsed on Shax's face last night. Understanding dawned. Demons must feel this grief and anguish all the time.

Poor Shax. And she meant it.

"Thanks. Be right there." Her voice was thick with unshed tears.

Emric looked concerned but kept their thoughts to themself. They stood aside as she walked to the kitchen and picked up the receiver from the table.

"This is Kheone."

"Lieutenant," Michael said, voice all business. "Anything to report?"

She'd met with a demon. Said demon had found a book that might hold the secret to opening the Gates. Oh, and she had every reason to suspect one or more of her gathering had something to do with Serel's death.

"No, Archangel."

Suspicions weren't worth reporting without evidence. The misrepresentation came easily, perhaps too easily, but it was better than what would happen if she spoke the unvarnished truth. If he didn't kill her outright at the accusation, Michael would demand proof. They had none, yet. Until she and Shax found something useful, Kheone would keep their arrangement to herself. No need to mention the way her heart raced and skin burned whenever Shax appeared. Perhaps that, too, had something to do with her recent headaches. Fatigue, maybe, with a touch of anxiety.

He grunted in acknowledgment. "I have found a healer. My next stop is Nairobi. The language expert I know resides there."

"Understood." A wave of relief washed through her. She hated to think of replacing Serel, but the simple fact was they needed a healer. The angels' ability to heal themselves was swiftly fading.

The dial tone greeted her ears before she could say goodbye. Michael rarely observed human niceties, but his abruptness seemed cold-blooded considering their recent interactions and his obvious concern for her.

How did Michael do it? It was difficult enough keeping her gathering in line. Keeping all the balls in the air for every gathering must be a gargantuan task. He made it look effortless. Of course, Michael was an archangel. Obedience was his due, a fact not even worth debating among the angels. Kheone had no such claim. She had to earn the loyalty of the gathering, had to earn their respect, and prove her leadership day after day after day.

Today had been challenging so far, and it was only half over. Besides Emric and Maj, she had dealt with the petty concerns of the gathering. Complaints about the patrol schedule, complaints about the food, questions over who got to move into Serel's room.

The last had sent her to her room. Kheone had a good cry while sharpening her curved, kopis sword. A poor substitute for the Guardian Angel's blade she had once wielded, but the repetitive action and rhythmic scrape of metal on stone soothed her.

She made a sandwich in the kitchen and took it to her room for lunch, eager to get back to examining the book. She wanted to have something, anything, to report to Shax when they met tonight. All these questions kept her from sleep. It had nothing to do with the lingering heat of his touch. Nor the new insight she had into his psyche.

Kheone pulled out the book, hoping the text would be clearer in the full light of day than it had in the dimly lit library last night. She was disappointed. The blasted book should make sense, but it was a mess. She had learned Latin over two thousand years ago and spoke it regularly for centuries. This wasn't even bad Latin, just Latin words thrown together without rhyme or reason. Something else was going on with the book, something she needed Serel to make sense of.

Or someone like Serel. Kheone tucked the book under her arm and returned to the kitchen. Picking up the receiver, she dialed Father Fauci's number. It rang, then went to voicemail. She left a vague message, hoping the priest would be there this evening before she met with Shax. Perhaps she would finally have some answers instead of all the questions that kept turning up.

Maj ran into her in the hall, tears dripping down her cheeks and chest heaving with sobs she wouldn't let escape.

"Oh," Maj said, freeing the sobs.

Kheone didn't have time for this, but Maj was her friend. She made the time, anyway.

"Come on," she said, guiding the other angel into her room.

Maj headed straight to the bed and plopped down. With a small sigh, Kheone sat next to her friend and pulled her into her embrace. Maj leaned her head on Kheone's shoulder and cried.

She took Maj's hand, reminded of Shax by this simple gesture. The warmth of his touch had lingered long after their parting, and the thought of him caused a warm spark of something to flicker to life deep inside. Kheone had never entered into a blood oath before. Perhaps this was a residual effect of the magic, a little of his blood remaining in her, flaring to life whenever she thought of him. Perhaps. It was better than the alternative. The only time she had felt anything like this before was under Michael's healing touch.

Maj's sobs quieted, and the angel wiped away her tears. She took a bracing breath.

"I feel like I'm always crying these days. Em thinks we need a break," she said.

"Do you want to talk about it?" Kheone asked.

Maj shrugged, and a tear drew a wet trail down her cheek. "I guess it's not a bad idea."

"Emric's a fool."

Her friend smiled, a pathetic thing, but a smile, nonetheless. Michael would not be happy with their relationship, but Kheone vowed she would make him understand it was easier to accept than to find replacements for them both.

"Be on time from now on." She smiled back at her friend.

"Thanks, Kheone."

"What's the saying? That's what friends are for."

Maj nodded and glanced in the mirror, brushing a stray strand of hair out of her face. Squaring her shoulders, she strode into the hall. Soft voices filtered in. Slowly but surely, their gathering was returning to normal. Pretty soon, Serel would only be a faint wisp of a memory.

Kheone took a deep breath. She would hold on to him as long as she could.

Six chimes sounded from the bell tower. Already? She pulled out the book and created a rift to the basement of the history building. Bracing herself for the pain, she let go of the magic, holding it open. Nothing, thank God. Fatigue must have caused her headaches yesterday.

Leaping up the stairs, she found Father Fauci's office again. He leaned against his desk and checked his watch, waiting for her.

"Good evening, Kheone," he said, looking up.

"Good evening, Father."

"You found something?"

Kheone hesitated. Serel had left no instructions, nor had he told the priest about the book. Who was she to share it with him? But the words were all jumbled, and she needed help. Serel had trusted the priest, and something told her she could, too. She gave the book to the priest.

He put on his glasses and flipped through the book, his brow wrinkled in concentration and a small smile on his lips. Satisfied with what he saw, Father Fauci returned it.

"He was crafty, wasn't he?"

Kheone glanced down at the book and back at the priest. "How so?"

"Serel told me he'd taken measures to prevent the information from falling into the wrong hands. It seems he found a method to scramble the words. The runes inscribed inside the cover, maybe?"

"Maybe, but one of the runes means demon, probably to keep them from being able to touch the book." She did not want to tell Father Fauci this was more than a guess.

The priest chuckled. "Ah. Two layers of protection are better than one. You have quite the puzzle."

"There's nothing else you can tell me?"

"I'm afraid not. For whatever reason, Serel kept this from all of us. He seemed to trust you, though. Find his notes, and you should have some answers."

"Thank you, Father."

"I didn't do much, but you are most welcome, Kheone."

Disappointment flooded through her as she walked to the dorm, the cold evening sending shivers through her body. She had hoped the priest would have some answers for her. Instead, he left her with more questions. She hadn't had this many questions since she woke up naked in a snowdrift last year.

The bells of the clock tower struck half-past seven, their music ringing across the campus. Blast it all. Kheone rubbed at her temple. She had no time before her meeting with Shax, but she couldn't risk taking the book with her. The demon would have to wait. Unless he had found something more interesting than she, their meeting was going to be short and not-so-sweet, anyway. From all those murder mystery shows, she thought crime solving would be easier.

So intent on the questions tumbling over and over in her mind, Kheone didn't see the great, spinning hurricane that was the Archangel Michael until too late.

He stormed up from the direction of the dorm, bent on sweeping her out to sea.

"You should not be out alone. Where have you been?" he thundered.

Michael stopped mere inches from her, his chin level with her forehead. She stared straight ahead, her training as a Soldier of God kicking in.

"I wasn't expecting you back, Archangel. If I had known—"

"Answer the question, Lieutenant."

"I found something Serel left behind and went to consult an expert."

He withdrew a step, staring down his nose at her. "I thought you said you had nothing to report."

"That was this morning." The ease with which she lied scared her a little.

"What did you find?"

Kheone held out the book. Michael snatched it with his gloved hands and thumbed through the pages.

"This makes no sense. Who did you show it to?" His voice was glacial, menace threading through it like a crack in the ice.

Without even planning to, she lied again. "No one, he wasn't there."

This lie felt right, felt protective.

He peered at her as though sensing the lie. Kheone readied herself to accept the consequences of her actions. His shoulders dropped, and when he spoke, the ice melted from his voice.

"You cannot show this to a human, Kheone. Not if it contains the secret of rebuilding the Gates."

"I understand."

"I do not think you do." Michael tucked the book under an arm. "The demons do not want the Gates rebuilt. If they suspect you have found a way, they will kill you like they killed Serel. I will not place the humans who have offered us shelter in danger. And I cannot lose you, Kheone."

"Me?" Her eyes widened in surprise. There was nothing special about her. She doubted anyone here would miss her much. Maybe Maj.

"I have never had a more loyal, more courageous warrior under my command. You have always impressed me, Kheone. Always. Why do you think I took you off guard duty so quickly?"

Only to an archangel would a thousand years be quick. She suppressed the smile which threatened to break her stoic soldier veneer.

"I assigned you to the hardest hearts. You were the only one with a chance to break through, to steer them toward righteousness."

Kheone shook her head. "I lost so many of them, Michael."

"No, you *saved* so many of them. Multitudes would now be consigned to perdition if you had not saved them. No angel has ever been more capable than you, more compassionate. You have earned your place at my side. I do not know what I would do without you, Kheone. I cannot risk losing you."

He raised a hand to cup her cheek. She held her breath, waiting for a rush of heat, for the desire to rise within her. Nothing happened. They stood there, painted by the golden light of the streetlamps, neither daring to do what seemed inevitable.

Kheone broke the spell and raised her hand to his chest, nestling it on his sternum. Softly she asked, "Why? Why can't you lose me?"

Michael removed his hand from her cheek and plucked hers off his chest. He heaved a great sigh and let go. Frigid air blew away the lingering feel of his cool caress, so unlike the warmth that dwelled long after Shax's simple touch. Kheone waited for whatever fate the archangel decided to dole out. He raked his hands through his shorn hair and fixed his gaze on her. His brown eyes were full of pain and shame.

"I cannot lose you because you mean more to me than is fitting. I have desired you, Kheone, since long before the Second Fall. It was easy enough to deny when we were in our celestial forms, but with each passing day, these feelings become harder to refuse. You are the best I have ever trained. You are my pride, Kheone, but you are also my shame. A part of me, the part I am most ashamed of, is glad you were caught outside Heaven's Gate, so I was not alone."

"There is nothing to be ashamed of, Michael," she said forcefully, taking a step toward him. "Desire is not shameful. Neither is caring. And not wanting to be alone, that is human. We are corporeal now, and every day we become more and more human. God would not give us these feelings if they weren't part of the plan, even though we can't see the plan."

Enough of this. Kheone closed the distance between them and took his hand in hers. Michael pulled her in and wrapped his arms around her. Her other hand slipped over his lower back, his muscles firm under his jacket. He groaned at the contact. Heat rose to her cheeks, and her breathing quickened. He lowered his golden-crowned head and pressed his lips gently, ever so gently, against hers.

Her heart raced. She wanted this, had wanted it since she first understood the demands and desires of her corporeal body. His lips were soft against hers. Michael groaned again, pulling her body hard against his, and the kiss changed. No longer gentle, this was the kiss of a man in pain, a man in the throes of desire. She opened her mouth under the onslaught, and his tongue invaded. She wanted to like his kiss, wanted to feel the fire blaze within her. Instead, something inside shriveled with the cold touch of his lips.

The memory of Shax's touch, hot and electric, rushed through her. That was what she truly wanted, the thrill of unholy need, the burn of a desire so deep she had no words for it. God help her. She wanted to feel Shax's lips on hers, not Michael's.

Kheone tore away from the archangel. He gazed down at her, his pupils dilated, eyes hot with need, and his lips wet from their kiss. She had always thought the biggest *what if* would be, *What if he didn't feel the same*? Kheone had never considered, *What if I didn't*?

"I did not mean for this to happen, Kheone. You must believe me." His voice cracked, and the fire in his gaze diminished.

"I do. I wanted it too." How did one let an archangel down easy? "But this is wrong. We shouldn't—"

He scowled at her, but before he could argue, a piercing ring came from Michael's pocket. He pulled out the phone and transferred the scowl to the piece of technology.

"Yes?" Michael listened for a moment. "I will be there shortly. My business here is concluded."

He tucked the phone into his pocket and studied her for a moment.

"I cannot stay, but this is far from over, Kheone. You told me not five minutes ago desire was not wrong, and yet now you say it is? We must finish this conversation at a later date."

Before she could protest, the Archangel Michael opened a rift and stepped through. With her book.

"Curse him," she muttered to herself.

The bells struck eight. She was late again.

What was she supposed to do, now she knew her own pounding heart's desire? Kiss a demon? The thought should have turned out the contents of her stomach or ruptured a blood vessel in her brain. Kheone should have felt something other than the excitement coursing through her or the flush on her cheeks at the anticipation of seeing Shax once more.

Kheone opened her own rift and went to meet her demon.

Chapter 18

What. The. Fuck?

Shax trembled, and his whiskers twitched, millennia of pent-up longing swirling through him with nowhere to go. He did not deserve anything Kheone had to offer. Not the truce they had, not her friendship, and certainly not her kisses. He was a demon, marked for eternity by Lucifer's rebellion. Untrustworthy, unsympathetic, and unlovable, yet he still yearned to be more than what he was.

He had waited by their tree at the museum, hands shoved into his pockets to keep them warm, breath fogging in front of him. He had expected her right around seven. Thirty minutes later, with no sign of Kheone or a note from her, Shax had pulled out the Judas coin. It would get him close to her, but he might land in the heart of the angel enclave. To do something so risky bordered on brainless, but he was still going to do it.

As soon as he materialized on the campus, a large building looming over him, he changed into his cat form and found a shadow to hide in. He scented her before he saw her coming out of the building. Thudding footsteps drew his attention as Michael stalked down the walkway as though he owned the place. He bolted under a bush and resisted the urge to arch his back and hiss as much as he fought the strong desire to turn tail and run.

Shax had forgotten how much the archangel looked like his brother, Lucifer. Even the grim expression gracing the archangel's brow reminded him of the Prince of Darkness, the spectral, orange light from the lamps heightening the resemblance. The cold fury radiating from Michael was truly the icing on the cake. Lucifer had it in abundance. A tremor of dread, or maybe desire, rushed down his limbs.

He was far enough away that only snippets of their conversation reached his very sensitive kitty ears. Something about a book, something about danger. Shax caught enough to jog something loose from the confines of his memory. Michael's voice had called for retreat at the moment before the

Gates crashed down. What in the nine circles was he supposed to do with that tidbit of information?

Kheone's smell of earth and rain mingled with the sharp scent of lemons and old wine. The conversation grew heated, and then Michael's entire demeanor changed, softened. He kissed her, and all the breath left Shax's body, freezing him under the bush.

Shax took advantage of the archangel's momentary distraction and scurried off. Staying out of Michael's path had served him well in the past. He did not see the need to change the behavior now.

Michael, with his iron will and pure heart, was supposed to be better, do better. Yet, here he was, giving in to the desires of the flesh, exploiting Kheone's understandable infatuation with him. After all, Michael was God's right hand, the infallible leader of the Heavenly Host, and the object of awe and obedience from every angel.

It was how Lucifer had secured loyalty before his rebellion. Shax had idolized the radiant Morning Star, oblivious to the destruction his mentor wrought. He would have followed Lucifer anywhere. And he did. Shax found the price well worth paying when the Prince made a place for him in his court.

He understood from hard experience how to exploit vulnerabilities. His gut told him that was precisely what Michael was doing with Kheone.

Why was he even worrying about this? Who she kissed was of no concern to him. Just because he dreamed of her did not mean she was his. Just because every move he made since the Second Fall had something to do with Kheone meant nothing, not really. His concern was holding up his end of the bargain, so he could leave behind the machinations of both angels and demons.

Shax ran the entire way to his motel, putting as much distance between himself and the angels. The entire lot of them were giving him indigestion.

He rushed to his motel and burst into his room. Sitting in the desk chair, legs crossed like a Goddamned princess, was the same petite, curvy figure from the other night. Oh, Christ. His night was about to get a whole lot worse.

"Hello, Shax," she said with a bright smile. It didn't reach her eyes.

Taking a step backward, he bumped into a solid wall of flesh. Shax looked up into the round face of a massive demon whose mouth turned down in a permanent scowl under shaggy, black hair. His hands were solid weights on Shax's shoulders.

He sighed, resigned to this fresh, new Hell. At least she had saved him the bother of finding her.

"Hello, Aeshma."

The Duke of Lust was short. A few strands of her honey-blonde hair escaped the soft chignon and artfully framed eyes the color of a stormy sea. Those eyes were just as uncaring and just as dangerous as any ocean. The curves revealed by her skin-tight dress would make a monk think about sex. Shax was no monk.

A tall, brawny woman with short, muddy brown hair took up a position outside his room. The first demon shoved Shax into the room, shut the door, and stood against it. The only way he was getting out of here was if Aeshma allowed it. Good news was, if she wanted him dead, he would already be shaking hands with Hinndal.

"Been gone from Pandemonium long enough to forget courtesy?"

Shax suppressed the urge to tell her to shove it up her lovely ass. That would get him killed before he could take another breath. Aeshma was a Duke of Hell, and if she insisted on the use of her title and pleasantries, Shax was in no position to argue the point.

"Good evening, Your Grace."

"You even kept the venom out of your voice. You're good at this, Shaxie."

He hated the nickname, Aeshma's petty way of reminding him of what he had given up when he turned down his own title. Shax was the only demon to refuse something from Lucifer. Ever. His defiance had amused the Morning Star but scared the shit out of everyone else. Those who thought they could get away with it used a diminutive of his name to make themselves feel safer.

"Thank you, Your Grace."

A sweet giggle greeted this simple statement.

"Have a seat," she said, patting the bed across from her.

Shax sat, their knees almost touching. Her eyes flashed with dangerous hunger.

"Now, what brings you to my city?" she asked.

Son of a bitch! There went his hope she was merely passing through. His mind raced, trying to find a way out of his predicament. Maybe the Gate would miraculously rebuild itself in the next thirty seconds, and he could return to Hell.

"The fountains," he said, remembering some weird touristy poster declaring Kansas City the City of Fountains. From the little he had seen, there was a shitload of the things.

She smiled, amused rather than angry at his smart-ass reply.

"I wondered what happened to you. I saw you fall but heard not a peep. The thought of your death saddened me." Aeshma even managed a pretty little pout. "And now, here you are, spying on me from trees and thinking I wouldn't find you to ask about it later. Care to explain?"

Damn, he had forgotten the duke knew his second form.

"I did not realize Kansas City was yours, Your Grace." If Aeshma insisted, Shax would beat the honorific until it was dead. "I'm just passing through. I'll be out of your hair as soon as possible."

With dead eyes, Aeshma reached up and cupped his cheek, rubbing her thumb against his lower lip.

"You're cute, Shaxie, thinking you have a choice, now. It so happens I have a recent opening in my horde. You remember Hinndal?"

Shax nodded, expressionless, keeping his heart rate slow.

"I sent him on one little mission, and the bugger went radio silent. Can't trust anyone these days."

"I'm sorry. I thought Hinndal a dependable sort."

"As did I. Your arrival is timely. I have a job I think you are well-suited for."

"Honestly, Your Grace—" He tried to protest, but her steely glare cut him off.

"You never were a joiner, were you?"

"No. The one time I did, the results were not as I'd hoped."

This brought a musical laugh out of the slight demon. At least Aeshma had a sense of humor. Most of the Dukes did not, and Shax had often run for his life after an unwelcome joke.

"I always said you were the comedian among us."

"One must have...talents...to survive in Hell."

"Ah, yes. Speaking of talents, I am thrilled you still have your ability to transform. So many of us lost our remaining gifts that it's hard to find anyone suited to the particular mission I have in mind. If memory serves, you've always been more curious than was good for you. Let's see if I can put that curiosity to good use. Mine."

Aeshma stood up and straightened her skirt.

"If you are not in my car in fifteen minutes," she said, "I will send Asag and Orax looking for you. If they find you, they will drag you back so I can renew our acquaintance. The last time you pissed me off, you lived to regret it. This time you won't."

Her sweet smile belied the vicious punishment she referenced, sending disgust rushing through him. He could not sit comfortably for days, waiting for the skin on his back and buttocks to regrow. She leaned in, her ample cleavage almost falling out of the low-cut blouse, her spicy perfume mixed with the taste of the bile he fought to keep down. He wanted to puke on her shiny black stilettos.

"Goodbye, Shaxie."

Shax was out of choices for the moment. If he didn't join them, he would join poor Hinndal in death, probably after spending a day or two begging for such release.

The door closed behind the duke and her bodyguard. As soon as her tapping heels and the tromp of boots faded down the walkway, Shax gathered his things and stuffed them into his duffel bag.

The good news: he'd kept his promise to Kheone. The bad news: he'd kept his promise to Kheone.

Chapter 19

Exactly fifteen minutes later, Shax showed up at the black sedan idling in the motel parking lot. The dark-haired heavy waited beside the car.

"You cost me twenty bucks, motherfucker," he said.

"Which one are you?" Shax asked.

"Orax."

The demon yanked the bag out of Shax's hand and opened the door.

"Hey, be careful."

In reply, the demon swung the bag at his head. Shax ducked, and the bag sailed over his head and landed in a puddle of slush six feet behind him.

"Fuck you."

Okay, that's how this would be. Shax got into the car while Orax loaded his soaked bag into the trunk. There was a bloodstain in the middle of the back seat, probably from the man he had watched them abduct.

Aeshma sat behind the driver, her other bodyguard. The duke noticed where his gaze lingered.

"I needed his help, too," she said, looking pointedly at the bloodstain. "Navigating these modern accounting systems takes a special talent, which, unfortunately, I do not possess."

Shax swallowed, knowing what she wanted him to ask. He hated giving it to her, but he must play along for now.

"What happened to him?"

Aeshma held her hand palm up with her fingers spread. A crackling ball of blue and purple flame burst into existence, and a sulfurous smell filled the sedan.

"Ashes to ashes, pet."

She closed her hand, extinguishing the flames. Orax climbed into the car, and the other, Asag, he presumed, put the car in drive.

It was one thing to make a promise to Kheone to find the Duke. It was quite another to come face-to-face with her. In the end, a perverse desire to undermine any plans Aeshma was cooking up overruled his flight or fight response. If he could pass along any details of her plans to Kheone, the angels might run a spike into Aeshma's scheme. The fact that if he left the city, he would also leave Kheone had absolutely nothing to do with his decision. Really.

A smile touched her lips, sugar laced with venom, and hunger darkened her eyes.

"I am glad you made the right choice," Aeshma said. "I've missed you. My current horde is unimaginative at best, and not one of them is nearly as pretty as you. My stay in Kansas City just got much better."

He returned her smile, suppressing the skin-crawling disgust he felt.

"As long as your hotel is better than that dump, so has mine."

"You think I would settle for anything other than the best?"

"Of course not, Your Grace."

Aeshma reached into the expensive leather purse on her other side and pulled out a small flask. She offered it to Shax.

"Have a drink. Then we'll discuss business."

Shax considered the flask, unable to hide his suspicion. Even odds she'd poisoned it.

"Oh, come on. Why would I offer you a job only to poison you?" she asked, her smile slipping a fraction. Aeshma took a sip from the flask. "There. I certainly wouldn't poison myself."

Out of options, Shax took the flask. She would, in fact, poison herself if she had the antidote. But Aeshma, unlike the other Dukes, usually needed a reason to kill someone, especially someone who might be useful to her. As far as he knew, he hadn't given her one. He was probably safe.

He was going to need this. Shax raised the flask.

"To Your Grace."

Aeshma took the flask back from him.

"You know, all this 'Your Grace' shit gets old after a while. Call me Aeshma when we're alone. You always used to."

In Hell, Lucifer had enforced his freedoms, bought with thousands of years of loyal service and other favors. Without the Prince, all bets were off. Aeshma had extended a serious olive branch. Shax grabbed hold of it.

"Thank you, Aeshma. Now, would you care to tell me why I'm here?"

"You still look good, Shax," she said, not answering his question. She would get to it when she was in the mood.

"As do you, Aeshma. Haven't aged a day." Vanity, thy name is Aeshma. Some things had not changed.

She preened under his attention, a wide smile gracing her lush lips. Shax toed a careful line. They had worked together, occasionally, when Lucifer had no other use for him. Although he and the duke shared a penchant for using sex to get what they wanted, he did not want to be pulled so far into her sphere of influence he could never escape. He would have to work against Aeshma every minute of every day in order to make that happen.

The duke's look turned calculating. "I have a proposal for you."

His flattery worked. Shax forced his body to relax, dropping his shoulders and releasing all of his tension. Every fiber of his being told him danger awaited but running now would be far more perilous.

"What could you possibly need from me?"

"With Hinndal gone, I find myself in need of a new spy. Although you can't turn invisible as he could, a demon disguised as a pussy cat might be almost as good."

A sly grin drew her red lips up into a beguiling smile. She put emphasis on the word pussy, giving away where her mind had wandered, and the gutter was a level or two above that.

"I can't drop everything because you can't keep track of your minions." Shax was pushing it, but if he gave in too easily, she would suspect his motives.

"Do you now?" Her voice was sweet, too sweet. "Figured out how to communicate with Lucifer? Some other miraculous feat I should be aware of?"

He held up his hands in defeat. It was a token protest, anyway.

"You caught me. I don't have anywhere to be, nothing to do. I'm having the time of my life doing jack shit. Forgive me for trying to keep it that way."

Better thought lazy than be suspected of betrayal. He hoped to ditch the only assignment left to him. After their recent encounters, killing Kheone for Lucifer was the last thing he wanted to do. He did not allow his mind to linger on the things he did want to do to her, with her.

Aeshma's giggles brought him back to reality. Chills ran up and down his spine, replacing the heat the simple thought of Kheone conjured.

"Poor Shaxie. Just when you thought you were free and clear, old obligations come calling. Sorry to rain on your parade, but I have need of your talents. The Gate is gone, and I'm the last duke standing, so I get to call the shots. Do well in my service, and I'll make it worth your while. Money, whores, food, drink, drugs. You can have *anything* you want."

Her voice dropped into a husky thrum, lingering on the *anything*, imbuing it with as much meaning as her pouty lips and heaving breasts could. That was what he'd been waiting for. Aeshma was desperate. She needed him. He steeled his face into bland acceptance and let her get the win, even though she had no authority to give him what he truly wanted.

"Fine. How can I be of service, Your Grace?"

She smiled wickedly at him and licked her lips. Another reason he did not want to be here. Aeshma was invariably looking to get him in her bed. Keeping her hands off him was going to take some finesse. He might miss the power of being a demon, but he did not miss the politics.

And he didn't miss the feeling of drowning in despair and corruption, poisoning his soul over and over with every kill he made on Lucifer's behalf.

"Hinndal was spying on a gathering of angels in the city for me. I need you to take over. My other source has become somewhat...unreliable of late."

He kept his muscles relaxed as his brain kicked into high gear. Irony was coming home to roost. She wanted him to spy on the angels who wanted him to spy on her. Jesus. Forget mortals being fools. Shax was at the top of the list.

Something else caught his attention. Aeshma had a source. Who? If she had another shifter, he wouldn't be sitting here having a nice, civil conversation with her. Could be a what, not a who. Maybe an eavesdropping spell gone wonky. Or they had mastered some of the newer technology and placed a fancy bug in the building. Whatever it was, Aeshma wasn't pleased. So now she wanted him.

"I can do that. When do you want me to start?"

"First thing in the morning should suffice. Hinndal disappeared a few days ago, and I know those angels are up to something." Pot meet kettle. "You need to find out what it is. I'd rather not leave Kansas City, but I will if need be. I like it here."

Here was his opportunity to put his amazing spy skills to work and pretend he knew nothing.

"Great. Where are they?" Shax asked.

"Hurst University. Have you run across it yet?" she asked, her voice all too innocent.

He shook his head. "As I said, passing through."

Aeshma smiled, a feral thing one step removed from a threat.

"I'll give you directions tomorrow. Use your discretion, but report to me immediately upon your return. If I am not in my room, I have one of these damned devices." She pulled out a cell phone and wiggled it in front of him. "Orax will give you the number."

The car stopped.

"We're here," Asag said.

She got out and opened the door for the duke. Shax retrieved his bag from the trunk. At least it no longer dripped.

He stared up at the hotel's ritzy Art Deco facade. Definitely an improvement from his one-star digs of late. If only the company he kept was better, like, in any way possible. He would rather sleep next to an alligator than here with the demons, but Aeshma hadn't given him much of a choice. Run and be hunted or join them.

"Is there anything else I need to know?"

There was a whole Goddamned mountain she was not telling him, but he could not tip his hand yet. Perhaps she believed she was sending him into a trap. Or she hoped he would get himself killed by something he didn't expect because she withheld vital information. Both scenarios were as likely as her request taken at face value. Good thing he already had an in with the angels.

Aeshma did not answer, cold cunning in her eyes, the feral grin still plastered on her red lips. She typed something into the phone.

"I have three suites on the top floor, and there's a spare bed for you. Let's get you a key, and then you can get some sleep. Unless you'd rather do something else?"

Her voice held the faintest hint of seduction. This was not the first time Aeshma had tried to lure him into her bed. It wouldn't be the last, either. Shax shook his head.

"I would hate for fatigue to lead to my discovery, Your Grace. Sleeping in a decent bed for once would be nice."

"Pity."

A flash of anger lit her face, and she strode into the lobby, forcing him to follow. He would have to tread carefully.

Compared to the rest of the clientele, he was vastly underdressed. His ratty jeans, frayed t-shirt, and worn duffle full of his worldly possessions screamed he did not belong. Only his fine, well-kept leather jacket and the woman he accompanied prevented the doorman from calling security.

The young woman at the desk watched them like a hawk. She wore what seemed at first glance to be a pleasant smile. Shax knew the look well. It was the look humans always got when confronted with someone or *something* they knew could eat them alive. Their hindbrains told them to look as non-threatening as possible, to be as submissive as possible, to avoid a confrontation they had no hope of winning.

"Good evening..." Aeshma let her gaze linger for a few seconds too long on the clerk's name tag, conveniently located above her right breast. "Nina. I'm afraid we need another room key for 2004."

"Of, of course, Your Grace."

Nina looked half-relieved to focus her gaze on the computer, avoiding Aeshma's gaze. The clerk tapped away, her fingers moving rapidly and hitting the keys harder than necessary. Sweat beaded at her brow. Shax had a few ideas of what must have put the fear of Aeshma in the hotel staff, none of them pretty.

The clerk grabbed a key card and ran it through the little machine. Fingers trembling, she offered the key to Aeshma.

"There you go. Is there anything else I can do for you, Your Grace?"

The young woman impressed Shax, keeping her voice smooth, polite even. Aeshma gave her a toothy grin as she allowed her fingers to graze those of the clerk. When Nina flinched from the contact, the grin only widened. Bastard enjoyed torturing random humans, even those doing their best to help her. Shax needed to keep that in mind. No matter how far back their relationship went, no matter how often they had worked together, Aeshma was a demon. Her entire purpose was to torture and be tortured. Since she much preferred the former, she held onto whatever power she could with an iron fist. And with Lucifer locked in Hell, the duke thought she had all the power.

"That will be all, pet," she said, saccharine dripping off the words. "This is my friend, Mr. Shaxie. Please extend him the same courtesies you do me."

"Yes, of course. Welcome, Mr. Shaxie."

Shax rolled his eyes. Now every employee of this Godforsaken hotel would call him by that awful nickname. There was no taking it back, and he certainly didn't blame poor Nina. She would be lucky to still be alive when Aeshma and her demon horde finally checked out.

"Thank you, Nina," was all he said.

They followed Asag to the elevators. She punched the button for the top floor. Of course, Aeshma would have the penthouse suite.

The duke pulled out her phone and tapped on it in the miasma of silence filling the elevator. When the doors opened, the fug of deadly intentions followed them down the hall. Aeshma handed the key card to him, her fingers lingering on his. Cold dread washed through him.

"Are you certain you don't want company?" she purred.

He pulled the card away gently. One did not offend a Duke of Hell without considering the consequences.

"You know my rules about mixing business with pleasure, Your Grace," Shax said. He never had sex with anyone he worked for. Not anymore, and he made sure word spread.

"A girl can dream." Another pretty pout graced her red-painted lips. "Perhaps I might change your mind."

Shax gave her a bone. "Perhaps."

Duke Aeshma sashayed down the hall. He swiped the key card and ducked into his room before she changed her mind. Shax leaned against the wall, his heart rate slowly returning to normal. He was in such deep trouble, and what he was going to do next would probably mean his head on a silver platter should anyone find out.

He tossed his bag into the closet and pulled out the silver coin in his pocket. Kheone needed to know what had happened. Closing his hand around the coin, he whispered her name, the feel of it on his tongue causing his heart to race once again, for an entirely different reason.

Chapter 20

Guilt wormed through Kheone's dreams, tormenting her. Serel's dead eyes stared at her, unseeing yet knowing how she had failed. His blood dripped from her sword.

"I'm sorry. I'm sorry. I'm sorry," her dream self said, stabbing him with it, over and over.

Strong arms grabbed her from behind and twisted the sword out of her hand. Michael pulled her into his hard body. In her dream, she lost herself in his liquid kisses and the warm shelter of his embrace. Pulling away, the embers of desire smoldering deep inside her, she looked up. It wasn't Michael. Shax's golden gaze mirrored her desire, amplifying it, until the flames within escaped and lit the world on fire.

Torn from her arms, she watched helplessly as he burned in the inferno they had created. Shax smiled at her, unaware of the pain she'd caused until nothing remained except ashes scattered by the wind. Gone.

A pattering, like rain on concrete, woke her. Kheone slammed against the limits of her physical body. The deep fatigue caused by nights of grief and days of chasing clues with no end to the business of the gathering made opening her eyes a near-impossible task. And the deal she had made with a devil. She must not forget that ill-conceived abomination of a decision.

The noise repeated. Kheone forced her body to obey her commands. She swung her legs out of bed and stumbled across the small room toward the window where the noise seemed to come from. Kheone opened it just in time to catch a face full of pebbles.

Shax was a contrast in dark and light, his black leather jacket and blue jeans blending into the night. His hair glowed in the dim light cast by the lamp in the middle of the courtyard. He was beautiful, ghostly, dangerous.

"Hey, Blue," he said. Shax dropped the next handful of stones and waggled his fingers at her with a goofy grin. She almost didn't recognize him without his usual smirk.

She used to hate the nickname he had called her since the day they'd met. Hated it liked she had hated nothing else in this world or the next. But the way he said the name now—she didn't hate it, not even a little.

"Shh," she hissed at him. "Do you want to get us both killed?"

He shrugged. "I have news, and you weren't at the tree."

"Shut up." She jerked her head toward a dark patch on the far side of the building. "I'm coming out."

Kheone closed the window as quietly as she could. She bundled up and threaded her curved sword onto her belt. Its heavy weight hung at her hip, offering reassurance she could handle anything the demon threw at her. She yanked her door open, looking up and down the hall. No heads poked out into the silent hall, and the noises from the common room didn't change in volume or tone. Breathing a sigh of relief, she hurried outside and sprinted toward the dark thicket.

"Shax?" she whispered.

"Here."

Shax stepped out of the shadows, only his snow-white hair indicating he was anything other than a shade himself. Shax, who had not been at their tree, either, when she'd showed up an hour late. Kheone had waited for another two hours, just in case, but returned to the dorm, worried about him. The damned demon had made her worry about him. And now that he was in front of her, safe and sound, she wanted to—

Kheone walked right up to him and shoved his shoulder. Hard. It was the only thing she could think of to keep from kissing him. His arms windmilled, keeping him upright. She suppressed the chuckle that burbled up at the ungainly sight.

"Did you lose your last brain cell in the Second Fall? Why in the nine spheres of Heaven are you here?"

Shax cleared his throat. "You know, I think your insults are getting better."

Kheone brushed her jacket away from the sword on her hip and placed her hand on its hilt.

"Try me, demon."

He held up his hands in surrender, but a small grin creased his eyes.

"And here I thought we were becoming friends."

"We'll never be friends, Shax."

Her voice was icy calm, and Shax jerked away as though her words were weapons. Perhaps they were. Weapons to keep him from finding out how much she wished they could be more than friends.

"Allies, then," he said in a fake, cheery tone and pasted on a phony grin.

The idea left her cold. She wanted something else from the demon who wanted to be her friend. Kheone wanted him. It would never happen, no matter the heat in his touch or how often he appeared in her dreams.

Kheone nodded and removed her hand from her blade. She could live with being his ally, at least until they found Serel's killer. She had agreed to this bargain, but after they fulfilled it, they must go their separate ways for both their sakes'.

"What in God's sweet name couldn't wait until tomorrow?" she asked.

"I found Aeshma." A wry grin crossed his face. "Well, actually, she found me."

"Really?" That was an odd bit of luck.

"We have a bargain. I won't lie to you while it is in effect."

Kheone considered his words. He had done nothing yet to lose her trust. And as often as demons lied, they generally abided by an agreement once locked into it.

"And? What are the demons up to?"

Shax's shoulders tightened, and whatever amusement lingered vanished.

"I don't know yet. I am here to tell you I found them. And I'm supposed to spy on you."

"Spy on us? Why not kill us?"

He shrugged. "They don't trust me enough to tell me yet. But my guess is they know Michael hangs around. No demon is going to challenge the Archangel Michael."

It made as much sense as anything else these days, which was to say, none whatsoever. A pulsing pain hit her temple. She didn't need any of this. When could she return to hunting down demons and reading books?

"Your turn," he said.

"Serel put a spell on the book. It's unreadable."

Kheone neglected to tell him the object in question was no longer in her possession. That was a problem for another time. Once she proved her theory, she could get the book back from Michael.

He whistled. "Must be a doozy of a spell."

"Yeah, but I think he hid some notes on the book somewhere. Maybe those will tell us how to break the spell."

Two layers of protection on the book. There might be more. After all, Serel had hidden it in the library, the letter to Father Fauci in his dresser, and the notes who knew where. Her friend had been more scared than he had let on the night before he died.

"Any ideas where to look?" Shax asked with a shrewd look. He caught the edge of his lip in his teeth and worried at it a moment, lost in thought.

She shook her head. "I haven't had the chance to think about it, let alone to start poking around the dorm. For all I know, Serel hid them somewhere far from here."

"Next move?" he asked.

"I'll try to turn up the notes. If I can't, I'll try to break the spell."

"What do you want me to do about Aeshma?"

"Lie. Isn't that what demons are good at?" Her bitter words made him flinch.

For Heaven's sake, frustration with her situation was no excuse for hurting Shax. He deserved better from her. And so did she.

"I'm sorry, Shax. You've been honest with me."

"No, you're right. I need to lie to her, but Aeshma won't buy just any old shit I make up. There has to be a kernel of truth to it."

He wasn't wrong.

"Tell her we're wary after losing an angel, but don't mention the special circumstances. And yes, I know that makes me sound more like one of you than one of us."

A mocking grin spread over his face, and he gave her a salute. "Yes, ma'am."

Kheone fought her own smile. "I need to get back. Michael doesn't want me out by myself while he's gone. He's afraid whoever went after Serel will come after me next. There will be Hell to pay if he finds out."

Crap, she hadn't meant to tell him Michael wasn't around. It was too late to take back the words.

"I'll be the judge of that," he said, a rich, warm chuckle following his words, sending shivers down her spine. The good kind.

Her brain definitely told her she couldn't trust him, but her foolish body didn't listen. At least it appeared Shax had not caught her little slip up.

"Who would have thought the loyal Kheone capable of disobeying Michael? Before you know it, you'll throw your lot in with Lucifer."

She snorted. "I'm not alone. You're here."

"I am." Shax's lips curved into a genuine smile this time. "I'll help however I can."

"Thank you, Shax."

"You're welcome, Kheone."

The use of her name earned him a genuine smile as he faded into the night. She had said they would never be friends. It was madness to think they could be anything other than what they were, but her heart was telling her it might be possible. Kheone pulled her thoughts from that path, and with a heavy heart, headed inside.

Chapter 21

Returning to the hotel was much harder than leaving. Shax snuck in through the back entrance and took the stairs up all twenty flights, not wanting to risk running into Aeshma or anyone else. All he wanted to do was sleep, but his mind raced.

Serel, like the good angel he was, wrote notes. He hid them somewhere. No, Shax knew exactly where. In the kitchen pantry, at the dorm full of angels, who would kill him if they spotted him.

He ordered a bottle of vodka delivered to his room. Fuck the cost. Aeshma was paying. Drinking more than he should, Shax plonked the bottle down on the dresser to remove the temptation to drink himself into oblivion.

The alcohol afforded him the ability to sleep, though he tossed and turned. The image of Michael and Kheone kissing played over and over in his mind. Her words on repeat, saying they would never be friends, but belied by the warmth of her smile, the liquid heat of her eyes when she thought he wasn't looking.

Slipping into a restless doze sometime before the sun rose, nightmares of all kinds plagued him. Chased by Michael, who changed into Lucifer wielding the obsidian dagger. Screwed by Aeshma, and not in the good way. Worst of all, Kheone lying dead in a pool of her own opalescent blood, a sword through her heart. A sword he knew, somehow, was his.

When bugs began crawling down his chest, Shax assumed he was still dreaming, another horror after a night filled with them. He tried ignoring them, but they didn't stop. What was worse, they ran directly south, tickling at his stomach. With a groan, he tried to brush them away. Instead of hard chitin, his fingers met smooth skin. His eyelids popped open.

Aeshma's steely gaze met his, her pink lips curved in a seductive smile. Her fingers danced over his abdomen, inching lower. He grabbed them, stopping their progress. The smile vanished, replaced by the perfect little pout.

"Come on, Shaxie, I was only having a little fun. Thought you'd enjoy a more pleasant wake-up call than Asag pounding at your door."

"I appreciate that, Aeshma, but I prefer to be conscious before engaging in foreplay."

"You're awake now."

He heard the smile in her voice, soft and seductive. Far more subtle than her peers, the Duke of Lust used sex to get exactly what she wanted. A trait they shared. Until he knew what she wanted from him, it was best to keep their relationship less...charged. Although he was attracted to her lovely exterior, the rest of her was much like biting into a decadent chocolate only to discover shit in the center.

"As I said last night, I don't mix business with pleasure." Shax sat up and swung his legs over the edge of the bed, keeping his naked back to her.

His head turned at her sharp intake of breath. Aeshma stared at his back, hand half raised.

"They're beautiful," she whispered.

He had taken a long look at the wings inked onto his shoulders only once, in a cesspit of a motel room in Florida. The brilliant color in the cracked bathroom mirror had caught his attention, and tears of relief streamed down. For ten thousand years, he had worn leathery demon wings, the color of dried blood, but his cardinal red angel wings had returned to grace his skin. He had no explanation and, until recently, no one else to compare his wings to since he spent every waking moment avoiding both angels and demons.

Aeshma's fingers reached out, brushing his skin below them, outlining the trailing edge.

"So few of us have wings, Shax, and I've seen none like these. How did you end up with *angel* wings?"

He shrugged and inched away. "I woke up in Florida with these tattooed on my back. That's it."

The duke choked out an unhappy sound. He heard rustling on her side of the bed. Soon enough, she crossed the room, hips swaying in form-fitting hot pink yoga pants. His red t-shirt dangled from a finger.

"Are you certain you don't want a little morning pussy?" she asked.

"I have work to do, Aeshma, unless your unreliable source has reversed course in the last few hours."

Disbelief flitted across her face, but she either accepted his statement or chose not to pursue it for the moment.

"Get dressed." The duke tossed the shirt at him. "Come see me when you're ready."

Aeshma glided into the hall, and only then did Shax take a deep breath and relax his muscles. Staying out of Aeshma's bed would be a tricky proposition if she continued her seduction campaign. There may come a time when he couldn't refuse her without raising all kinds of misery, but today was not that day. He wanted a drink.

It was too early. Besides, he was still a little drunk from the vodka last night. He settled for a hot cup of coffee and a cold shower, finally getting his traitorous body under some semblance of control. His hook-up in St. Louis felt very long ago.

A middle-aged woman opened the door to Aeshma's suite when he knocked a half-hour later, her long, brown hair threaded with silver and worn in a braid over one shoulder. She was tall for a human woman but still several inches shorter than Shax. Despite the silver in her hair, her face had few wrinkles. She exuded a mystical power, though definitely not a demon. A pet witch, perhaps?

"You're late," she said in a tired voice, her mouth twisted in annoyance as she backed away from the door.

"I didn't know I had an appointment."

She looked at him sharply but said nothing as she led him past a small bathroom and a kitchen, walking into a well-appointed sitting room. A TV took up most of a wall. Large, overstuffed chairs surrounded a comfortable-looking sofa. The sight would have been more inviting had he not recognized the figure sitting in a chair.

There was nothing about him that would stand out in a crowd, except for the skin-tingling, creeping sensation anyone with a brain felt when standing anywhere near the motherfucker. His average height, average build, medium-brown hair, matching brown eyes, and a placid, forgettable face were Peth's greatest assets. His extraordinary ordinariness caught most people off guard, usually just long enough for the demon to strike.

Shax suppressed a shudder. He preferred to make his kills clean. Perhaps a quick stab to the heart or a clean cut to the throat. No muss, no fuss.

Peth was a messy bastard, enjoying nothing more than torture followed by the painful death of his victim. He was the Dukes' favorite freelance torturer. His victims lasted days, sometimes even weeks, begging for death. Peth's presence told him all he needed to know about the kind of duke Aeshma was.

"Hello, Peth," he said, noticing the woman kept herself as far from the other demon as possible. He didn't blame her one bit. The only mercy Peth granted was killing you before he ate you.

Peth grinned at him, a malicious thing full of hatred and jealousy.

"Go fetch Her Grace while I acquaint myself with…" Shax said.

"Irena," the woman whispered.

"Duke Aeshma is otherwise occupied, Shax. She won't appreciate your interruption," Peth sneered, glancing at the door to Shax's left.

Lusty moans drifted out of the room, giving him hints as to what occupied Aeshma. She had insisted he report to her as soon as he could, probably hoping he would join in. Shax sighed and shut out the distraction.

"Would you rather I tell her you failed to inform her I was here?"

Peth's grin faded, replaced by uncertainty. He could see the gears turning in the monster's head. Shax outranked every demon except the Dukes and Lucifer. If Peth challenged him now, he could very well end up dead. And if Aeshma wanted to know when Shax arrived, and he failed to perform that task, well…the Duke of Lust was not famous for her mercy.

"Fine, but if she's upset, it's coming out of your hide, not mine."

Peth heaved himself off the chair and walked into the bedroom, the moans invading the quiet of the sitting room. Shax glimpsed Aeshma's naked body writhing on the bed before the door shut.

"Was that wise?" Irena asked.

Shax shrugged. "It was necessary."

Early in their acquaintance, Peth had tried to claim a soul Shax had corrupted as his own victory. Shax had beaten him nearly to death in front of Lucifer and all the Dukes. The other demon had given him a wide berth ever since.

"The best way to deal with Peth is to teach him a lesson he won't forget. I merely reminded him of the lesson I taught him eons ago."

Irena peered at him.

"You're not like the others, are you?" she said, coming to some sort of conclusion.

"I'm exactly like the others," he said, giving her his best boyish grin laced with iron. "Except when I'm not."

He walked over to her, and she flattened against the wall attempting to keep some distance between them. Shax placed a hand flat on the wall, next to her head, and leaned in close. She watched him warily, yet she was not afraid. *Curious.*

"I wouldn't do that, Shaxie," Aeshma said, exiting the bedroom. Shax withdrew his hand and took a step away, looking over at the duke. She placed a rather large vibrator on a table next to the door, and the curve of a creamy breast disappeared under a silky dressing gown. "My sorceress is highly intelligent, unlike most of her species. She devised a spell of some sort, which makes touching her agonizing for our kind. Well, your kind. I find it a good reminder if I wish to lay a finger on the bitch, I best be prepared for some pain. Shall I demonstrate?"

Ah, that explained Irena's lack of fear. He wondered if the woman realized she was only safe from Aeshma as long as Aeshma allowed her to be. Probably, if she was smart enough to devise the spell. No need to feel sorry for the evil sorceress; certainly no need to make friends with her. He wasn't even sure why he'd given her the best advice he had to offer.

"That won't be necessary, Your Grace," Shax said.

"Oh, no, I insist."

Aeshma closed the distance and grabbed Irena's arm, digging her fingernails into the other woman's flesh. The duke hissed in a breath, but after a moment, a joyless smile formed on her lips. Irena went pale, then green. The demon released her.

"Off you go, Irena, unless you'd like to wait for Peth?"

"No, Your Grace."

Irena inspected the blood oozing out of the half-moons Aeshma's fingernails left in her skin. She looked as though she wanted to say something else but thought better of it. Irena left, her steps quick, but she did not run. Running only encouraged the predator to chase.

Shax opened his mouth to ask about the sorceress. Although not unheard of for a demon to hire a practitioner of magic when called for, Lucifer generally gave his Dukes enough power to take care of anything they might encounter. A moment's thought answered his unvoiced question.

With their connection to Hell gone, so were many of their powers, even the duke's. Having a sorceress available would allow Aeshma to operate near her normal capacity. Shax shut his trap before he could embarrass himself.

The duke sat on the sofa, the split in her robe showing off her rounded thigh. Shax swallowed. Getting involved with Aeshma was nearly as bad an idea as making a blood oath to an angel. That did the trick. Any lust he felt for the duke disappeared at the mere thought of Kheone, replaced by something he chose not to poke at. He might not like what he found. Or, worse, might like it too much.

"Coffee?" he asked, heading to the kitchen.

She trailed a pink fingernail along the edge of her dressing gown, drawing his gaze to the swell of her breasts. Her full lips, the same color as her nails, pulled up into a sultry smile, but she made no mention of his obvious attempt to distance himself from her. Aeshma looked as much of a coquette as she had ever been in Louis XIV's court. Shax took another deep breath, pushing down his natural and annoying attraction to her.

He made another cup of coffee, her predatory stare leaving a dead weight in the pit of his stomach. Leaning against the counter, he sipped at it, the warmth dispelling the dread clawing at him.

"I thought you wanted me to spy on the angels first thing," he said, voice calm and even.

"I do, but what kind of friend would I be if I didn't let you renew your acquaintance with dear Peth?"

Maybe Aeshma had learned a lesson or two. This was a much more subtle reminder of her power than she usually gave. Or maybe she merely wanted another chance at him. Before the Second Fall, he rarely turned down a good time. Until he found himself in Kansas City, he hadn't turned down a single opportunity to get his rocks off.

"And Irena? Is she your recently unreliable source?"

Aeshma waved a finger at him. "Uh uh. A lady never reveals all her secrets."

Shax snorted, unable to keep his cynicism to himself. The duke glowered beautifully at him. He needed to watch his tendency to assholery. It would get him killed.

"What am I doing here, Aeshma?"

"I thought you might want to put off your new career as a spy. I find it's hard to start my day without an orgasm or two. Care to join me?"

This question he could answer one hundred percent honestly.

"Thank you, but soonest started, soonest ended."

A pretty little pout graced Aeshma's lips. "Suit yourself."

He stood and offered her a hand, like a proper demon would for his duke. The robe gaped open as she stood, mostly because she meant it to, offering a taste of what he was giving up.

"Goodbye, Your Grace."

Aeshma said nothing, merely waggling her fingers at him as she slipped into the bedroom, smiling coyly as she let the robe drop. Shax turned away. He didn't know if the contempt sweeping over him was for her or for himself for being attracted to her despite everything.

Chapter 22

"Meow." The plaintive cry greeted Kheone as she walked into her room, hair damp from her shower. Her cat sat on the outside window ledge, scratching at the clear panes. She hurried over and opened the window.

"Well, hello there. Did you miss me, Machka?" Kheone asked in the affectionate voice she reserved for the cat.

He bumped his head against her hand, and she obliged him with scratches under his chin and behind his ears. Machka jumped down and twined himself between her ankles, purring loudly.

Kheone scooped him up into her arms, leaving the window cracked. The little cat let out a squawk of protest. She stroked the sleek fur, and the cat's firm muscles relaxed under her touch. Kheone laughed, carrying him to the cabinet in her room. She pulled out a can of plain tuna.

"I thought you might be back." Kheone opened the can and spooned some onto a paper plate.

Machka squirmed out of her arms and trotted over to the food. She stroked his back as he gulped down his treat. The cat licked his lips and stretched. Instead of making a beeline for the window, he jumped on the bed, turned around a few times, and curled up. His tail covered his nose, and he closed his amber eyes.

Grateful for the quiet company, Kheone sat down at her desk, staring at the only decoration in her room. The poster of her favorite painting from the Nelson-Atkins Museum usually brought her joy, but not today. Too much was going on today. Shaking her head, she took a deep breath and reached to the small of her back, massaging the knot of discomfort. Kheone rearranged the calendar and papers on her desk, procrastinating the task at hand. She needed a new patrol schedule before noon.

Kheone crumpled up her first attempt. She forgot to take sleep into account. Though the angels could work on less sleep, if needed, they performed better with a good night's rest. Once she completed the second draft, she put it to the side and stood up.

Machka opened his eyes and mewed at her, a question in his pitiful voice.

"It's been a long week," she said.

He blinked, stretched, and jumped off the bed. Rubbing his cheek on her legs for a moment, once he received his due attention, he leaped onto her desk. The cat batted her pens off the edge and messed up all her papers. She laughed in spite of herself.

"I agree. Work is pointless when there's a cat to play with."

Kheone picked up a pen and swished it back and forth on the edge of the desk. Machka flicked a paw at the pen, tail twitching. Then he stopped. The cat's nose twitched at something undetectable to Kheone. He arched his back, and his fur stood on end, suddenly seeming much larger. Machka hissed and dashed straight to the window, clearing the sill with marvelous grace.

She smelled the ozone, then. A split second later, a red line grew in the middle of her room, expanding until it framed a broad figure holding a sword. Michael stepped into the room, leaving the rift open behind him, a grim look darkening his face.

"What's wrong?" Kheone crossed the room and grabbed her sword.

"Has anything occurred since we last talked?" He surveyed the room, tension in the crease of his brow. Michael held the rest of his body in relaxed readiness, a perfect warrior's stance.

One did not lie to an archangel lightly, but she had no way of explaining to him how she knew what she did. Aeshma was in town, and her only source was a demon she wanted to kiss. That would go over well, just before Michael sent her to the afterlife. If such a thing even existed anymore.

"No, it's been quiet," she lied. "Why?"

"Gather everyone you can, Lieutenant. Tailash is missing."

Yes, she remembered Tailash. He had spent several weeks here training before assuming command in Nairobi. A good fighter with an easy-going leadership style. The angels liked him, but she'd had doubts about how effective he would be. He was more successful than she feared, fortunately.

"How heavily do you want us armed?"

"Carry as much as you can. Are you able to open a rift that far?"

Kheone nodded, belying her doubt. She hoped she could. If not, she would make a pit stop in Morocco to keep her gathering safe. What Michael didn't know wouldn't hurt him. Only results mattered.

"Good. Bring them to Nairobi as soon as possible. I will meet you there."

Steel entered her voice, hard, detached.

"I'm not staying here while you go back. This could be a trap. You need me."

"Are you questioning my orders, Lieutenant?" Michael's voice iced over.

The thought of allowing him to go into danger without her rankled. The thought maybe he didn't trust her to have his back stung even more. But millennia of discipline kicked in.

"No, Archangel. I thought—"

Michael's voice rang out even more serious than usual and filled the small room.

"I am the right hand of God, and all my powers are still intact. I can kill dozens of demons and barely break a sweat. I am not worried about me. I am worried about you."

"I'm perfectly able to take care of myself." Her voice, too, rang with authority.

"I know. I trained you. But if whoever killed Serel did so to send me a message or provoke me, you are the next likely target. You are..." He cleared his throat before continuing, his voice softer, more intimate. "You are too important to your gathering, too important to me. Come when you have all the backup possible, and not before. I cannot concentrate on the enemy if I have doubts over your safety."

The words stunned her. Perhaps they shouldn't have. Michael had made his feelings clear the other night when he kissed her.

"Of course, Archangel." It was the only appropriate answer to a direct order, though it still rankled.

"Good. I will see you soon. Call the Nairobi gathering should anything unexpected occur."

"Understood. Anything else?"

With a quick, fierce grin, Michael closed the distance between them, hunger in his eyes. The red light of the rift lent an air of danger to the simple movement.

"Do not think I have forgotten our conversation, Kheone. Once this business is concluded, we will resume where we left off."

He placed a lightning kiss on her forehead and ran into the rift. It vanished with a snap.

Kheone stared at the spot for a moment, gathering her thoughts, making sure the past few minutes had not been a delirium dream she would wake up from any moment. She set aside her personal feelings. This was no time to wonder how that conversation with Michael would go.

She bolted out of her room, all thought of the cat chased away by her new mission. Running down the hall, Kheone banged on all the doors she passed.

"Grab your gear. We leave in twenty. Let's move, angels!"

A flurry of activity followed in her wake. Doors opened, and weapons clanked. She raced up the stairs and repeated her actions for the second floor. Once assured everyone was moving their butts, Kheone went back downstairs.

"What's going on, LT?" Emric asked, standing next to the common room.

"Michael needs us in Nairobi."

She squeezed past. A few angels had already gathered, strapping on swords and twirling daggers.

"What about Maj? She's still on patrol."

Crap.

"Call her," Kheone said. "Tell her what's going on. She's to return here and hold down the fort until our return. Grab your sword and join us as soon as you can."

Emric sprinted to the kitchen, their voice a murmur in the background. Kheone waited in the common room for the angels to gather. She stood on a chair, and the room quieted.

"Tailash is missing," she said. A few mumbles greeted her announcement, followed by a few elbows jabbed at the perpetrators. "We're heading to Nairobi. Michael will brief us further once we're there. Be prepared for anything. Questions?"

Nothing but silence. Not like she could have answered their questions, anyway.

Kheone took a few deep breaths, preparing to open the rift. Although she had no further incidents since the other day, she did not want to take any chances. Open too many rifts in quick succession, and she could find herself senseless. Open one too far away, and she could be lost in the between place, a void without time or sensation. She shuddered.

Fixing Nairobi in her mind, the red line and sharp ozone of a rift ripped into existence, bathing those present in a hellish light. It had worked, but her hold was tenuous.

"Go, go, go," she ordered.

One by one, the angels drew their weapons and ran through the rift. A pulsing ache began at her temples. Kheone couldn't hold the rift for much longer. Emric ran down the hall, their sword sound over their shoulder, and, without slowing down, leaped through the rift. Kheone pulled her own sword from its sheath and followed.

Chapter 23

A hush settled over the dorm. Shax twitched his sensitive ears around, searching for any noise indicating he was not alone. He had heard everything from the bushes outside Kheone's window. Now, the only sounds were the creaks of an old building and the wind blowing. Cautiously, he poked his nose out, whiskers trembling. In her mad dash to aid Michael, Kheone had left the window to her room open. Discretion being the better part of valor, Shax jumped inside and hid under the bed.

When he heard nothing but silence, he scurried to the kitchen, still wearing his cat suit. Changing in an instant, he quickly pulled out the soda and felt around again. Nothing. Taking a deep breath, he employed his sneaky-ass demon brain. If he was trying to hide something in a place with shelves, what would he do?

Inspiration struck him. Shax felt around on the bottom of the lowest shelf, where somebody could stash a flat object. His fingers encountered a large envelope taped there. He ripped it off, stuck it down the back of his jeans, and replaced the things he had moved. Shax returned to his cat form and trotted to Kheone's room.

All he had to do was make the leap through the open window. His reluctance to leave confused him. He was already pushing his luck, a commodity he did not have in any significant amount. But this place, this small room, felt like home. Kheone showed affection for him here, all traces of suspicion gone. It had been too long since anyone had expressed affection for him. He had others' fear, respect, even lust, but nothing remotely resembling love since he had followed Lucifer.

What was he going to do? Wait around here for Kheone to return? No, he had the next piece of the puzzle. Besides, he still had to report to Aeshma. Since he was supposedly in his room all night, he had not passed along the information Kheone wanted him to. It was time to rectify that oversight.

Shax leaped out the window and ran. A few blocks away, he changed, pulled out his phone, and summoned a ride.

A short drive later and a mad dash up the stairs, again, he ducked into his room. Too nervous to pull out the unopened envelope in the car, he spared it only a quick glance before stuffing the envelope under his mattress. Careful handwriting spelled out Kheone's name.

Of course. She was the leader of the Kansas City gathering and had been Serel's friend.

Nothing else on the envelope showed what might be inside.

Putting all thought of it out of his mind, he went to face his next task. Orax answered his polite knock.

"Her Grace sleeps," he said.

Waking Aeshma was worrisome. Keeping his news from her was worse.

"I'll tell her I beat you to a pulp if you're afraid," Shax said with a grin.

"Your funeral."

Orax let him in and disappeared through into the connecting room, leaving Shax alone. Shax rapped on the Aeshma's bedroom door. When there was no answer, he tried again.

Only silence greeted him. He inched the door open. The last time he had entered a duke's chambers without an invitation, someone had nearly taken his head off. Since he had been there on Lucifer's orders to take the life of the Duke of Greed, he considered it fair. The duke's minions had fought brutally, afraid for their positions in Hell's hierarchy, but in the end, Shax had delivered the duke's heart to the Prince on a gold platter.

The sultry air was heavy with sex. Aeshma slept alone, on top of the covers, clothed only in a black lace negligee. She had probably kicked out her companion, or companions, not long ago. Shax stood at the foot of the bed, considering the duke's soft curves. Soft where Kheone was firm; short while Kheone was tall. Cruel while Kheone was kind. They were so unalike. Most might choose Aeshma's silken allure and lusty appetite but not him. Shax would take Kheone's fierce beauty and her compassion for a wayward cat any day.

Lifting his hands to show he was no threat, he took a deep breath and cleared his throat. In a heartbeat, Aeshma rolled out of bed and confronted him, heedless of her state of dress, hands glowing blue with demon fire.

"Hello, Your Grace," Shax said, keeping his voice calm.

The glow vanished, and Aeshma reached over to turn on the bedside lamp. Her eyes were stormy with rage, her color high. She stalked over to her wrap, draped carelessly over the chair. Thrusting her arms in, she tied it tightly around her waist. He'd be getting no invitations to stay and share her bed today.

"You have one minute to explain before I call Orax in here to tear your tongue out of your lovely mouth. I'd hate to do that. Tongues can be quite useful when in the right place." She dropped on the chair and smiled cruelly.

Shax bowed and kept his sarcasm to himself. He played a dangerous game. He had defied Lucifer twice. First, by refusing to kill Kheone. Then by refusing to pursue her after the Gates fell. The consequences of those decisions haunted him. His compulsion to find her was constantly at the back of his mind. All he had to do was allow his concentration to slip for an instant, and it returned. He was only spared the buzzing irritation in his brain when he was in Kheone's presence. Their bargain to search for Serel's killer bound them together more tightly than before. Part of him chafed at the cords that tied them together. Part of him delighted in them. He was all kinds of fucked up.

Now embroiled in some sort of twisted spy fantasy, Shax balanced his growing desire for Kheone with his obligation to her and his need to stay alive while fulfilling his agreement with Aeshma. When in the nine circles of Hell had his life fallen apart? The answer came almost immediately. All his plans had collapsed once Hinndal found him in St. Louis. The only thing to go his way was Kheone's reluctance to kill him outright.

He took a breath. Time to play his hand.

"An angel died."

She forced a laugh. "Ha, ha. Very funny."

"I'm serious, Aeshma. There's a dead angel, and the gathering's in turmoil."

The duke hissed in a breath as she contemplated the news. Silence fell, heavy with malice.

"Son of a bitch. Did you do it?" she finally asked.

"No, Your Grace." Short answers were best. Less chance for him to stick his foot in his mouth.

"Why not?"

"I didn't have the opportunity."

"Do they know you're there?"

Shax rarely lied. Not because it was wrong, but because he hated to keep track of his story. Too many stories to keep straight, and he might as well slit his own throat. So, when he did lie, he made sure it was airtight. He kept his lies simple and as close to the truth as possible.

"No." *They* didn't know he was there. Only *Kheone* did.

"Who was it?"

"Serel, I believe." He would never forget it. The agony in Kheone's eyes every time she mentioned him etched the name into his memory.

"Hmm, Serel. I'm afraid I never had the pleasure."

Aeshma seemed remarkably untroubled by this news. What could kill an angel could usually kill a demon. Either she had not made this connection yet, or she knew something she was not telling him. Shax would bet good money on the latter. The duke was not foolish.

"The angels are adjusting their routines, increasing patrols."

"Michael has a protective streak a mile long. It seems fortuitous I found you when I did."

So far, so good. She believed everything he told her. It was the truth, mostly.

"What killed him?" she asked.

Now it got tricky. He could not tell Aeshma about the book, especially after meeting Irena. If he said he had left the book in the library, the duke would send her human servant and discover his lie. And there was no way in Hell he was going to tell her he gave it to Kheone. That would paint a target on the angel's back even she might not survive. He had vowed to help her find Serel's killer, not send a killer after her.

"Not sure. I inspected the library where he died. Found a ton of angel magic." He shivered at the memory, only partly for show. "Just a whiff of demon."

Her pretty, painted fingernail lingered on her bottom lip as she thought.

"Could an angel and a demon be working together somehow?"

Not the question he had expected. And she asked it with a certain sincerity which made him doubt she knew the answer. The duke was either a good actor or was genuinely ignorant. Even odds on which. Aeshma was the most likely candidate, but not the only one. A pair could have built the bomb, taking blood from an angel they had killed.

Shax smiled and replied as truthfully as he could. "In an infinite universe, all things are possible, Aeshma. But if so, why did the angel end up dead? And why wasn't there more demon magic?"

"Good questions. Keep spying, and perhaps you'll find answers for them. Anything else?"

He swallowed. Shax worried what Aeshma might do if she found out the angels' residence was all but deserted. If her other source reported back, he would be in deep shit. Here went nothing.

"Michael's out of town." That was true. "I got the sense it wouldn't be for long, but I don't know for sure."

Aeshma's face split into a smile as cold as Hell.

"Hmm, interesting. I will think on it. We may have an opportunity to act before he returns. Any idea where he might be?"

"Nairobi."

She pressed her lips together, and a flash of outrage flickered in her eyes.

"You have been a busy boy." Aeshma stalked over to him. She drew a red-painted fingernail up his chest, a sly grin on her lips. "What would you like as your reward?"

Shax had to play it like he didn't know exactly what Aeshma offered. She would not take an outright rejection well right now.

"A good bottle of tequila would be sufficient, Your Grace. I've been drinking some real dreck lately."

Her lips made a perfect pout, but she chose not to pursue her original intention.

"Very well. I'll have it sent to your room. When will you return?"

"After dinner, I think." He knew. He had a standing appointment with an angel.

Aeshma nodded.

"I am utterly exhausted, so unless you are joining me, shoo."

He did not wait for her to change her mind. Shax shooed, leaving her to crawl back into her bed, alone. He brewed a cup of coffee in his room and sat down to work. Between himself and Kheone, they had three clues: the book, the runes on the pottery fragments, and now Serel's notes. Shax lifted the mattress and retrieved the envelope he'd found in the angels' dorm. He tore it open with a pocket knife he had lifted from some dude at a mall once. The knife was too useful to pawn.

Shax pulled out five pages covered in tiny, precise writing which looked vaguely recognizable. He was a timeless being and had spoken, read, and written hundreds of languages over the millennia of human civilization. What in Christ's name was this particular form of gibberish? The nucleus of a massive headache pricked his brain.

He sipped the coffee and stared at the first page, hoping it would progress from a fuzzy feeling of familiarity to sudden insight. After several minutes of futilely searching his memory, he downed what was left in the mug and put his head in his hands.

Shax hadn't been Lucifer's favorite because of brains, at least not the kind that translated languages. He'd been cunning, persuasive, and, above all else, beautiful. The perfect instrument to tempt kings and queens, religious leaders and powerful bureaucrats, and the odd hero. He was an equal opportunity tempter, but his favorite sin to lure his marks was lust, sex being one of the few ways to rid himself of the pain of damnation, at least temporarily. And he had used these skills to become the perfect instrument to kill those Lucifer wanted dead and gone, demons, dukes, and humans alike.

Linguistics was not a natural talent for him, but this writing wasn't modern. Although it would be more difficult to pull on the required memories for an ancient language, there were fewer to choose from. He could rule out Latin, Greek, and Hebrew. He had used those for centuries at a time, and their modern counterparts had enough similarities for him to recognize their ancient forms.

This was a bunch of lines and triangles, and Shax knew he had seen it before. He just had to figure out where or, more precisely, when.

He put the pages aside. Maybe he should try something easier first. Fishing around in his jacket pocket, he found the scrap of paper with the runes on it. The silver coin fell out, spinning on the carpet like a normal coin wouldn't. It spun, flashing in the light. Shax stepped on the coin. When he removed his foot, the engraved portrait leered at him, judged him.

Picking the cursed thing up, he glimpsed smoke and fire consuming a low, brick building. A strong, slender hand held a familiar, curved sword, and shouting voices called her name. *Kheone*. Shax blinked, and the vision vanished. Well, that was new and different. New and different were not usually good things with the Judas coins.

He didn't know if his vision was the past, the present, or the future. He couldn't go to her aid, either. The only way he could help her was by figuring out some of these lousy clues. Shax returned the coin to his pocket and studied the scrap of paper. It was the same writing as Serel's notes, except for the symbols used for angel and demon. The rest still looked only vaguely familiar. Something he should recognize but couldn't quite remember. He tucked the scrap into the envelope.

On to the third clue, the book. Shax pulled out his smartphone and typed the title in. The results surprised him, even though he hadn't known what to expect.

Shax found a short article on a rare books blog. Only a dozen copies of *Ancient Rituals of Sumer* survived. The number had been shrinking over the past year as many books burned in suspicious fires or simply vanished. Finding an unwarded copy would take skills Shax simply did not have.

Brewing another cup of coffee, he added a small amount of vodka, knowing it was the only thing that would make what came next anything close to pleasant. Damn Serel and his book...and damn himself for not putting it together. It was there in the title of the book. He had lost too many brain cells in the past year. This writing was Sumerian cuneiform.

The last time Shax had spoken Sumerian was three thousand—no, four thousand—years ago. This was going to take a while to translate, and it was going to be boring as fuck.

Shax worked the rest of the day, painstakingly drawing from dusty memories. The longer he worked, the more frustrated and downright resentful he became. If he continued to bash his head into the wall of cuneiform, he would have to come up with more ways to say how Goddamn hard it was. The words came slowly and sometimes still made little sense. He lost a lot of context by translating in this manner.

All he had wanted since the Second Fall was to get so good and lost no one, angel or demon, would ever find him. He had almost forgotten his torment. And then, Kheone had walked back into his life, forcing him to confront his one failure. To top it all off, he was caught between an angel and a Duke of Hell. He sure knew how to get himself entangled in lose-lose situations. By dinner, he had a headache and maybe a quarter of a page which made sense. Even that much made him want to drink.

He poured a mug of vodka. The tequila still had not arrived.

On the banks of the Euphrates River six thousand years ago, a group of priests believed demons would take over the world from their pantheon of gods. The era had been a fruitful one to be a demon. A whisper in the right ear could set off a chain of events giving Lucifer enough human souls to torture and entertain him for a few decades. The assassination of the right leader at the right moment could change the course of history, guaranteeing a path that bent away from justice, kindness, and all the other junk the angels sang about. It was the first time the demons seemed to have the upper hand, the first time they almost made the archangels pay for their exile. The priests developed a method to destroy the Gate to Hell should the forces of evil be on the verge of winning. In the end, the angels had prevailed, and the priests never deployed the solution to their demon problem.

Shax could not remember why the angels won, but he remembered who Lucifer blamed. As the Morning Star's assassin, he had spent most of the next year with black demon blood on his hands as the Prince cleaned house.

According to Serel's notes, somewhere in the book was a spell to destroy the Gate to Hell. The angel had likely hoped if he could find the spell, he could undo the damage it had wreaked. But why was Heaven's Gate destroyed, too?

The answers were likely in the rest of the pages, now strewn on the desk. Lucifer help him. If he had to do one more minute of translation tonight, he would turn himself over to Michael to save himself the bother of death by boredom. He grabbed the bottle of vodka and upended it over the glass. A drop fell out.

For Christ's sake, time for a break.

Shax returned the notes and his own translation to their hiding place under the mattress. He picked up the pad of paper the hotel left on the desk and began scribbling. He resisted the temptation to write the entire saga of his day and kept it simple. Kheone needed to know how important and potentially dangerous the book in her possession was. If she missed tonight's meeting, he would leave the note.

He grabbed his jacket and tucked the note into the pocket next to the silver coin. The cold smacked him in the face as he walked out the front entrance of the hotel, and the air smelled of storm and snow. It was not a night to be out in, but he had no choice. The sooner Kheone knew what she had in her possession, the better. He was only keeping his bargain, after all.

Yeah, right, and I'm the Prince of Hell.

Chapter 24

Kheone peered around the corner of the red brick building. Smoke poured from its windows, and the flickering flames lit up the night. She held her sword at her side, waiting for the signal. A piercing whistle rent the night, and she reached through space to open a rift. Kheone jumped in first, her gathering following her and spreading out inside the smoke-filled building.

A mountainous she-demon stood at the far end, holding the sharp edge of a Bowie knife to Tailash's kidney. Strung up by his arms, the rope looped over a hook on the ceiling, and his body hung limp. His head rolled back and forth, though, giving Kheone some hope he still lived.

They needed to get the angel and get out. The flames consumed the building, and the smoke made it difficult to see and breathe. A bright red flash behind the demon meant Michael had joined the fray. Hope and fury warred within her breast, and she led her gathering in a frontal assault. Part distraction and part desperate gambit, the onrush of nine angels armed to the teeth was a sight to behold.

The demon bared her teeth and drew back the hand holding the knife. Kheone put everything she had into getting there before the demon could strike. She failed. Instead of stabbing Tailash with her knife, the demon tore his throat out with her teeth.

It was the last thing the demon ever did. Michael loomed behind her, and swinging his great sword, lopped off her head. Her body collapsed to the ground, and the head rolled to Kheone's feet. Too late to save Tailash, but the demon would never hurt anyone else again.

With another swing of his sword, Michael severed the ropes holding Tailash. Kheone swooped in and caught the angel as he fell. Blood gushed from the wound in his throat, and his head wobbled wildly.

"Shh, Tailash, we are here. You're not alone."

A MEMORY OF WINGS

She looked up at Michael. The archangel kneeled next to Tailash, his hands shining with golden healing light. At Michael's feet, though, sat a rough ceramic cylinder. A sigil glowed brilliantly red. Holy shit, it was another bomb.

"Michael! Bomb!" Kheone nodded frantically at the cylinder.

He looked down at the device and over to Tailash. Michael picked up the bomb.

"I am sorry. The needs of the rest of the angels must outweigh the life of one."

Michael opened a rift and stepped through. The archangel placed the cylinder on the ground and held his sword over it. An instant after the rift closed, a strange note pierced the air.

Kheone waited for the bright flash of light and the darkness to follow. And waited. When nothing else happened, she examined Tailash. He was dead. Gently placing his head on the floor, Kheone rose and made her own rift, following Michael.

The archangel stood in a circle of flattened grass, the remnants of the bomb at his feet. She approached cautiously.

"Michael?"

He knelt and bowed his head. "I had no choice, Kheone. Had I not destroyed the thing, all of you would be dead."

She placed a hand on his shoulder. "I know. Thank you."

Kheone knelt next to him and examined the pieces of pottery in the center of the circle.

"It would seem we have located our murderer," Michael said.

She stared at the evidence. The remnants of the device were all too similar to those found in the library, but something felt off.

"It would seem so."

"You do not think it is the case?"

"How did the device come into the demon's possession? And why would she have killed Serel?" she asked, mostly to herself.

Michael answered anyway. "She was a demon. That is all the reason they need. Perhaps Serel forgot demons are not to be trusted. Perhaps she surprised him. We will never know for certain, but we have found our killer."

He rose, towering over her, and held out a hand. Taking it, Kheone pulled herself to her feet.

"Now what?"

"We return to the gatherings and announce our findings. Then, we go home."

His finger brushed her jawline. She pushed it away.

"Michael—"

A flicker of anger crossed his face. He withdrew his hand and opened a rift to a spot a hundred feet from the burning building. The other angels stood in a silent circle around Tailash's body, heads bowed, ignoring the light and noise of the rift. Michael and Kheone joined them.

Emric looked up at their approach. "Archangel. Lieutenant."

The others raised their heads, murmurs rippling through the gatherings.

"I destroyed the device. The same kind killed Serel. We found our murderer, and justice was served," Michael said.

In unison, they turned to regard the building, where the demon's headless corpse lay. A few ghastly smiles appeared, and a few angels turned away in disgust. The rest showed no emotion, grimly focused on the task at hand, including Michael.

"Those of the Nairobi gathering, see to your dead and wounded. Those of Kansas City, your duty is complete. Dismissed."

The Nairobi angels carefully lifted Tailash's body and carried it through a rift.

Her own gathering congregated around her. Michael stood a few yards distant, watching.

"I know this isn't the outcome we wanted, but you all performed admirably," Kheone said. "Tonight, we mourn Tailash's passing. Tomorrow, we celebrate our victory. All the cheesecake you can eat!"

Wry smiles greeted her announcement, but the mood lightened considerably. They would be okay. She opened a rift home, and her angels walked through. Before she could join them, Michael pulled her aside.

"You and I still have a conversation to finish."

"Come join us tomorrow. We'll talk after."

He gave her a sharp nod and walked away. She followed her gathering through the rift.

Kheone rubbed her temples, the beginnings of an ache informing her she had made too many rifts today. Unable to do anything about it right now, she pushed aside her worry. Although the headaches seemed to be accelerating, they did not stop her from performing her duty. With any luck, it wouldn't come back to haunt her.

Her angels dispersed to their rooms, except for Emric.

"Hey, LT, I'm going to find Maj," they said, bouncing up and down in anticipation.

"Go," she said with a kindly smile.

The smell of smoke and blood sent her running for the showers. Kheone had one more meeting today, and she did not wish to smell like a funeral pyre. The hot water streamed down, easing the ache of her muscles and washing off her cares for the moment.

All her work, all her worry, her short-sighted bargain with the annoying demon, all for nothing. Some other demon had acquired a bomb and used it as demons often did: indiscriminately, without thought of the consequences. With the immediate threat dead, they could finally relax a little.

That left the question of what to do about her demon problem. Shax had done everything in his power to help her. Kheone considered their bargain fulfilled. It was time to free him from his obligation, so he could finally do what he had wanted all along: save his own skin and run. Grief washed over her, grief she had not felt at Tailash's death. She could not miss Shax, miss his arrogant face, miss his warm voice, miss the fevered desire he kindled within her. This was for the best. Kheone couldn't take much more of her conflicted feelings.

She shoved her arms into a jacket and opened a rift to the museum as the bell tower struck seven. Bracing herself for the headache and vertigo which would follow, she failed to notice the rather large puddle and stepped right into it. The water soaked her sneakers.

Slow claps greeted her. Shax stood by the tree, a smug grin on his lips, and his eyes twinkled with amusement in the dim light. He was much better dressed for the weather than she, his heavy leather jacket a strong bulwark against the piercing winds. The demon was even smart enough to wear gloves. No longer impervious to the elements, she really needed to think more like a human when it came to weather.

"Damn you, Shax," she murmured to herself.

"That ship sailed a long time ago, Blue." He had sharp ears.

The vertigo hit hard as soon as Kheone took a step out of the puddle. She fell to her knees on the concrete walkway, pain shooting through her legs. Clutching at the matching agony in her head, she failed to notice Shax rushing over. His firm arms held her, his body pressed against her, soothing the pain. Kheone looked up at Shax, the smirk he constantly wore gone, replaced by something she would call worry. Could a demon worry?

She pushed him away and stood, regretting it in the next breath. Gone was his warm support, replaced by the brisk night air. Her vision blurred from the rumbling truck trying to take up permanent residence in her skull.

"What's wrong?" he asked.

She shrugged. The demon did not need to know how weak her power was nor how much she regretted pushing him.

"Just tired. I haven't slept much since Serel died."

He gave his lips a wry twist. "I know the feeling."

The Midwestern winter wind blew against her neck and face and turned her feet, still encased in wet sneakers, into icicles. She should have picked an inside place to meet. Turning up her collar and tucking her hands into her pockets, Kheone sat down on the bench. Shax joined her at the far end, removing his gloves. He offered them in an odd gesture of chivalry, but she shook her head. He draped them over a leg and leaned in, giving her his undivided attention. His dark eyebrows drew together as the worry he showed earlier returned.

They sat in silence for a moment. She had come here to give him his freedom, and yet, she dreaded the upcoming conversation. Kheone nudged the feeling. Somehow, even knowing what he was, he had become important to her. Heaven help her.

"What do you have to report?" she asked, meeting his gaze.

Warm eyes for such a cold heart. He reached behind his back. Kheone tensed, reaching for the knife on her belt. The warmth dimmed as he pulled out an envelope.

"I found Serel's notes."

"But how?"

He waved away the question. "You're freezing. We don't have time for how. The important thing is Serel translated the entire spell to destroy the Gate to Hell."

"But Heaven's Gate was destroyed, too. Something must have gone wrong."

"That is an understatement."

Kheone laughed half-heartedly. She needed to tell him now.

"Thank you, Shax, for your work on this, but it doesn't matter anymore. The demon who killed Serel is dead. It was pure coincidence she found Serel in the library. Serel was a scholar, not a warrior, and lost the fight. We were wrong."

"Are you sure? Because it's awfully convenient."

Anger rushed through her. "Are you calling me a liar?"

He held up his hands and leaned back. "That's not what I said. I just wondered if you got the whole story before the demon died."

Mollified, she shrugged. "It doesn't matter. She's dead, and we can move on. What else does Serel say?"

"I haven't finished the translation."

Shax studied the envelope before handing it over as though he regretted having to do so. Why? It should thrill him to quit this bargain and flee the city. Perhaps he could find a place with no demons or angels and build a quiet life for himself. As long as he kept his head down, Michael would have no reason to go after him, and Kheone was disinclined to tell the archangel of her recent working relationship with the demon.

Her finger grazed Shax's as she accepted the papers. A fiery tingle shot up her arm. She yanked it away, and the heat rippled through her body. Kheone risked a glance at Shax. Those amber eyes of his flashed with the same fire she felt. He looked to the side, and when he returned his gaze to her, the spark had vanished.

Had she imagined it?

"I'm not good with reading and writing languages, especially ones I haven't used in a few thousand years," he said with a cool dispassion, belying the inferno they had shared a moment ago. "I hope you're a better scholar than I am."

Kheone gave him a half-smile while she looked at the pages. "I'll manage."

She tucked the papers into her own jacket before rising from the bench.

"Thank you, Shax, truly. I didn't know if I could trust you, but you proved yourself to me. You don't need to run afoul of Aeshma. Go now, before my brain kicks in, and I let Michael know you're in his city."

Kheone tried to soften the last with a smile, but the amusement in Shax's eyes died with her words. He took a deep breath before he stood, too. He pressed his lips together and looked away. She got the feeling he wanted to tell her something else but was unsure how she would take it. Straightening his back and squaring his shoulders, he held out a hand.

"It's been a, well, let's not say pleasure. It's been an experience working with you, not against you, for once, Kheone. Good luck."

She looked at his hand and back up at his face. He'd had ample opportunity to thwart her while still fulfilling their bargain. He could have held onto Serel's notes. If he had betrayed them to Aeshma, the duke would have attacked long ago. Kheone ignored his hand and wrapped her arms around him in a firm embrace, surprising both of them.

The tension in Shax's body melted, and he leaned into the embrace, encircling her with his arms gently, as though he knew he couldn't hold on to her.

"Godspeed, Shax. May you find what peace you can."

Kheone pulled away. Shax reached over and tucked an errant strand of her hair behind her ear, sending burning tendrils of need through her. Her eyes locked on his lips, and she wondered what they would taste like, how they would feel. She would never find out, now. An awkward silence later, Shax cleared his throat and walked off without another word, his white hair a crown of light drifting through the dark night. She watched until he disappeared behind the museum.

Kheone opened her last rift of the day and stepped into her room. Another wave of sorrow filled her chest like she had left a part of herself behind. Fighting off the knife blades in her head, she stumbled to her bed and collapsed upon it, falling asleep with her cold, wet shoes still on.

Chapter 25

For once, Shax had no words. Walking away from Kheone was hard. Not looking back was harder.

Hell, for a split second, he had thought she wanted to kiss him. What kind of fool was he? The molten line of her touch cooled. For the first time in ten thousand years, he had felt like someone actually gave a damn about him. Even now, the thought of her fierce form against his body sent a rush of desire coursing through his veins. When she withdrew from the embrace, he had resisted the urge to hold her tighter for just a little longer. Had he kissed her, he never would have been able to walk away.

He ignored the tears as best he could, telling himself the breeze caused them. Perhaps the end of their arrangement was for the best. Kheone distracted him, invaded his thoughts and his dreams. Kissing her would have made it all the worse. Neither side would tolerate their relationship. This was how it had to be for both of them.

Now all he needed to do was escape Aeshma's influence. Once free, Shax could easily disappear into the teeming masses of humanity and drink, fuck, and party his way across the globe.

Shax ducked into a liquor store and picked up a bottle of cheap tequila with his remaining cash. He carried the bottle wrapped in a paper bag into the hotel lobby. A familiar figure caught his attention. Irena was on an intercept course. Shax picked up his pace, but so did the sorceress. He arrived at the elevator a second before she did, poking at the button in the slim hope it could magically transport him to the top floor and spare him the tedious conversation he foresaw.

Alas, his magical rescue was not meant to be. No magic portal opened to save him. Instead, they stood, awkward and silent, waiting for the infernal elevator to arrive. Shax did his best to ignore her. It lasted until the doors finally closed on the two of them.

Irena glanced down at his paper bag.

"Planning on drinking that all by yourself?"

"Yep."

Shax stared at the metal doors in front of them. He hoped the sorceress got the hint. She did not. After a moment's painful, blessed silence, she spoke again.

"I wanted to thank you for the advice about Peth. It worked. I grabbed him and watched him scream the next time he insulted me in front of Duke Aeshma."

Guess he had done his good deed for the millennium. After helping one troublesome angel, he did not have the emotional capacity to worry about somebody else.

"Peth is a bastard and a careless one to boot."

"You're not."

Irena did not need to get any ideas about his soft, squishy interior. He had not even known about it until recently.

"Oh, I am, but not in the way you think."

"You don't seem to take any joy or pleasure in the pain the others inflict. Why?"

The sorceress was observant. It was true. He never had taken pleasure in pain, his own or others'. All demons seemed to do was cause pain and chaos. But then, he had not become a demon for the joy of it. No, he'd become a demon for the most naive reason possible: love.

Shax gave her the only answer he could under the circumstances.

"It's a long, sad tale, and I'm too sober to share it with you. Talk to me once I've finished this bottle, and maybe, *maybe*, I'll tell you."

Irena regarded him, sharp intelligence on her face. Coming to some sort of conclusion, she took a deep breath.

"I want out, Shax."

I bet you do.

They had two floors left to go. He wasn't touching her statement with a ten-foot pole.

"I'd keep that to yourself, Irena. If you want to hear my sob story, you're welcome to knock on my door in a few hours. Otherwise..."

The elevator opened, thank Lucifer. He cut off what he was going to say and strode down the hall. She followed more slowly. Shax swiped his key card and disappeared into his room before the witch could ask any more awkward questions. He poured himself a healthy shot of the cheap-ass tequila and downed it in two gulps. Irena might show up to his room soon, and he would have to deal with it.

The tequila wasn't doing its job. There was still an aching hollow inside him, an emptiness that had been there for a very long time. Eons, maybe, and he had never noticed. He had walled off his heart after it broke, figuring he would never have use for that particular piece of emotional real estate again. And it had only taken nine thousand years for him to realize how wrong he had been.

Kheone had ditched him as soon as she could, tearing down his walls. He did not blame Kheone, not really. An angel and a demon barely worked as a crime-solving duo, let alone as friends or, God forbid, lovers. It still hurt like Hell. He should know. He would take a session with Lucifer's most infamous torturers rather than go through this dark agony again.

Maybe another tequila would fill it. The drink burned as it traveled down his throat and spread fire through his body.

Shax had avoided death by angel. By fulfilling his bargain, he had gained a measure of freedom, at least from her. It was everything he had wanted a few days ago. He could go anywhere once he figured out how to ditch the duke and her retinue. He was miserable.

Shax was sure he was missing something from the whole, sad situation. It had been too easy, Michael finding the demon who murdered Serel while he and Kheone closed in on the spell.

Another thing bothered him. Aeshma was playing her cards close. She was obviously waiting for something, but Shax didn't have a single clue what it might be. That was out of character. Although she was more subtle than her peers, she was not artful enough to keep a secret for long.

If he did not spot whatever she waited for, life would get even more complicated. He would rather die than be her plaything until the Gates were rebuilt, or she killed him out of boredom. Shax would bet on the latter happening first. He had traded off his reputation as Lucifer's favorite for millennia, but there was no one to protect him now. When had his life become so complicated?

The answer was obvious, of course. It had been the instant he saw Kheone again. The angel had brought him nothing but trouble since the moment Lucifer had given him her coin. She escaped his blade, and the Gates crashed down. He tracked her down, and a falling body had almost crushed him. He made a blood oath to her, followed by a bargain pitting him against his own kind. Kheone was bad news for him.

And yet, he constantly dropped into her orbit. She made him laugh, made him feel seen. Kheone was kind to his alter-ego.

Shax poured himself a last shot, finishing the bottle. He was now free to do as he saw fit. And he wanted to leave behind this city, start over once again. If he was smart, he could keep out of the archangel's way. If he was lucky, which was a shakier proposition, he could stay off Aeshma's radar, too.

Sweet Lucifer, he still needed to report to the duke tonight. She wouldn't be happy he returned so soon. What information could he give her?

His thoughts were thick and slow, molasses in winter, after consuming so much tequila. He made a cup of coffee, needing as many of his wits about him before facing Aeshma. Still intoxicated but feeling like he could handle a simple conversation with his boss, he walked down the hall and knocked on the duke's door.

A young man in a black leather collar and matching briefs greeted him.

"Who is it, darling?" Aeshma's voice called from the bedroom.

"A gentleman with white hair, Your Grace," said the young man.

"Oh, Shaxie. Let him in."

"Of course, Your Grace."

He bowed nicely to Shax and led him to the bedroom. Poor guy thought he was role-playing. He would run screaming if he knew how close to death she might push him unless he was into that sort of thing. Now Shax thought about it, that was probably why he was here. Shax shook away the thought and walked into Aeshma's bedroom.

Her back was to him as she put on a silky wrap that barely covered her. She turned around, having tied it loosely, leaving the swell of her breasts on display, painted red lips parted in a provocative smile.

"Will he be joining us, Your Grace?" the young man asked.

"We'll see, pet. It depends on if he's been a good boy or not." She sighed. "Wait in the other room and shut the door behind you."

He bowed and did as he was told.

"Where are Asag and Orax?" Shax asked, keeping his gaze firmly fixed on her nose as he tossed his jacket on a chair.

Aeshma rose out of bed and strode over to him. He looked past her, pointedly ignoring the glimpses of her luscious curves and heavy breasts, the triangle of hair between her legs flashing with every step.

"Orax is in the other room. I prefer privacy with my whore. Asag is running a little errand for me. Now, why don't you tell me something I don't know, Shax."

She ran a finger up and down his arm. He shivered at her touch, half in disgust, half in desire. Whether the disgust was at her or himself, he was still too drunk to determine.

"The gathering figured out who killed that angel a few days ago," he said.

The finger ceased its movement.

"Oh?" Aeshma said, her voice a lesson in practiced noncommittal interest. She did not want him to know she was very curious about the answer.

"Apparently, it was some random demon. She's dead, now."

Aeshma's already pale face grew positively ashen. Not the reaction he'd expected. She grabbed his arm, her fingernails digging into the skin. He couldn't pull away without suffering further injury.

"Are you all right, Aeshma?"

She swallowed and looked up at him. "Yes, yes, I'm fine. That is...rather unfortunate. I could have used someone with enough skill to kill an angel."

Aeshma shrugged, her color slowly returning to normal. She released her death grip on his arm, leaving behind small, half-moon marks. Tiny drops of black blood oozed from out of the wounds.

"Oh, dear, I am sorry," she said.

The duke stepped into his personal space, pressing her body against his. She used the corner of her wrap to dab at the blood, loosening the tie. It gaped open, revealing soft, full breasts and the curve of her hip, causing a normal but inconvenient reaction. Aeshma sighed prettily, her breasts heaving, and gave him a practiced, saccharine smile as she ran her hand over his crotch.

"I want to see them again, your beautiful wings."

As angels, their wings had been sacrosanct, and touching someone's wings without their permission was a serious violation. As demons, wings became a tool of control, and pleasure or pain were doled out as needed to buy loyalty or punish betrayal.

Shax had lost count of how often his wings had been used against him, even though the only demon who could command him was Lucifer. The Prince of Darkness preferred tempting with pleasure or punishing with pain to outright orders, reveling in his subordinates becoming complicit in their own corruption.

Aeshma licked her red lips.

"Take off your shirt and show me."

He could refuse this simple request. Unlike ordinary demons, the magic which bound him to Lucifer protected him from the dukes. He should refuse this request. And yet, both his tequila-addled brain and his cock were telling him fucking Aeshma could be an excellent deal, indeed. No one else wanted him, after all.

He dragged up the hem of his shirt and removed it with a flourish at the end, keeping his eyes locked on hers. She smiled wickedly and rotated her finger in the air. Shax turned around.

Her fingers were cool against his skin, but she avoided touching his wings, stopping an inch below the tips of the inked feathers. He imagined them wrapping around him, protecting him, comforting him long ago, before the first Fall had turned them to leather.

The breath of her sigh drifted over his back. His shoulder muscles twitched in reaction.

"You always had some of the most glorious wings among the angels, and even as a demon, they were impressive."

"Do you still have yours?"

"Impertinent."

She removed her hand, and he looked over his shoulder. Aeshma had retreated a few steps and stared at him, a dangerous spark in her storm-blue eyes.

"Apologies, Duke Aeshma."

She waved his apology away. "Oh, I have a very good idea of how you can make it up to me."

Her smile turned vicious as she stalked toward him. Shax backed up until he hit the door, the soft thunk the only sound in the room. His obvious discomfort only made her laugh.

"Your body knows it wants me, Shax. Your brain needs to catch up."

Aeshma unknotted the tie to her wrap and slipped out of the silky material, which drifted to the floor. Leathery black wings, tipped in sharp claws, reached around her rib cage, perfectly tattooed. The stark contrast with her pale skin drew attention to her full, rosy-tipped breasts.

Heartbroken and unwilling to admit it, Shax braved Aeshma in all her unholy glory, and his resolve crumbled. His best chance at survival now was earning the duke's trust, so he would have an opportunity later to break it and run.

The duke hooked a finger into his waistband as the fight left him and pulled Shax to her. He did not resist.

"That's better," she purred as her breasts pressed into his chest.

Shax claimed her mouth, shutting her up. His cock did not care at all, hardening at Aeshma's touch through his jeans. He wrapped his arms around her, brushing the wings inked on her back so gently only the swift intake of her breath let him know she had felt it.

"Don't stop," she said as she grazed her own hands down his back.

The electric touch of her fingers against his wings almost dropped him to his knees. Shax had only slept with humans since the Second Fall, whose touch upon his wings felt good but normal. He had almost forgotten how it felt when a fellow demon touched them.

As he kissed her and ran his palms down her back, trying desperately to lose himself in the moment, a faint notion kept rattling around in his brain. He had felt something similar to this recently. Crawling through the red, lust-haze of thoughts, it finally hit him. When Kheone had taken his hand, it had felt like this. No, it had been better.

Kheone. Lithe, graceful, and strong. Fierce and brave.

The soft flesh Aeshma offered paled compared to Kheone's taut, powerful body. Lust was all the Duke had to give. It would never be enough. He would yearn for Kheone for the rest of his days, no matter who else shared his bed.

He imagined Kheone's warm, golden-brown skin in place of Aeshma's ivory. Her sleek, blue-black hair in place of the Duke's soft, blonde locks. Long, supple legs wrapped around his waist and silver eyes, liquid with desire, not Aeshma's steely gaze. He tried to imagine the duke was something she was not.

He failed.

Shax broke the kiss and moved his hands down to Aeshma's rounded hips.

"No," he croaked.

Aeshma growled at him. "If you want pain, Shax, you're on the right track."

"I told you, I don't mix business with pleasure." He would die on this hill.

She traced a perfectly manicured fingernail over his wings, then dug it into the sensitive flesh. He hissed as fiery agony radiated from the point.

"This is the last time you refuse me, Shaxie," she said, the warm honey of her voice now frozen over.

Aeshma shoved him. His back hit the wall with a thud. She glared at him as she jerked her robe on.

"I understand, Your Grace," Shax said.

He grabbed his shirt and jacket.

"Send in my whore. I don't pay him to wait in the sitting room."

"Yes, Your Grace."

Shax bowed and fled the room. The young man watched porn on the large TV, his own cock straining against his leather underwear. He looked up, eyes widening in surprise.

"She's ready for you," Shax said cooly.

The young man turned off the TV and walked through the door. Shax beat a hasty retreat to his own room, breathing hard.

He had just chucked his golden opportunity to fuck his cares away into the trash. He stumbled over to the desk. No tequila fairies had refilled the empty bottle, so he settled for a hot shower. The water hit his body, and the punishing heat turned his skin pink. Shax scrubbed himself with the floral hotel soap to rid himself of Aeshma's scent. It lingered and, no matter how hard he scrubbed, he couldn't rid himself of the memory or the shame. The bastard had almost manipulated him into sex, teased and taunted him, and he had enjoyed it too much.

What in Christ's name was wrong with him?

Shax dried off and pulled out the coin, hoping for another glimpse into her life. It was warm in his fingers, like a cup of coffee. Its warmth flowed through him, setting his skin tingling. The voice which had egged him on for the past year was silent, leaving a contradictory sensation. This hypnotic calm coupled with a prickling need. Holy Hell, he was falling again. For a damned angel.

A demon believing he was in love with the Prince of Hell was, if not ordinary, at least understandable. But this? This was insane.

His cell phone vibrated, the sound amplified by the wooden nightstand. He ceased his pointless speculation. The only thing that mattered now was getting out of Kansas City alive.

He pressed the green circle. "Yes?"

"Your car's extended warranty will expire—"

Shax pressed the red circle and hurled the phone into the wall. It hit with a satisfying bang. He suspected Lucifer had a hand in inventing the infernal devices.

He needed a plan. Too drunk to think of one, he crawled into bed. He dreamed of luminous silver eyes under warm sunny skies and soft skin. If only he could stay there for an eternity.

Chapter 26

When Kheone awoke the next morning, the smell of bacon and fresh bread greeted her. She poked her head out of the door, the boisterous laughter of her gathering echoing down the hall. The noise originated from the kitchen. Kheone went to investigate.

An angel she had only met a few times stood in the middle of half the gathering, dishing out plates of eggs from a large pan on the stove. A tray full of bacon sat on the table, alongside the remains of at least two loaves of fresh-baked bread. For the life of her, her sleep-addled brain could not come up with her name.

"Hey, LT!" Maj said with a wide smile. "Michael dropped off our new healer late last night. Em tried to wake you, but you were dead to the world."

"Hi, I'm Mriluda," the new healer said.

Right, Mriluda. That was it. "Welcome. Glad to have you on board."

"I was so sorry to hear about Serel. We served together many times. Care for some breakfast?"

"Yes, please."

Kheone gave the angel a tepid grin. Her head still hurt. Hopefully, a hearty breakfast and a nice hot cup of tea would do her good.

"Did Michael stay?" she asked Mriluda, the rest of the gathering drifting off.

"No. He brought me and left. But he said he'd see us tonight."

"You'll join us?" Kheone asked their newest member. Even more reason to celebrate.

"I'd love to."

"Excellent. Seven sharp."

Mriluda nodded and poured herself a cup of coffee. She leaned against the wall and peered at Kheone.

"Sure you're okay, LT?" she asked. "Michael was concerned when they couldn't wake you last night. Frankly, so am I."

Kheone shrugged. "Just fatigue, I think."

"Nothing else?"

"Nosy, aren't you?" She softened her words with a quick grin.

"I'm a healer. It's part of the job description." Mriluda chuckled.

"I've been getting some severe headaches when I make a lot of rifts in a day. Yesterday was one of those days. Could be why I slept so soundly."

The healer nodded. "Could be. Come see me in the next couple of days, or if it happens again."

"Will do. Need any help settling in?"

The other angel shook her head. "I'm good, thanks. Maj and Emric have offered to show me around today. I'll see you tonight."

Putting her cup in the dishwasher, Mriluda left. Emric's voice floated down the hall, and the outside door crashed shut. Kheone started the dishwasher and returned to her room. She had some interesting reading to catch up on.

Seeing her name written in Serel's neat hand on the envelope Shax had given her last night, a shiver of sorrow raced through her. At least his killer would never hurt anyone again. Michael's sword sent his adversaries to oblivion. There would be no resurrection for Serel's murderer.

Kheone opened her window, hoping Machka would visit sometime today. She had not seen him in a couple of days. A small part of her worried for him.

Her skill in Sumerian cuneiform still intact, she took turns looking at Serel's originals and Shax's translations. The demon had not done a terrible job. The translation was much more literal than necessary, but the meaning was clear.

The extraordinary spell had brought down the Gate to Hell, destroying Heaven's Gate along with it. With the exception of angel blood, the unusual ingredients would take tremendous time and effort to procure. Soil from the Garden would be nearly impossible under the current circumstances.

Most of the magic Kheone used was innate and instinctual, like the rifting. Kheone had rarely performed spells, and those had been simple ones to communicate with the celestial realm.

If they were to have any chance of restoring balance, she had to figure out what had gone wrong and why. She could not do that without the help of someone far more versed in spell casting than she. Once she translated Serel's work, she would need to tell Michael what she had discovered. No, to be fair, what Serel and Shax had discovered.

Idly, she wondered what happened to the book Michael had taken from her. As much as she trusted Serel, it was better to have the original source. She tucked the notes in the envelope, placing the drawing of the device in with them, and slid it into her sock drawer. Afraid working on a translation would bring back her headache, Kheone turned her attention to more mundane tasks.

Those tasks ate up her day, and before she knew it, the bell tower on campus struck six. Confusion swirled through her. So many nights, she had armed herself physically and shielded herself mentally in order to meet Shax at the museum. A small part of herself missed the preparation, missed the banter, missed—

No, she did not miss the demon. She merely associated the demon with her investigation. Since the investigation was no longer necessary, neither was their relationship. No matter how often she told herself that, something still tugged at her, pulling her towards Shax. Even the thought of his name sent coils of need circling low in her belly.

Kheone shoved the thoughts away and grabbed her jacket. She was walking to The Cheesecake Factory. Maybe the cold air and exercise would help her get her priorities straight. Her long strides ate up the distance, and she soon joined her gathering in the bar.

"Hey, I did not say all the beer you could drink," she said with a chuckle. "Just cheesecake."

"Beer and cheesecake are proof God exists, LT," Emric said.

"But not together," Maj added, elbowing her lover in the side.

"No, not together," Emric agreed, their smile widening.

Kheone spent many minutes visiting with her gathering. She had a quick conversation with the bartender and told him she was only paying for the cheesecake. The angels sat around four tables. Some had cheesecake of many kinds. Some had drinks, also of many kinds.

A little before eight, a hush fell over the restaurant as a large, golden-haired man strode in like he owned the place.

The first time Kheone had seen Michael, his head crowned with golden curls, he had wielded a sword of light, the blade sharp enough to separate a soul from its body and leave both intact. His strength of conviction, his honor, and his leadership had made choosing sides easy, really, when Lucifer had rebelled. It didn't hurt he was the most beautiful of the Archangels. How could anyone deny the Commander of the Heavenly Host?

Except a third of the angelic host had done so and paid for their hubris with eons of agony. She had helped Michael force the Fallen horde into Hell. The archangel had led a macabre parade, dragging Lucifer by his own golden locks. The fury on Michael's face had been truly awesome.

Kheone became the best at every task she undertook, hoping to impress the archangel. He had sent her on the most difficult missions, turning the hearts of powerful men and women toward goodness and compassion, leading gatherings to defend the souls of warriors on the battlefield, and guiding the souls of the virtuous dead to their final rest in Heaven. She had been the first to step forward every time, hoping Michael would notice. And, one day, he realized he did not have to ask.

When the chaos of the Second Fall brought her plummeting to Earth, his powerful arms had pulled her up off the streets of Kansas City, half-frozen in the depths of winter, the pain of her vanished wings branded in her skin. He had healed her physically and given her purpose in her despair. Kheone had loved Michael since her first glimpse of him. And she still did, but it was the love warriors carried for their compatriots. A familial bond of sorts. She must make that clear to Michael tonight.

The gathering raised their glasses as the archangel joined them. He pushed through to the bar and ordered a beer. Once in hand, he raised his own glass.

"To missing friends," he said.

"To missing friends."

The bar stool Michael sat on looked like it would collapse under his muscular frame. The barest hint of a smile graced his usually stony face. His eyes locked onto her, and he beckoned her over. Kheone joined him at the bar, placing her jacket over the back of the chair and sitting next to him. He covered her hand with his cold one.

Whenever she touched Shax, pure lightning, immediate, blazing, deadly, shot through her. Nothing of the sort happened with Michael's touch, confirming her suspicions. As much as she had once dreamed simple, human-like desire would bind them together, her true feelings were worlds away.

"I see you have met Mriluda," Michael said.

"Yes. She's already won them over with bacon and eggs. She'll fit in fine."

"Good. So, what is this cheesecake I am supposed to consume?"

Kheone laughed. "They only have a million choices. Here."

She handed him a menu and turned it to the dessert section. As he looked over his options, her angels began leaving. First, Maj and Emric stopped by to bid farewell to the archangel. They escorted Mriluda home, the newest member still finding her footing in the new city. Then, in twos and threes, the rest came by, also taking their leave. Soon enough, only Michael and Kheone remained.

"Finally, we are alone," he said, running a sword-calloused finger along her jaw.

"Not here," she said through gritted teeth.

"Yes, you are right. This is not the place." His grin was wide, with a hint of the wild in it. "I cannot choose based on these descriptions."

"They have all the cheesecakes in a case by the entrance."

"Then I will select one for us to share."

He walked away. She stared after him. Two weeks ago, she would have admired the way his muscles moved under his tight t-shirt and jeans. Now, she thought of someone else, someone she could never have. How was she going to let an archangel down easy?

"Whew, honey, I don't know what you're still doing here with *him* to look forward to tonight. I could feel the heat from the other end of the bar." The bartender had snuck up on her and gazed appreciatively at Michael's butt. "He is beautiful."

The man did not know how much of an understatement that was. Kheone had seen Michael in his full, angelic glory, glowing in the light of Heaven and God's love. He had been magnificently, divinely, terrifyingly beautiful.

The bartender fanned himself. "You are a lucky woman."

No, she was not. If she was lucky, she would have fallen for the angel who so obviously wanted her, the being she could build a future with. Not the demon whose very presence in her dreams should be an affront to all that was holy and yet set her aflame with desire. She was screwed.

Kheone didn't notice Michael return. He brushed his fingers across her shoulders, lightly pressing the wings beneath. The gentle touch did nothing for her. It should have set her skin on fire.

Michael frowned slightly, as though noticing her lack of reaction. A smile quickly replaced it.

"As it is my first visit to this restaurant, let us order an original."

His voice rumbled as he ordered from the bartender. She paid little attention. Why did she not have a reaction to Michael's touch? That was...weird was the best word she could think of. Before she could chase down likely answers, the dessert arrived, and Michael fed her forkfuls of decadence.

"We still need to have our conversation, Kheone."

She nodded, her mouth full.

He ran a finger up her arm. Goosebumps trailed after it.

"Cold?"

Kheone shook her head. There was something else, something she couldn't put a finger on.

"Come, we will find someplace more private to talk."

She paid the bill, shrugged into her jacket, and followed Michael outside. Wintry air slapped Kheone in the face. She shivered again.

Michael pulled her into his arms. The shivers only got worse.

"What is wrong, Kheone?"

"I, I don't know."

Michael opened a rift behind her to his room. He swept her under a protective arm and escorted her through. No sooner had the rift closed behind him than he enveloped her with his massive physique. Michael bent his head and claimed her mouth as his own. He traced the outline of her wings, and the spiky, gnawing tension inside her tipped toward the breaking point. Great, wracking sobs escaped her.

"Stop, please," she said.

"What is wrong, my beautiful Kheone? I thought you wanted this."

He did not release her, trapping her in his arms.

"I did."

"Good. Now that is settled…"

Michael lowered his head once more. Kheone pushed against him and leaned as far away as the too-tight embrace would allow.

"I did want this. I don't anymore," she said.

"But you are mine, Kheone, my perfect angel."

He had no right to demand that from her. She owed him her loyalty and her obedience for fighting the forces of darkness. Not this.

"I...what?" Maybe she'd misheard.

"You belong to me, Kheone, from this night and for always."

Bitter outrage replaced the confusion. She belonged to no one, not like this. She shoved against his chest, but the rock-hard muscles didn't budge.

"Let me go." Her voice was glacial.

He blinked at her, confusion roiling through his brown eyes, ones she had once thought beautiful but now were needlessly aloof.

"I want you, Kheone. And you want me. You belong with me." Michael sounded like a lost little boy, unable to comprehend how what he wanted was not what he was getting.

"I don't—" She shoved again. His grasp only tightened.

"Of course you do. Your modesty becomes you, Kheone. There have been other angels who have waited all eternity to be in your shoes."

"You're not listening, Michael. I don't want you anymore."

His expression turned, rage clouding it where once there was desire. "Who are you to deny me? You owe me everything."

"I don't owe you this." She yanked her arm out of his grip and retreated a few steps. "Who I sleep with, who I'm attracted to, that's entirely up to me. And I don't want you."

"Get out." His voice was an arctic blizzard.

Kheone stood frozen at his bitter anger, wondering what she had done wrong. She had not meant to lead him on, but this had been their first real chance for a conversation. Michael's assumptions about their conversation differed vastly from her own.

"If you will not leave, then I shall."

A line of red light opened to his right. He turned on the balls of his feet and stepped through without another word.

Gathering her wits, Kheone ran out of the room, down the stairs, and into the night, pushing past several angels. She took great, gulping breaths of the cold air and ran until she reached the bell tower in the middle of campus. Icy tears flowed, and she leaned against the white walls of the tower. What the Hell had just happened?

Chapter 27

Tired of staring at the four walls of his room since he woke at midday, Shax dragged himself out for a cup of coffee. He needed to do something, anything, to pass the time until he could sneak back to Kheone as Machka. She had not ended things with the cat side of him. Lost in the warm thought of curling up with his favorite angel, he did not see Peth until it was too late.

The smaller demon smacked into him in the hall, pushing him to the side. Shax bumped into a table, knocking a flower-filled vase to the ground in a splendid crash. Peth cackled. Shax grabbed the other demon by the jacket, his movements supernaturally fast, and lifted him to his toes.

"Watch where you're going, dickwad."

He dropped Peth to the floor and turned to go. Shax froze when Peth placed a hand on his back, directly below his wings. His response was as cold as the winter winds blowing through the city.

"Remove your hand before I do."

It fell away, and Shax whirled around to put Peth in his place. Instead, he confronted a demon so broken he was no longer a threat, at least not to Shax. Sure, he wouldn't trust the demon in a room with an ordinary human, but the Peth standing in front of him now wouldn't challenge anyone with even a drop more power than him. And Shax was just below the dukes. An argument could be made he was right at their level but with no followers.

"Did Aeshma tell you? My wings burned off in the Second Fall and were just...gone. I'll never fly again, Shax, whether or not the Gate is ever rebuilt."

He stopped himself from feeling sorry for the demon. Although every demon was petty and cruel, Peth would win some kind of prize if any existed. Shax had never seen evidence of anything resembling mercy within the other demon. The cosmos shuttered in fear when Peth was on a rampage, only the Dukes and Archangels safe from his brutality. It was a good thing he would never fly again. If the angels could not find a way to open the gates, none of them would ever fly again, with or without wings.

"What did you expect, Peth? There are consequences to our choices, and you chose Lucifer."

"Don't get all pious on me. We made the same choice, backed the losing side. Why is the price I pay higher than yours?" The demon flashed his teeth at Shax, a ghastly grimace.

Shax shrugged. He had often asked himself the same thing. Why had he been able to hold on to some form of compassion while no others had? Only one answer was clear. Love. He had made his choice for love. That answer wouldn't make Peth any less bitter.

"This conversation is going nowhere." Shax pushed past the other demon.

"It's only a matter of time, Shax, before she uses you up and spits you out," Peth called out. "How much longer before she grows bored and moves on to a new pretty? You better make damned sure your information is important to her. If it isn't, she will rain down holy Hell on your perfect body. And I'll be there to help."

The demon cackled, the sound following Shax down the hall, only disappearing once Peth shut the door to his own room. He stepped into the elevator and pushed the button for the first floor. Peth had said nothing Shax had not thought. He was only here until Aeshma tired of him. Kheone did not want him around, either. Stuck in this twisted situation unless he could find a better ally or a way to slink away unnoticed. He didn't want to spend the rest of his life running from the duke or her horde. He needed an escape.

Shax walked to a coffee shop near the hotel. Settling into a pleasantly soft armchair, he pulled out his phone. He had taken pictures of Serel's notes, expecting Kheone to ask for them. If there was an answer to his predicament, maybe he would find it in these pages.

The translation was still slow, too slow, but he finished a bit more despite his limitations. Besides the spell, he had a paragraph on the logic behind it. With this and access to the original book, he might figure out how to reverse the damage, reopen the Gates, and send everyone back where they belonged. It might take a few days, a few months, a few centuries, but he was sure with the knowledge in that book, someone, somewhere, somewhen would be able to do it.

Was it in his best interest, though? He did not want to return to Hell, or Lucifer, or his old life. If you could call what he did living. Having the information might earn him some sort of get-out-of-jail card or keep him alive long enough to come up with a better plan.

He spent the early evening in his room, idly flipping through the channels on the TV, hoping no one cared where he was, waiting for a chance to return to Hurst University. Orax's thudding footsteps lured him to watch the hall from the peephole in the door. Irena paced up and down, reading from a book and mumbling to herself. Orax and Peth traveled between their rooms and the duke's several times. There was still no sign of Asag.

His phone rang around eight.

"Join me. Now," Aeshma said without preamble.

When a Duke of Hell snapped her fingers for you, you ran. He tucked the pages away and crossed the hall. Aeshma answered the door herself, dressed in a business suit. A few minutes later, room service delivered dinner for two. Apparently, she had invited no one else in her little horde.

After the server left, Shax removed the cover from his plate. Steak, almost bloody, with vegetables and potatoes and an expensive bottle of red wine. He poured for both of them and waited for Aeshma to get to the point.

He didn't have to wait long.

"Michael still absent?"

"To the best of my knowledge, Your Grace."

"And when is he due back?"

"My source is uncertain but expects it to be a couple of days."

She took a bite of steak, chewing thoughtfully.

"This is sinfully good, wouldn't you say?"

Shax took a bite and chewed, but everything tasted like sawdust. Until he could figure out the duke's next move, nothing would sit right with him.

"Yes, it's delicious."

She trilled a musical laugh at him.

"You are a terrible liar, Shaxie. Eat up. We have a busy night ahead of us."

He swallowed the bite, and it sat in his stomach like a lead weight. Aeshma was up to something.

"Where are the others?"

"On an important errand."

"Where are they?"

She tutted him. "You're spoiling the meal. Can't we just enjoy ourselves for fifteen minutes?"

"Where are they?"

Aeshma sighed theatrically and laid down her fork and knife.

"Fine. I'll tell you. It's really rather lovely."

She leaned across the table and crooked her finger at him. He leaned in, and she spoke in a whisper.

"They're preparing an assault on the angels as we speak."

Shax swallowed, and his usually sharp tongue failed him. Alarm bells went off in his brain, and his first thought was to warn Kheone. He should have planned for Aeshma to act on his intel long before now.

His extremities grew cold as his body prepared for fight or flight. The fork and knife clattered to the table. Too late to seem casual, he took a few deep breaths.

"Are you sure it's wise?"

Aeshma covered his hand with her own, her sharp nails digging into his skin.

"Why would you say that?"

His thoughts seemed to bubble up through syrup.

"There are still eleven of them, and Michael's chosen leader is powerful in her own right. Three demons and a sorceress won't last long against them."

"What on Earth makes you think I only have three demons to send against them?" Aeshma smiled widely and watched his reaction carefully.

The blood drained from his face. He stopped breathing, and his vision narrowed. Her eyes sparked with malice.

"Oh, poor Shaxie. His pet angels are about to get their asses handed to them by my horde of dozens. You are not as good at hiding your feelings as you think you are. I knew you felt strongly for at least one of them. Did you not know my favorite whore is putting himself through college at Hurst? Imagine my surprise when he saw a black cat jump into the window of—who was it now? Kheone."

His breathing quickened as adrenaline flooded his system. He needed to get out of here and warn Kheone.

"You know, I heard a rumor she's banging Michael?" Aeshma shook her head in mock censure, and a wicked smile crossed her lips. "If Lucifer knew, he'd be livid his brother was getting away with something he couldn't."

He took a deep breath. He could not help Kheone if he raised Aeshma's suspicions before he could run to her aid. Shax took a sip of wine as if his world was not crashing down on his head.

"How do you think I was getting my information, Your Grace?"

Her eyebrows raised in surprise. Whatever she had expected, this was not it.

"Angels are trusting creatures, especially of a harmless, little pussy cat. The fool took me in, and I overheard many conversations they never would've had in front of a human, let alone a demon."

"But she is *fucking* Michael."

Her information was a little off, but it wouldn't be long before her words were true. After all, Kheone had kissed Michael. She would not turn down an invitation to his bed. What angel would? He gestured in dismissal.

"I told you, I was only using her to get information. Why would who she slept with bother me?"

Aeshma looked at him and deflated. Her pink lips formed a perfect pout. He needed to throw her a bone before she decided she hated being tricked. Make it seem he withheld information to benefit himself, something to stroke her ego.

"My apologies, Your Grace. I did not want to reveal my methods, so I would remain valuable to you. Forgive me, Aeshma?" He extended his hand, palm up.

Take it. It would have been a prayer if he thought anyone would listen.

The Duke tented her fingers together and tapped them against each other while she considered his words. Her smile told him all he needed to know.

"Perhaps you're a better liar than I have given you credit for, Shax. Eat up. We have a busy night. The attack will begin in an hour."

Which meant he had an hour to figure out how to escape Aeshma, warn Kheone, and return before anyone realized he was missing. He was well and truly fucked. And if he did not figure out a way to do it, so was Kheone.

Chapter 28

Kheone gasped for breath, the wall of the bell tower the only thing keeping her upright. The great archangel, the literal golden boy of Heaven, did not listen to her. He had assumed her attraction, had pressed the issue, and when she had told him no, the rage pouring from him broke something inside her. At best, Michael had confused love with possession. At worst—

The tower marked ten o'clock, a startling cacophony. Kheone took a deep breath and wiped away the tears, her hands trembling in the cold. She needed to get home, warm up. Her feelings would wait until tomorrow.

Five paces from the tower, Machka ran out of the bushes surrounding the Commons like a cat out of Hell. His name froze on her lips as he transformed between leaps into the demon, Shax.

"What the—" Kheone got out before he placed a hand over her mouth. The usual heat from his touch streamed through her body, vanquishing the cold of the winter night.

"Shut up, Kheone. I have two minutes before they realize I'm missing. There's a horde of thirty demons ready to assault your dorm. Get there, now."

He took his hand away and looked around as though expecting someone to come crashing through the bushes after him. Kheone crossed her arms over her chest and stared at him.

"Why—"

"I could've killed you any number of times since I found you. Trust me or don't. I'll do what I can to delay and distract them."

He took a step toward the dorm, then spun around and framed her face in his palms, planting a quick, fierce kiss on her lips. She should have pushed him away, but his kiss ignited a firestorm inside her, flames of desire licking through her, stealing her breath. It was over before she could react.

"Go, Kheone."

He let go and took off running, changing back into his cat form before darting beneath the bushes again.

Holy Mary, Mother of God. She touched her lips where his had been an instant before. An all-consuming, frightening maelstrom of desire roiled through her. The kiss had been everything she had hoped. And she wanted more.

She shook aside the turmoil Shax had caused. A single question filled her mind: did she trust him?

If anyone had asked her before the Second Fall, she would have said no. For Heaven's sake, if anyone had asked two weeks ago, she would have said no. He had been her enemy, her foil, her opposite. What she tried to save, he attempted to destroy. Where she had preached mercy, he had lured the humans to their dooms. When she had chosen God and Michael, he had taken Lucifer's side. He even lied by pretending to be her cat. That one really stung.

But she had spent the last several days working with the demon. He had taken a blood oath to prove his innocence. He had helped when she asked. And now, released from their bargain, he risked his life to warn her. Her head told her demons were untrustworthy under the best circumstances, but her heart said she trusted Shax. To take a demon at his word was madness, but it was true. In the end, Kheone followed her heart. She would not chance losing her entire gathering over the possibility Shax lied to her. Kheone opened a rift to her room.

Silence greeted her. Dead silence. The hairs on the nape of her neck stood on end. Kheone pulled her sword off of the hook next to her door.

She opened it a crack and listened. Not a sound. She held in her breath. Her thundering heart filled her head in the quiet. Closing her eyes, she let out her breath in a whoosh. The thump of her heart receded, replaced by nearly inaudible chanting. No wonder she hadn't heard it before.

Latin, she thought, after listening a moment, the word for sleep sung over and over. The lethargy began at her toes and moved up her body.

"Hey, dickheads, anyone home?" A child-like voice called out, bringing Kheone back to reality.

Shit. They were going to attack when they were sure every angel was at their most vulnerable. Cowards.

Mumbling admonitions greeted this taunt. The damned demons were about to be gravely disappointed. She pulled the fire alarm in the hall and waited.

The mumblings outside grew into shouts while inside, one head poked out of a room, then another, and another. Footsteps tromped on the floor above.

"Arm yourselves! Everyone to me," Kheone said.

A booming thud sounded against the steel dormitory door as her angels gathered around her. Cackles and shouts rose outside now the jig was up. This was a bad place for a fight. Outnumbered at least two to one, not enough space to spread out. They would be quickly overwhelmed. Time to move this outside.

"What's going on?" Emric asked.

"Demons," Kheone said.

She opened a rift in front of her, and the small grove of trees on the far side of the gym filled her vision. Kheone stood to the side and motioned her angels through.

"We're not running, Kheone. This is our home," Maj said.

"We're not going far. We need a better fighting position. Go. There is no time, and I can't hold this rift forever."

Maj nodded and ran for the rift, the others on her heels. She stood guard on the other side as the angels poured out. As soon as the last was through, Maj turned and gestured at Kheone, urging her through. Kheone shook her head.

"Flank them. I'll be the distraction."

"No, Kheone—"

The rift closed with a snap. This was not up for discussion. She could escape. The others could not.

Kheone pulled her knife out of her boot and crouched into a ready stance, her sword held in the other hand.

She did not have long to wait. Three more booms later, the front door crumpled inwards with a metallic shriek.

"Honey, I'm home," a feminine voice said, gobs of saccharine dripping off it.

"Come on in, bastards!"

A small demon stumbled forward carrying a penknife, the others cackling behind her.

"You first, Charun, since you told them we were here." A low, growly voice taunted the demon.

"They were supposed to be asleep!" Fear leached out of every word.

Kheone waited for the obvious sacrifice to move closer so she did not have to give up her advantageous position in front of the stairs. The demon inched closer, waving the knife around wildly. When she was close enough, she lunged at Kheone, no discipline to her strike. In a fluid motion, Kheone disarmed the little demon before planting a roundhouse kick firmly on her chest. Charun went flying and knocked over one of the other demons now swarming the hall. That was two she did not need to worry about for a bit.

With her foot, she slid the demon's knife to her, knowing she may soon have reason to be grateful for an extra knife, and waited again. The new crop of demons was more confident while still maintaining a healthy sense of caution as they approached Kheone. The hall only allowed two at a time. Any more, and they would simply get in each other's way. Kheone gave the two facing her a grimace.

They charged. She kicked the legs out from under one demon and parried a clumsy strike from another before knocking them into the wall. The two behind those tried to get into the fray and tripped over the demon on the floor. Kheone kicked a newcomer in the head, knocking it out cold. The other she stabbed through the hand, pinning the demon in place, howling screams echoing through the hall.

Another pair approached but halted out of the reach of the flailing limbs, taking in the chaos. Their compatriot extricated itself from the knife, and hot, black blood spattered across her. Howling in pain, they tried to scramble away, but the two behind them and the threat in front kept them in place.

An arm closed around her windpipe from the demon she had knocked into the wall. Kheone opened a rift, slicing the legs off a demon in front of her, and used her leverage to toss the one behind her through. The rift closed with a snap, and the pop of light reflected off her sword as she prepared to challenge the rest.

The two waiting outside the combat zone looked toward the exit, hoping for escape. Several sets of two demons lined the hall. Boxed in, they could not go back, and they didn't wish to move forward.

In the kitchen and common room, the tinkling sound of glass breaking filled the sudden quiet. More were coming through the windows. Soon, they would realize they could get up to the second floor, exposing her back. Kheone had to make her stand here. She needed them to focus their effort on her so her gathering could outflank them.

"Now, what are you going to do, angel?" snarled a voice.

She shrugged. "Kick your ass back to Hell?"

"Who do you think you are? Fucking Michael?" This sounded a lot like the first little demon she had encountered.

Screeches and howls rose from outside, the dull thuds of fists hitting bodies and the ringing sound of steel on steel telling her the calvary had arrived.

"No, but I have friends."

The two closest to her charged, swiping at her with their blades. She dodged and hit one demon on the side of the head, sending it into the wall. The demon slid to the floor, eyes unfocused. The other sliced at Kheone again, ripping her shirt and leaving a shallow cut. She plunged her sword into its heart and yanked her blade out. Kheone turned to meet whatever came next.

The acrid stench of gasoline filled her nostrils. No, they would not set fire to the building, not with their own still in here. The looks on the demons' faces told her that yes, they would. She looked down the hall. A demon near the entrance carried a large, red canister and poured the gasoline against the wall and on the floor.

A wave of terror rippled through the demons, the cold stench of it competing with that of the gas. None of them focused on Kheone any longer, only on their own skins, stabbing and pulling at each other to clear a path to safety. They flung their companions to the floor or into open rooms in their desperate attempt to escape. Kheone had done her job, and it was time for her to join the other angels outside. She had one last thing to do.

Kheone dashed into her room, locking the door behind her to buy her some time. Even a few seconds could make a difference. Shouts echoed in the halls. She did not have more than a minute before demons swarmed this room. She grabbed Serel's notes from her dresser drawer and tucked them into the back of her jeans. An uncanny quiet fell over the building, followed by a rushing whoosh as someone lit the fire. Kheone opened another rift and ran toward the commotion, fighting the searing pain shooting through her head.

A flaming demon tumbled from the building, screaming, while fire licked up the sides of the dorm. Red firelight danced in the first-floor windows. The demon collapsed on the ground, and its screams died off while the rest of the horde scattered. Out of the corner of her eye, a tall, white-haired man and a buxom, short blonde walked away. Torn between chasing after Shax and tending to her gathering, Kheone chose her angels. With Michael gone, they needed her.

She let Shax go. He would answer for his betrayal later.

Chapter 29

The chaos of the fire painted the courtyard in a hellish palette, all shadow and red light. The flowers and bushes planted next to the building blackened as flames licked the windows and doors and wherever else the gasoline had splashed. Shax sensed the duke before she spoke, a presence larger than her current form suggested. Aeshma slipped her hand into his, giving it a squeeze as though they were innocent lovers at a beach bonfire.

"It's beautiful," she said, breathless.

"Yes," he lied. "We should leave. Someone will call the fire department."

Aeshma sighed dramatically. "I suppose. I was hoping for a houseful of crispy angels. You don't think any died, do you?"

She looked up at him, and he saw the flames reflected in her eyes, like twin sparks of hope. Shax lifted his shoulders.

"I don't think so. Charun gave up the game too early."

Aeshma pouted, a pretty little moue of her lips belying the viciousness behind her sweet, harmless facade. "I must have a discussion with the little shit-weasel. She cost us our victory today."

Shax sent a prayer of thanks out into the universe. Flinging a well-timed pebble, he had started a fight between two lesser demons. Leaving Orax and Aeshma to deal with the blood lust, he made a show of checking on the preparations around the angels' dormitory. He slipped off in the confusion and took off to warn Kheone. Gone five minutes, tops, Shax had made a show of coming around the far side of the building, giving him an excuse for being out of sight. So far, no one had called bullshit.

Watching the angels' home go up in a conflagration Lucifer himself would appreciate, he gave thanks to the shit-weasel's poor timing. He would be having that *discussion* with Aeshma if Charun had been any smarter.

A flash of red light caught his attention. Kheone ran out of the rift and straight to the fight. She glanced back, and their eyes locked for an instant. The heat of their kiss rose in him again, rivaling the fire consuming her home.

She made her choice and turned toward her gathering. Deprived of her life-giving attention, he reluctantly forced his own back to the immediate problem.

"Shall we, Your Grace?" He tugged gently on Aeshma's hand, their fingers still interlaced, leading her away from the flaming building.

"You are dismissed," the duke called out to the horde. "Shoo!"

A few started passing along the word. The sirens from the fire trucks in the distance hurried the process along. Shax led Aeshma to the idling car where Peth waited.

"Back to the hotel, please," Shax said as they slipped in.

Peth glanced at Aeshma and did not drive off until she nodded her assent. Okay. He was still being tested. A few minutes later, Peth dropped them off at the hotel entrance. Shax opened doors and pushed buttons for Aeshma, waiting for the other shoe to drop. If saving Kheone's life cost his own, he would count it a fair trade.

As soon as the door to her suite closed behind them, the duke pressed herself into his body, snaking her sharp-nailed fingers under his shirt. When he thought he would be fucked after this little raid, he did not think it would be so literal. Dread filled him. He couldn't refuse Aeshma now, not without repercussions. So, the question wasn't whether he would face the music but which music he chose to face. Sleep with the Duke of Lust or deal with whatever retribution she felt appropriate for refusing?

Aeshma bit her lower lip and smiled up at him.

"I must admit, pet, tonight turned out to be completely different from I'd expected."

"What did you expect, Aeshma?"

"I expected you to run to your precious Kheone and warn her. I expected to never see you again. I was pleasantly surprised when I saw you hadn't left.
"

Heart racing, he answered in a voice as calm as a placid pond. "She means nothing to me." The worst lie he had ever told.

"I'd like to reward you for your loyalty tonight, Shax." She licked her lips.

Once, that would have been enough. Once, he would have done anything for a break from the agony of Hell, the agony that kept him company every hour of every day. Sex had been his favorite remedy. Since the Second

Fall, though, he had enjoyed the more subtle aspects of desire. A pair of beautiful eyes, the curve of a hip under his hand, a lovely laugh, sometimes even a kind gesture. Only now did he realize all those things reminded him of a specific being, and she was not the one standing in front of him.

Aeshma pulled him over to the couch by the waistband of his jeans. His rational mind screamed this was a horrible idea but could not come up with an alternate plan.

Hammering at the door saved him from making a decision.

"Christ on the cross." Aeshma let him go and looked angry enough to spit venom. "Go get the fucking door."

Shax did not envy whoever had interrupted their interlude. Orax greeted him when he yanked the door open, the demon Charun slung over a shoulder, bound hand and foot. Shax stepped out of his way, and Orax strode in, followed closely by Peth. Still no sign of Asag. What errand had Aeshma sent her on?

"Where do you want her, Duke Aeshma?" Orax asked.

"I don't want her," Aeshma said, pouting once again.

Orax turned on his heel and moved as if he would take Charun somewhere else.

"Ugh. Fine. Put her in the bedroom, then summon Irena. Peth, I require your services. Fetch your kit."

A light sparked in Peth's eyes, and a cruel smile split his face. He disappeared into the adjoining room. This was about to get ugly. Perhaps now would be a good time for Shax to excuse himself.

"Your Grace, I should leave you to your business. Come find me when you're done, and we can pick up where we left off." With any luck, he could come up with a third option, one better than the two he had right now. He bowed low before taking a step toward the exit.

"Oh, no, Shaxie, you're not leaving yet." She grabbed his arm, digging in her sharp fingernails. "I make it a point to show the newest member of my horde what happens when you disregard my orders. Charun knew stealth was important tonight. Instead, we got one burned building and zero dead angels. You can go when I have made my point."

Well, balls.

"Of course, Your Grace." It was the only thing he could say.

Aeshma pulled him into the bedroom. Charun lay in a heap on the four-poster bed as Orax removed her bindings. Her left eye was swollen shut, and blood leaked from her nose and mouth, staining the white bedding with black droplets. Her chest heaved, but she made no other movement, not even when freed from her bonds. She had given up and accepted her fate. Her death would be long, bloody, and painful.

"Stand there, Shax," the Duke ordered, letting him go and pointing at a chair in the corner.

He took his place next to the chair, assuming Aeshma would sit there through the torture. Mostly for the view, but directing it as needed. For now, the duke stood next to Charun and stroked her cheek.

Irena entered, a brisk, no-nonsense rhythm to her stride, carrying something resembling a toolbox.

"What do you require, Your Grace?" she asked, keeping her gaze purposefully glued to the duke.

Shax did not blame her. He wished he did not have to watch what was going to happen to Charun, either.

"This room needs to be soundproof."

With a sharp nod, Irena got to work. Opening her box, she pulled out salt, a jar, some herbs, and a weird-looking silver ball, punctured with holes and mounted on a stick. The sorceress thrust the jar at Shax.

"Go fill this with warm water. Leave some room for the other ingredients."

He glanced at Aeshma, who was whispering to the demon on her bed, too softly for Shax to hear. The duke paid no attention to anything else. He took the jar and did as he was told. Irena took the jar from him, added salt and herbs, and screwed on the lid.

Peth walked in, carrying a folded plastic tarp, a length of rope, and a long piece of leather rolled up and tied with a string.

"Tie the little shit to the frame, Orax," he said, tossing the rope to the bodyguard.

Orax looked to Aeshma for confirmation. She nodded and stroked Charun's cheek once more.

"I'll enjoy the show, Charun. Know in your last moments that you will bring your duke such pleasure." She rose and walked over to Shax. "Watch and learn, Shaxie. Should you ever disappoint me, this could be your fate, too."

"I understand, Your Grace."

Aeshma made herself comfortable on the chair.

"Go fetch me a drink."

Shax left as Irena bent down to talk to the duke, and Orax bound Charun to the bed. The shakes started as soon as he closed the door. He took a ragged breath as he walked to the bar cart. Leaning on it, he cleared his head and stopped the shaking with a few more deep breaths.

Christ, he had forgotten the viciousness of demons in the past year. He was a chucklehead to throw his lot in with Aeshma, even if only temporarily. He should have run when he had the chance. Except...No, he could not think of Kheone right now.

He poured the duke's whiskey. His hand shook, scattering a few drops. Shax steeled himself, knowing he was going into the room to watch someone die, in the slowest, most humiliating way possible, as a message to him and all the other demons in the horde. And he had to do it or risk being the next lesson.

Shax walked into the room and handed the drink to Aeshma. Irena sprinkled water from the jar around as she chanted in a language it took him a while to place. It might be Old German or something else from before the printing press but after the fall of Rome. Pressure built in the room, making him feel as though someone stuffed cotton in his ears. Irena clapped once, and the pressure lifted. She packed away her supplies.

"As long as the door is closed, no sound will escape this room," she said. "The spell will last four or five hours. Call me when it wears off."

Aeshma glowered at the sorceress. "Can't you do any better?"

"Not with the materials on hand, Your Grace. Should you care to wait until morning, I can shop for ingredients to make a longer-lasting spell."

"I guess it will have to do."

Dismissed, the sorceress bowed and left the room. Shax doubted the duke had noticed. Aeshma's focus was now entirely on Charun and Peth. Now bound to the bed frame, the smaller demon's body was pulled so taut she stood on tiptoes. Peth undid his knife roll and pulled out a scalpel and a sharpening stone. The metallic scritch-scratch filled the room as he dragged the blade against the stone.

"Get on with it, Peth," Aeshma commanded, licking her lips in anticipation.

"Yes, Your Grace." The toothy smile Peth shared with her sent chills down Shax's spine. This was Peth's happy place.

The demon no one ever noticed until too late sliced the scalpel down Charun's back. Her scream filled Shax's ears, and bile rose in his throat. With a swallow, he suppressed the urge to vomit. If he showed any weakness today, he would be next, sure as Lucifer's wrath.

Chapter 30

The demons scrambled off, leaving Kheone to deal with the chaos they had created. A few bodies littered the courtyard, but none were angels, thank God. Sirens wailed in the distance.

"Gather the bodies and take them to the basement next door," she ordered.

Kheone opened yet another rift. This had to be her last. She did not have the energy left to open another safely. A throbbing ache beat in rhythm with her heart.

Blank faces looked at her. "But the demons—"

"I don't want to explain why we have half a dozen bodies littered around our dorm. Do you? Do you think Michael would appreciate the human authorities investigating our presence? Or our hosts? Gather the bodies. Now."

Once shaken out of their confusion, the gathering removed all the bodies quickly and efficiently. By the time the fire trucks and police arrived, the angels milled around the courtyard. To an uninformed observer, it would seem like they had heard the alarm and evacuated.

Kheone gave a statement to a police officer, something believable and mostly true. Strange sound in the hall. Someone pouring gasoline inside the building. Fire alarm and evacuation. Thank goodness no one had been injured. She made sure the angels' keen hearing picked up her story.

The police interviewed the rest of her gathering. Kheone watched from a short distance and jumped when a heavy hand rested on her shoulder.

"It is only me, Kheone," Michael said softly. His voice carried both sadness and anger, but nothing like the rage she had glimpsed earlier. "I came as soon as I heard. Is everyone safe?"

"We're okay, Michael." She stepped away from him.

He frowned down at her.

"I am sorry for my earlier behavior, but now is not the time to discuss it."

A little of the tension bled from her. With everything that had changed in his life this past year, he deserved the benefit of the doubt. He was not used to dealing with the vagaries of attraction and desire. Kheone gave him a nod, accepting his apology. After all, nothing bad had happened, had it?

"You were fortunate to hear them," he said, his voice lighter.

Here it was. Here was her opportunity to come clean and tell him about Shax. She took a breath and readied herself.

"It wasn't luck."

Michael raised his eyebrows and opened his mouth to ask for more information, but the gathering began mustering around them.

"Let's get everyone settled for the night, then we'll talk," she whispered.

He nodded and faced the angels. "We shall shelter in the gym tonight. I will call around and find some bedding."

The crowd of police and firefighters slowly thinned, and the angels gathered near the annex. Kheone threaded through them and unlocked the building. In twos and threes, they shuffled into the gym and sat on the mats.

Michael took his place at the front of the room, Kheone to his right.

"I need to talk to each of you about what happened. Kheone, guard the door. I will begin with Maj."

"I need to speak with you first, Archangel. I pulled the fire alarm, and you need to know why."

He peered at her, his brow furrowed in confusion.

"It's important," she said.

"Very well." He gave a sharp nod. "Maj, you have the door. Come, Lieutenant."

Michael led her down to the basement, to the very room where she had briefly imprisoned Shax on the night Serel died.

"What is so important?" he asked.

Michael moved to the far side of the room, far enough away they would not touch. Even so, he took up most of the tiny space, most of the air. The heat in the room rose.

Kheone opened and closed her mouth a couple of times, trying to get the words out. It was her job to help him protect their gathering and all the other angels trapped here on Earth. He could not do that if she kept her knowledge from him.

"I've been working with the demon, Shax."

The color drained from Michael's face, and he glowered at her. He reached for the dagger at his side, hand resting on the ancient handle.

"Please, Michael, let me finish," she said, pleading. Her voice barely carried over the few feet between them.

"You will address me as suits my station." His voice was quiet death. In her heart, Kheone knew only their long relationship stayed his hand from plunging the dagger into her breast.

"Yes, Archangel."

"You are the reason we have lost our haven? You, Kheone?"

"Yes, Archangel."

"You have betrayed me and this gathering by working with the enemy. Why should I not drive my blade through your heart right this moment?"

"Shax warned me the demons were coming. He saved us when he didn't have to. I didn't misplace my trust. Neither have you."

"When did this start?" None of the tension left his shoulders, and his eyes still snapped with rage. The color had returned in spades. She recoiled from his terrifying anger.

"Since Serel's murder. He's been helping me put the pieces together," Kheone said in a small voice.

"How did you know he did not kill Serel?"

"I didn't. Not at first, but he took a blood oath. And then we found these."

Kheone pulled the notes out of her jeans and gave them to Michael. He took them with a grimace of disgust as though they still held a taint from being found by a demon.

"What is a blood oath to a demon like Shax?"

"The same as to me or you. Lie or break your oath, and you're dead."

"And these?" Michael waved the pages around. "I suppose he found them and just gave them to you?"

"Yes." His gaze narrowed in disbelief. "We both felt mine were better hands for keeping them safe. The translation isn't done, but the spell that tore down the Gates is in there. Our best guess is it went wrong the first time. I'm not sure what happened with Serel or the demon in Nairobi."

"Why did you not tell me?"

"I didn't want to make an accusation until I knew exactly what had happened. I realized one of my gathering could be involved. I lived with them, and I didn't know who was capable of killing a fellow angel. I worked with Shax because I knew he didn't do it."

"Why would he help you?"

"He only wants to be left alone. I promised if he helped me, I would make sure he survived to live out his life here on Earth. Shax kept his ability to transform. He became a small, black cat who followed me home. He had every opportunity to kill us and chose not to."

"This is madness, Kheone," he said, grabbing her shoulders and giving her a shake. "You cannot trust a demon, not even one you have known for ten thousand years. And you cannot trust *this* demon, ever. Shax is...Did he seduce you?"

Did he? No. There was no denying the desire between them, but not once had he ever tried to seduce her. Not even when he had kissed her. Kheone shook her head.

Michael's grip tightened on her shoulders. She deserved the bruises he would leave for lying to him.

"How can I believe you? You admitted to hiding a demon in our midst, to keeping secrets from me. Perhaps this has all been an elaborate scheme to undermine my authority so you could seize power for yourself, lead our angels to their own destruction."

"I worked with Shax to find out who killed Serel. I only found out he was Machka tonight when he came to warn me."

His disappointment broke her heart. How could she ever prove to him she would never betray him? Kheone searched her memory for answers, even while guilty tears dripped down her face. An idea wormed through the dark recesses of her mind. Oh, it was a doozy, but might be the only way to prove her loyalty to Michael.

"The Rite of Revelation," she whispered.

Michael froze, his eyes widening. No angel had invoked the rite since the Fall. Some of Lucifer's followers had attempted to hide their loyalties once the punishment for rebellion was apparent. A suspect angel could either accept their fate and join Lucifer in Hell or choose the Rite of Revelation. If one lied, even a lie of omission, during the grueling ritual, the soul would vanish. No Purgatory, no Heaven, no Hell. Just...nothing.

Even under the best circumstances, the rite left the subject weak, helpless even, for a long time, relying on the very beings who had tortured you to care for you. It was an act of trust as much as loyalty. If she had any hope of retaining Michael's trust, retaining her command, this was the only way.

He tightened his grip on her shoulders. Pain shot down her arms.

"Are you certain?" he asked.

"Yes. I invoke the Rite of Revelation."

"I will make the preparations. You are to stay here until my return."

Michael kissed her forehead gently, sadly, and released her. Kheone collapsed against the wall. He locked the door behind him.

Kheone sat on the floor, legs crossed, the concrete hard and cool on her buttocks through her jeans, patiently awaiting Michael's return. She breathed in and out, the ancient rhythm centering her in this moment, this truth. With every breath she took in, she prepared herself for the grueling ordeal she was about to endure. Few survived the Rite of Revelation. One lie, one misleading statement, one tiny bit of truth withheld, and the supplicant burned into oblivion.

The snap of the door lock drew her out of her meditation. She was either ready, or she was not. The next few hours would tell. Michael entered with a duffle bag slung over his shoulder. He bolted the door and placed the bag on a shelf. Grief dimmed the usual luster of his eyes.

"Are you certain, Kheone? Once the rite begins, there is no going back."

She stood. She did not want to meet her fate sitting on a concrete floor in a storage room.

"Will you ever trust me again if I don't go through with it, Michael?" When he shook his head, she continued. "Then, yes, I'm sure."

Michael emptied the rest of the contents from the duffle: a thermos, a vial of holy oil, and a plastic baggie filled with dried herbs. He handed her the thermos.

"Drink this, all of it."

Kheone unscrewed the cap of the small vessel and smelled the contents before she took a sip. The scent was more pleasant than she had expected, but the taste was bitter, like the rind of a lemon mixed with mustard. The tea would make her mind more suggestible and her skin more sensitive. It wasn't torture if it didn't hurt. She drank the rest as quickly as she could and gave the thermos back to Michael.

The archangel mixed the herbs with the holy oil and painted a circle on the floor, taking up almost all the square footage in the room. Light-headed as the tea began to work, tiny motes of color danced across her vision.

"Step into the circle." Kheone did so. "What do you seek, Kheone?"

"I seek the truth, Archangel."

"Speak only truth in this circle. Lies bring oblivion."

Michael chanted in a language long forgotten by the mortals of this world. He raised his hands out from his sides, palms up.

"Truth is light."

He flipped his hands over, shoving his palms down. Angel fire sprung up from the circle, enclosing them in a ring of rainbow flames. From now until Michael had asked his last question, he would be the only one able to cross the circle. The flames chased the chill out of the air. Sweat beaded on her forehead. The sparks of color from the hallucinogenic tea melded with the colors of angel fire, roiling her stomach. Kheone wanted to close her eyes, but she stood tall in the circle, determined to show she had nothing to hide.

"Each question will bring more pain than the one before," Michael said, his voice soft in reverence for the ritual. "Answer truthfully and fully. Hold nothing back. A lie or an omission will end your suffering immediately and bring oblivion. The truth will set you free. Do you understand, Kheone?"

A stinging sensation traveled up her left arm like she'd scratched herself on a nail. Kheone looked down, but the skin was intact. The pain would all be in her mind, not her flesh.

"Yes, Archangel."

The first two questions were straightforward. When did she first know Shax was in town, and when did she discover Machka was Shax? Those answers were simple and reaffirmed what she had already told Michael.

She ground her teeth together as more lines of pain scored into her skin. Imagining what the pain would be like ten questions in, she now knew why only a few survived. As the pain twisted in on itself, her ability to think clearly and give full answers, with no omissions, would become nearly impossible. The only way she would survive was to clear her thoughts as best she could.

"If you found the demon over Serel's body, why did you not suspect him?" Michael asked.

That was a harder question to answer.

"I did, at first. But then he made a blood oath, swearing he had nothing to do with Serel's death. And lived. I knew I would lose any chance of questioning him once you and the gathering arrived on the scene. I made a rift here and pushed him through it."

"But he has deceived you. He impersonated a cat in order to get close to you. Why do you still trust him?"

"He had every opportunity to kill me, kill all of us. He didn't. All he did was help me investigate Serel's death. Every clue we unearthed proved no single demon could have made and triggered the device that killed Serel."

"What have you discovered about Serel's death?"

She went through their entire investigation, every piece of evidence they had uncovered, every deduction they had made. A demon could not touch the book, so must have had help. No human could handle so much magic. The forces needed to perform the spell would overwhelm a single angel.

"Then you doubt the demon who died in Nairobi was working alone?" Michael asked.

The pain came like a knife digging into her kidney, adding a new layer of misery. Without a tool causing it, the pain surprised her every time, agony rocking her body. It took her a moment to gather her thoughts after he had asked the question.

"Yes."

"Who would have worked with her?"

"I don't *know*, but Shax and I have some guesses."

"What are your guesses?"

She panted, her thoughts escaping her, scattered by the pain.

"A duo or small group of angels and demons working together. They might have enough power to build and trigger the bomb. Maybe a Duke of Hell. You."

"Is that why you didn't come to me with this? You thought I did it?"

The rapid-fire questions flooded her with torment. Kheone moaned. It was the first sound of pain she had made since beginning the ordeal. A tiny voice told her one lie would make it all end. She shoved the voice down deep. Oblivion was not the answer, not yet.

"No. I wanted to come to you with actual answers, not more questions. And I knew you would judge me for working with Shax."

Michael continued the questions unrelenting. She spilled every secret she had been keeping, unaware of how much time passed. The pain dulled her other senses, and all she knew was she stood in a circle of fear and truth, pain and fire.

Disturbed by the information she spilled out, the archangel kept asking similar questions, almost as if he was trying to catch her dodging one. She was at her limit now, each question bringing an ocean of pain. Her knees were ready to buckle, and her body trembled from head to foot. Michael laid a hand on her shoulder, and she screamed.

"We are nearly finished, my angel. I only have two questions remaining."

Her shoulders slumped in relief. Michael stepped in front of her. Her vision still affected by the drugs he had given her, a pulsing blue aura hung around his head. Nauseated, she almost vomited. He placed his fingers over her heart, and she screamed again, done fighting her pain.

Michael leaned in and whispered in her ear, "Have you fornicated with Shax?"

After the echoes of her scream stopped reverberating in the small room, she answered, her voice raw and tears flowing freely.

"No."

His eyes widened in surprise as she opened her mouth to wail again, but the only sound she emitted was a pitiful, rasping wheeze.

"Do you love me, Kheone?" he asked.

When the pain subsided, she answered with one word, her voice a croaky mess.

"Yes."

At the moment of her creation, Kheone looked upon the golden face of perfection and loved. When Michael rejected Lucifer, she did, too. She owed him everything, including painful truth.

"But not the way you want."

Michael doused the flames. The pain swept her away, and she collapsed into his arms. Every minute, her agony decreased until it was a normal amount of pain for someone run over by a truck.

"Brave Kheone," Michael whispered in her ear.

Kheone tried to slip into sleep, the only escape from her pain now. He laid her gently on the floor and covered her with a blanket before walking out.

Caught between dream and wakefulness, Kheone appreciated the coolness of the floor on her bruised body. The blanket kept her from shivering. Lying there in pain, her name being spoken in Michael's rich voice caught her attention. The door must be cracked open.

"Kheone has been working with Shax," he said.

No voice answered him, but he paused as though listening. She wished she could move, get closer, see who he was talking to.

"She confessed everything, demanded the Rite of Revelation. She is too close to the truth."

What truth was she too close to? If she had ever known, Kheone had forgotten in the pain of her trial. She was weak from the agony, from the hallucinogenic tea, from the emotional maelstrom she had survived. She could not think straight if she had wanted to.

"This may be easy for you, Aeshma, but I do not do this lightly."

Aeshma? Who was Aeshma again? Somewhere in her fogged brain, alarm bells rang. She should know who Aeshma was. The edges of her vision darkened. It would be so nice to give in to sleep.

"Is there not another solution? Perhaps we can convince her of our cause."

Michael's voice faded, too. Kheone was so damned tired. She needed to rest. Everything would make more sense when she woke up.

"You keep that animal away, Aeshma. Kheone deserves a clean death, not whatever your monstrosity will do to her. I will handle it." Footsteps receded down the hall.

Death? Aeshma? Her exhausted brain finally put all the pieces together. Aeshma, Duke of Hell, was working with Michael, Leader of the Heavenly Host.

And he was going to kill her.

Why? Unable to move, she let her mind wander over what she had heard. Kheone was too close to something. Michael's cause. Holy Mother, Michael had destroyed the Gates. Michael had killed Serel. And now, he was working with Aeshma to keep the Gates from being rebuilt. He was going to kill her because she had nearly found them out.

Everything she had ever felt for the archangel came crashing down. Kheone had loved him, but not anymore. A weight lifted, duty and unquestioned loyalty vanished, and in these, her last moments, she was free.

There was nothing Kheone could do to save herself. She could barely even twitch her fingers and toes, let alone get up off the floor and run. When Michael came for her, she was doomed.

But Michael did not come. With eyes closed, Kheone breathed in and out, drifting, and still, he did not come. The pain lessened as the tea wore off, and she teased the edges of sleep. Maybe her death would be painless. Kheone was going to miss Earth. The food, the drink, the heat, the cold. The sex.

And in her last moments, Kheone finally admitted to herself she was going to miss Shax. She wished she could warn him, tell him to run, tell him she forgave him.

Chapter 31

For the last few hours, Shax had been doing his best to hear nothing, see nothing. Whenever his excellent sense of self-preservation failed, what he saw and heard made him want to run from the room and keep running. He would never forget this, which was precisely the point. Those who defied Duke Aeshma paid in blood, pain, and death.

Aeshma clutched his hand, her gaze fixated on the grizzly scene in front of them. Charun's blood spattered nearly every surface. The black specks faded every hour, covering Aeshma's flowered dress, replaced by more with each cut, each lash. A demon's rapid healing was no gift under these circumstances.

An insistent chime rang out, startling everyone in the room. Peth froze mid-slice, and Orax straightened up from where he leaned against the door, ensuring Charun had no escape. Aeshma blinked as though coming out of a trance and looked up at him, annoyance twisting her lips. On the table next to the door, Aeshma's phone blinked, buzzed, and chimed. Shax left her side and picked it up.

"Four hours." Holy shit, four hours. He could only imagine how long it felt to poor Charun.

"Already? That's a shame." She played with the hem of her skirt and looked thoughtful.

"Shall I continue, Your Grace?" Peth asked.

"No. Let the poor creature rest before the next round. It's no fun if she dies too quickly."

With a hideous smile, Peth put his blade down and stepped away. Choking sobs erupted from Charun, still tied to the bed frame. Her voice gave out long ago, and the sobs had escaped Shax's notice as he tried to tune everything out.

"Shax, fetch Irena." Aeshma stood and straightened her skirt, all business. "And knock on the door once you can hear through it again."

She approached her prisoner, examining Peth's handiwork. A wintry smile flitted across her face, and she turned to the vicious little prick.

"Such fine blade work, my dear." Aeshma caressed Charun's wounds. The other demon twitched in agony. "You've really outdone yourself this time. You deserve a reward. Go rest and think on what you want. Be back in an hour."

The weaselly demon's eyes gleamed, and he practically skipped in joy. Charun's sobs and groans followed them out until Shax closed the door, reactivating the spell. Peth crossed the living area and disappeared into the adjoining room. Good riddance.

Legs abruptly wobbly as the need to maintain indifference evaporated, Shax stumbled toward the kitchen. There was a reason he had kept out of sight for the last year. He filled a glass with water and walked over to the desk. He let his wobbly legs win, slumping on the chair. Sipping his water, he stared at his phone until his hands stopped shaking.

He called Irena.

"Yes?" she answered.

"Duke Aeshma needs you to do the spell again."

A long silence filled the line.

"Now?"

"Soon. The next session begins in an hour. You'll probably want to make yourself scarce before that happens." Bloodlust did peculiar things to demons, made it harder to control their worst impulses.

Irena cleared her throat and said in a quiet voice, "Thanks for the heads up. How long do you think...?"

Shax knew what she was thinking because it was the same thing he was thinking. He could be next. Once you crossed a Duke, your life was in their hands and was worth exactly as much as they decided. He answered the only way he could.

"As long as she wants it to last. What did you think would happen when you joined up with a Duke of Hell?"

"You think I had a choice?" Her voice was bitter and brittle. "When a demon shows up at your door to demand you serve them and threatens your children if you say no, there isn't one."

She was right. "My apologies. Even I can only say no so many times."

"Why?"

"It, too, is a long, sad story, best suited for another day."

"Will you say that every time I ask?" Her words carried a trace of humor.

She was smarter than he had assumed. The corners of his mouth twitched up, but he said nothing.

"That's what I thought," she said. "I'll be there in a few minutes if Her Grace asks."

"I'll tell her."

He hung up the phone. Shax grabbed a paper towel from the kitchen and ran it under cold water. He scrubbed off all the black blood he could find. Gone in an hour, no matter what, Shax didn't want to wear Charun's blood any longer than absolutely necessary. He kept scrubbing.

When he turned the water off, he heard Charun's pitiful sobs coming from the bedroom. The spell must be wearing off. Shax tried to tune them out as he poured himself something much stronger than water. Today, of all days, he didn't dare leave until Aeshma dismissed him. The strains of *Running with the Devil* drifted under the door.

"Hello, I'm busy," Aeshma said in a sing-song voice, too pleased with herself.

It wouldn't be long before she called him back in. He took some deep breaths and steeled himself for what awaited behind the door.

"I know it's you, darling. You're in my contacts. What do you need?"

He drank the last swallow of vodka in his glass and left it by the sink.

"Really? Now, that's surprising."

Shax moved closer, his interest piqued. What he heard next nearly stopped his heart.

"Looks like we both have messes to clean up. Pity. Shax is a rather useful creature, and he just got here. If I keep having to sacrifice members of my horde for this, I might have to reevaluate our arrangement."

Aeshma was going to kill him.

Shit, shit, shit.

His heart thundered in his chest, and he broke into a cold sweat. He needed to get out of here.

"Are you sure you'll be able to kill Kheone, Michael? I understand if you might need assistance. You're not one for casual fucking, and you've really fucked her this time."

He froze as Aeshma laughed at her own joke, a silvery giggle at odds with the words spewing from her mouth. The weight of what he heard sunk into his heart and stopped his breath. Michael. Aeshma was working with Michael. The archangel was going to kill Kheone.

His head spun from the sudden upending of his world.

"You don't have a choice. If you want to keep the gates closed, you must kill her. The last thing either of us wants now is Lucifer free to seek his revenge. If you can't do it, I'll send Peth over later. This might be the reward he needs."

Shax broke through the fear keeping him frozen and crept from the bedroom door. He did not have long to escape, let alone to rescue Kheone. His mind raced. He could run right now and have a better than fifty-fifty shot at saving himself. If he tried to rescue Kheone, go up against Michael, he put his odds as *a snowball's chance in Hell*.

He couldn't do it. He cared too fucking much. The angel had scaled the walls built long ago around his heart and made him care. Shax had no choice. There was only one way he could reach her before Michael—Jesus, Michael!—killed her.

He picked up a pen and jotted down a note. *Fetching Irena. Back soon.*

If he was very lucky, it would buy him a few minutes to get to Kheone first. Shax stuck his hand in his pocket and pulled out the coin. For the first, and hopefully only time, he sent thanks out into the universe for this cursed piece of silver.

"Very well—"

Aeshma's voice cut off mid-sentence as Shax whispered Kheone's name.

His best bet at staying alive was to run. Run far, run fast, and never stop. But Shax had figured out a very important thing about himself since he had saved Kheone from Serel's falling body. No matter the cost to him, he had to help Kheone first. He had to try. He could never live with himself if he left her to this fate. The only thing in his entire, miserable existence that made any sense to him was a very simple, very hidden fact. He loved Kheone. And she needed him.

The coin dropped him a hundred yards from the burned-out dorm. The darkened windows stared at him, no sign of movement inside or out. The barest blush of pre-dawn brightened the sky in the east. So much had happened in less than twelve hours, his whole world upended, in the best and worst ways. Shax had to be prepared for anything, even the possibility his mission would end before it had even begun.

Where would Michael hold Kheone? Motion caught his eye. Speak of the archangel. Michael strode out of the building next door and disappeared into the shadowed wreckage of the dorm. At least he knew where Michael wasn't. Shax ran for the building the archangel had left as though Kheone's life depended on it.

It was the longest damn run of his life, all ten seconds of it.

Shax pulled on the door, expecting it to be locked. It was not. His brain screamed at him to take off, leave this mess behind, and survive another day, another month, another year. The thought of living with himself should he make that choice filled him with disgust. His heart told him he could not. He would end up taking his own life, one way or another, should he stare at an eternity without Kheone.

Because it boiled down to some sick, cosmic joke. A demon in love with an angel. Shax imagined Lucifer's cruel, knowing laugh. And if God could see him now...

He followed his heart. Stalking silently like his alter ego, he passed the gym, full of sleeping angels, crept downstairs, and stopped halfway down the hall in front of a door.

There was nothing special about the gray industrial door. But behind this door was Kheone. His soul knew it, a certainty he had only experienced once before in his immortal life. That time had been a mistake. This time he was wiser. This time he knew what real love looked like. It wasn't some false idol, trapping him in torment of the body and the soul. It was Kheone.

Shax took in a deep breath, preparing for whatever lay behind the door.

She could be dead, said the realist in him.

Shut the fuck up, said his heart.

There was only one way to find out. He tugged the door open, crouching down to make himself a smaller target in case Michael had left a guard.

Kheone's body lay in the middle of a circle of ashes, covered in a ratty blanket. It took him a moment to notice the slow rise and fall of her chest as she breathed. *She breathed*. She was alive. Oh, thank God, she was alive.

Chapter 32

The door opened with a soft creak of its hinges, and the draft of air over her body brought Kheone out of her stupor. Her body was still boneless, and her mind untethered from reality. Without windows, she had lost touch with time.

Ten minutes or ten hours, it didn't matter. She took a breath, knowing full well this could be her last and wishing it tasted of something other than musty basement.

"Hey, Blue. Found yourself a bit of trouble, I see," a familiar voice whispered.

Not Michael. Shax.

That ludicrous nickname was now her favorite word in the entire universe. The way he said it filled an aching emptiness she had never recognized before. She opened her eyes and tried to smile, but it likely came out as a grimace. He knelt down next to her, brushing her cheek with his finger. Kheone flinched, but instead of pain, his touch was a warm balm, pushing aside a little of the anguish riddling her body.

"I know you don't have a reason to trust me, but you have to. Michael is going to kill you. We need to go."

Kheone opened her mouth and tried to form words, but an awful groan was all she managed. White-hot fire shot through her limbs.

"What the fuck did that dickwad do to you? Can you move?"

His eyes, brimming with tears, found hers. She tried to reach for his hand, to reassure him she would be okay if only they escaped. Her fingers twitched, but nothing else happened. Kheone felt warm tears of her own trail down her cheeks. Shax brushed them away.

"No time for explanations, anyway. I don't suppose you can make a rift?"

She tried to shake her head, moving it a bit.

"No, I thought not. Michael is next door, but I don't know when he'll return. I will be as gentle as possible, but fast is best. Try not to make any noise."

She blinked again, hoping he understood it as a sign of her consent. Shax tucked the blanket around her and picked her up in a smooth motion, cradling her close to his body. The warmth he radiated was far more comforting than the cool floor. Kheone gave a little sigh.

He carried her like a small child, though they were similar in build, out the door and down the hall. With his foot on the first step, he froze. Booted feet thumped on the floor above.

Michael.

Her heart sped up, feeling as though it would burst out of her chest. The tears came again. After millennia of loyal service, Michael had betrayed her. He had betrayed all of them.

Shax turned and began trying each of the doors down the hall. They were all locked, except the room they had left. He slid in and closed the door. Michael's boots tromped down the stairs.

"Shh," Shax said, placing her gently back on the floor where she'd been. "I have a plan. Trust me."

He turned into a cat and hid in the dark recesses of the room.

What plan? Hide until Michael killed her, then escape when his attention was elsewhere? That would have been a good plan for him, not for her. But if he wanted to escape, why had he shown up in the first place? He had asked for trust. She had no other choice but to give it to him.

Her eyes met his, wide in fear. In his cat form, Shax could say nothing. He blinked slowly and twitched his tail. She blinked back at him, comforted by his presence. Even if this ended badly, she would not die alone.

The door opened, and Michael's enormous figure filled the frame. Kheone squirmed under the blanket and tried to speak, even though her body throbbed and lightning shot through her organs. Anything to draw the archangel's attention to her and away from the cat hiding in the shadows. Michael leaned against the door with a loud sigh and crossed his arms.

"This is not how I had hoped things would turn out," he said. "I have made many mistakes in my existence, but none as monumental as killing Serel. If I had chosen another way to deal with his curiosity, neither of us would be sitting here now. I am truly sorry, my perfect angel."

Kheone kept her focus on Michael and tried to get her voice to work. She opened and closed her mouth a few times before sound came out.

"W...w...why?" she asked.

Michael laughed, a cruel, dry sound. "I suppose I owe you an explanation. It is more than Serel received. Lucifer was right, Kheone."

Blasphemy. Lucifer was jealous, and cruel, and so very, very wrong. For Michael to think he had a leg to stand on meant the archangel was corrupt, too.

"These humans are vermin. They do not deserve God's love. Yet, He forced us to serve them. I spent ten thousand years trying to get them to follow God, to be kind and merciful. I led armies of angels against the demon hordes to protect the ungrateful wretches. I guided kings and queens, generals and warlords, all to protect the righteous. I recruited Guardian Angels to help, to whisper in the ears of these creatures in hopes they would fill the gardens of Heaven."

Kheone knew this. She had been by his side through all of it, the first to volunteer. She did not see the humans as vermin. They were gloriously flawed, equally capable of so much good and miserable amounts of evil. A nudge in the right direction usually did the trick. Although she would not tell him so, Michael apparently needed the same guidance.

"All these years and all I had to show for my efforts was grief and exhaustion. I missed my brother. I spent centuries looking for a way to rescue him. Centuries. I found the spell to destroy the Gate. If I could get Lucifer out, no one could return him to Hell. We had a plan. I would free Lucifer minutes before the bomb exploded and call a retreat. It was supposed to look like the bomb killed me. No one would know we were free. After an eternity of servitude, we would kill whatever demons still lurked about and assert our dominion over the human race."

Lucifer roaming the Earth without anybody strong enough to toss him back into Hell, and Michael egging him on was a nightmare that did not bear contemplation.

"Something went wrong. I struck the chains holding Lucifer, but the bomb exploded before he could escape and before the angels were safe behind Heaven's Gate. Both Gates blew. So, I gathered the angels I could, killed what demons we found, and hoped we would adjust to our new lives. You certainly seemed to, fornicating with random humans."

"I...I was looking for c...connection," Kheone said, her voice quiet. Finally, a complete sentence. How else was she going to tell Michael to go to Hell?

"Had I known, I would have come to you earlier. And then Serel started digging into what happened. He would not let it go, so I laid a trap in the library with a small version of the bomb. I played on your obvious attraction to distract you from the investigation. You were the best lieutenant I had ever trained. For that alone, I am sorry I have to kill you."

"I loved y...you," she said, her voice a little stronger this time, the tears drying.

"I hoped to have you join us once you were mine. But I cannot risk it now. The Gates must remain locked. God would throw me into the pit to join my brother, and Lucifer does not take kindly to those who have betrayed him. And he would see my mistake as a betrayal. When I found Aeshma a few months ago, I proposed an alliance. I would stop any angel from trying to rebuild the Gates, and she would keep her demons away. Otherwise, we would be free to do as we wished. We sealed our bargain with a kiss which led to...other things. Ten thousand years of celibacy was foolish. I am a fool no longer."

"She will betray you, too," Kheone murmured.

"Of course she will. It is her nature, and I will kill her when she does."

Michael drew out a dagger about the length of Kheone's forearm. Its blade was the black of the deepest cave and glinted cruelly in the dim light of the storeroom. Its bone handle yellowed with age. A chill ran down her spine as he stepped toward her. The dagger sang of death.

"You have your explanation, Kheone. I am sorry this is how it must be."

Chapter 33

Shax did not, in fact, have a plan. His only thought had been to get Kheone out and run. When Michael had shown up, even that went to shit.

He hid in a dark corner of the room and watched. There would only be one shot to save Kheone, and he needed to wait for the right opportunity. Looking so like Lucifer, treacherous and cruel, Michael pulled the dagger out. How the Hell had the archangel found his dagger?

Shax knew this blade intimately, would recognize it anywhere, anytime. Lucifer had pressed it to his neck more than once in answer to his defiance. He had wielded the dagger himself, taking lives and souls for the Morning Star. Held it to Kheone's throat. The blade would doom her soul to oblivion. His moment had come.

Shax leaped from his hiding place, changing midair, tackling Michael to the ground. The knife clattered away as the two figures wrestled, each trying to get the upper hand. The only advantage Shax had was surprise. He needed to finish this quickly. Michael's size, strength, and sheer prowess in battle would soon negate Shax's temporary edge.

He pummeled the archangel, using every dirty trick in his book. Shax could not kill Michael with only his fists, but he could incapacitate him long enough to escape with Kheone. He had no idea how he would do that, but one step at a time. First, knock out Michael. Then flee with Kheone. He finally had a fucking plan.

He threw jabs to Michael's kidneys, butted his head, scratched, and bit. Shax even made a few attempts to kick the archangel in the balls. But he may as well have punched a wall. With every hit, Michael roared and hit back harder. Shax amassed a collection of bruises to make any boxer proud, and black blood oozed from his split lip. His opponent was in much better shape, despite Shax's best efforts. The scratches and bite marks Michael sported had barely bled, and the pearlescent ichor congealed and shone like diamonds.

"I weary of this, demon. Stand down now, and I will guarantee a painless death for both you and Kheone. Continue to fight me, and I will allow Aeshma to have you both before I send you to oblivion."

If he had been fighting for only his life, Shax likely would have surrendered then. A quick, clean death was better than what Aeshma would do any day of the week, as he had witnessed a mere hour ago. Even oblivion was better than what Aeshma would do. After ten millennia of torment, oblivion sounded peaceful.

But Shax was fighting for Kheone's life, too. The mere thought of a world without her in it made his blood run cold. Memories of their time together fueled his desperate attempt to inflict as much damage on the archangel as possible.

Kheone's anger at his insults across the wasteland. Her own faltering insults she had tossed at him. Their very first warrior to feud over. His half-assed effort at corrupting the soldier in some ancient Mesopotamian army and the joy when she had shaped him into a decent human being. The many, many warriors after she had helped. His efforts became more subtle, but her goodness won out more often than not.

Kheone was worth fighting for. Not only for her compassion toward a small, homeless cat but also for believing him, trusting him, when he was certain everything she had ever been taught screamed at her to kill him. If anything happened to her, it would be over his dead body.

Of course, that was looking more like the inevitable outcome every second. Michael had overcome his surprise at Shax's appearance and rained down blows on him. Black blood spattered the floor. He could not take much more punishment. Michael had knocked him to his hands and knees, and it was all Shax could do not to collapse to the floor.

"Michael, stop," Kheone cried out.

The next blow did not come. Movement drew his attention. Kheone struggled to sit up, but her voice was as powerful as ever.

"You don't have to do this," she said. "We won't tell anyone. Who would believe us anyway? Just let us go. We'll disappear. You'll never see us again."

"See, that is a problem, my angel. You keep using we. Do you not remember you are mine? I will not allow you to seek solace in another's arms, certainly not his arms. Do you even know what Shax is?"

Balls. He had hoped to tell her himself, soften the blow. It wasn't every day you found out Lucifer's infamous assassin was after you. Let alone he was the Prince of Hell's former lover. Not that it mattered. He may have loved Lucifer, but Lucifer had never loved him. He'd used Shax to get what he wanted, to soothe away the pain of Hell, to kill his enemies.

"He's my friend. That's all I need to know."

Warmth bloomed in his chest. All this time, she had insisted they were mere allies, a relationship of convenience in order to get a job done. Somewhere along the way, she had changed her mind. Thank the ever-loving Christ.

"He is a whore and a killer, Kheone. You deserved better. I am sorry I could not offer it."

Shax looked up at Michael, who had both hands clenched together in a great fist. The blow would knock him out, enabling the archangel to retrieve the blade and finish off both of them. He could try to scurry off, but that would only delay the inevitable. He had no tricks left.

The fist came down, and Shax closed his eyes. But instead of pain and darkness, a warm body covered his own, taking the blow for him. Kheone.

She muffled her grunt of pain in his shoulder before collapsing on the floor at his feet, unconscious. No more blows fell, and Michael took several steps back.

"No, Kheone, I did not mean—you were not—" the archangel said.

The sharp click of heels on concrete tapped down the hall, the softer clomps of boots right behind. The noise echoed through his head in the sudden silence of their defeat.

"Well, Michael," Aeshma said from the door, her voice dripping with contempt. "I see you've fucked up again."

Orax stood behind her, knives out. Demons liked combat and blood too much to use something as efficient as a gun. It might give Shax enough time to plan.

"I am not the only one," Michael said, annoyance clouding his face. "May I remind you that Shax still alive, and you ordered an attack on my angels."

"You killed Asag. Tit for tat, pet. She wasn't very bright, but she was loyal. I suppose we'll remedy the other situation together. Where's your fancy knife, angel?"

Michael looked around the room and saw it, the blade under a desk, the handle gleaming in the light from the hall. Shax moved before anyone else. Michael still got to the knife first, damn him.

The archangel held the blade to Shax's throat. A strangled laugh escaped his lips.

"I hold a blade of true death to your neck, and you laugh? What madness is this?" Michael asked, confusion making a crease in his brows, a frown on his lips. It only made Shax laugh harder.

"That's his blade, Michael, and you aren't the first to threaten him with it," Aeshma said with a knowing smile. She had been there for more than one of Lucifer's shows.

A flash of unease passed through the archangel's cold eyes, but his hand didn't waver. "I do not threaten, Aeshma. We must end this."

"I don't disagree, but I have a better idea," she said. "What if you didn't have to lie to your gathering?"

"I cannot tell them—"

"Not about the Gates, you half-witted fly fucker. What if instead of telling your gathering you killed Shax after he killed Kheone, you actually killed Shax after he killed your precious sex toy?"

"I never—"

"I never?" Her voice was mean, the sing-songy cadence of a middle school bully. "You were just supposed to distract her."

"Why do you get a whore, and I do not, Aeshma?" Michael's voice was cold as stone. If Shax had any chance at all, he was going to kill the douchebag.

"Did you pay her? Did she do whatever you asked as long as your money was good?"

Michael shook his head.

"Then she wasn't a whore. She was a lover. *I* am your lover, and I don't share."

She failed to mention what had passed between them, but he kept his mouth shut. This entire situation was absurd. An archangel trying to set Lucifer free. And failing. Killing his fellow angels. Fucking a Duke of Hell. At his most imaginative or under heavy drugs, Shax never would have believed it.

"What does it even matter, Aeshma? She dies today."

"If Shax kills her, I give my solemn oath as a Duke of Hell neither of them will suffer. Their deaths will be clean and quick."

"And if I won't?" Shax asked, knowing the answer but needing to hear it said out loud.

"Peth hasn't practiced his skills on an angel in some time. It would be a lovely treat for him. I'm sure he'll make slow work of her."

Shax couldn't suppress a shudder.

"You would trust him with this blade?" Michael asked.

"I think he cares for Kheone and doesn't want her to suffer any more than she already has." Aeshma approached Shax and cupped his cheek in her hand. "And I know he's suffered enough to prefer a quick end to prolonged torture. Poor Shax, always the hard choice."

He stared into her eyes, thunderheads ready to rain down destruction. There was no mercy to be found, no light he could tether his hopes to. He had two shit choices and had to decide between them for both himself and Kheone. This sucked. His life had sucked, and now his death would, too.

"I have your oath?" Shax asked.

"On the Gate, on the throne, on the Prince of Hell himself, I swear you will have a clean death after you kill the angel, Kheone," Aeshma said, not blinking, voice soft and clear.

"Give me the dagger," he said.

Michael looked at Aeshma. At her nod, he handed Shax the blade. Warm to the touch, the fucking thing vibrated in his hand, finally home after being lost in the Second Fall. *Guess I'll never know where Michael found it.*

Shax next to Kheone's unconscious form and held the tip of the blade over her heart, back to where he had been a year ago, ready to kill her at the behest of another.

He looked at Kheone, her blue-black hair stark against flesh made ashen by trauma. Her lips had paled from their usual ruby red, her breathing was shallow, and her pulse beat wildly in her neck. Love coursed through him, something he had long felt incapable of. The hand holding the knife trembled. Shax couldn't do it. He would not be the one to end her life, no matter who ordered it.

A nasty laugh escaped Aeshma's lips.

"You weak fool, you fell in love with her, didn't you? Imagine a demon in love with an angel. What could be more pathetic? You are the worst demon I ever met, Shax, though you're a better liar than I gave you credit for. I order you to kill Kheone."

What did he have left to lose? He was dying today. It no longer mattered if Aeshma knew of his special gift.

"Fuck you," he said as he dropped the knife by Kheone's outstretched fingers and stood up. "I will not kill her."

Aeshma's eyes widened in surprise. Few knew of his ability to say no to a duke. Oh, sure, rumors flew, but no duke wanted to confirm there was a demon out there who could say no to them. He had never denied Aeshma before. She usually phrased her orders as requests and was less likely to abuse her power than her colleagues.

"What does he mean, Aeshma?" Michael asked. Guess Heaven did not get many updates on the denizens of Hell.

"I'd heard—it doesn't matter. You know the consequences, Shax. Peth will carve up the pair of you, Kheone first, and eat your flesh. It won't be pretty, and it won't be quick. Can you stand to see that happen to your beautiful angel?"

"He won't have to," Kheone said, her voice a creaky mess.

In one hand was Lucifer's blade. With her other, she reached out and grabbed Shax's ankle. A rift opened below them, and he fell.

Dammit, he was tired of falling.

Chapter 34

Opening rifts had always been easy, a simple thought of wanting to be somewhere else coupled with the intention to open a way there. This was different, like reaching through a wall of viscous goo in order to open a window stuck tight with years of paint. Lances of pain shot through Kheone's head, adding to the torment already inflicted upon her.

They landed with a heavy thud, arms and legs entangled. Embarrassing if the situation wasn't so dire. The dagger clattered away. The blanket Michael—that son of a bitch—had covered her with made the journey with them, wrapped around her leg. Kheone kicked at it, suppressing the shiver threatening to begin at the base of her spine now the danger had passed.

The archangel she trusted had betrayed her, her age-old enemy saved her, and she had no time to figure out what any of it meant. Not if she wanted to live. On top of the pain that Kheone already felt, the fall knocked the wind out of her. She lay gasping on the cool, tiled floor in the oddly lit room.

"Oh, Christ, that hurt," Shax said with a groan from where he had landed, right on top of her. He levered himself up to look her over. "Where are we?"

"Museum," she wheezed. "Should be safe. Only Serel—"

God, it hurt to breathe.

"Are you okay?"

She nodded, finally taking in a deep breath. The pain in her body ebbed as oxygen flowed through her, replaced by pure rage.

"Get off."

Kheone shoved Shax away, unable to bear having him so close. He sprawled on the floor, his expression hurt.

"What did I do?"

"What did you do?" Kheone stood, towering over him, and spewed out her anger. Even as she did so, she knew Shax didn't deserve all of it. He was merely the closest target. "You lied to me. You betrayed me. You—"

"I saved your ass," he said, rising from the floor. They stood toe-to-toe, his amber eyes snapping.

"I saved yours."

Kheone jabbed him in the chest with a finger, the pain of the Rite forgotten in her anger. Shax grabbed her hand, and molten need swept over her still-sensitive skin, dousing her fury. His eyes flared, echoing her desire.

"You kissed Michael," he said, soft and accusing.

"Michael kissed me." Some of the heat left her voice.

"You wanted him to."

"Yes, I did."

Shax let go of her hand and turned his head, focusing on a point behind her. She missed his touch, though he stood within easy reach. A blanket of regret she wished to toss off fell over her heart.

"I don't anymore," she said. His gaze snapped back to hers. "You kissed me, too."

"I did."

"Why?"

"I'm a demon, Blue. Why not?"

Kheone grabbed his jacket with both hands and pulled him to her. No more lingering gazes, no more smoldering caresses. No more games. She had to know if what she felt was real. She had to know if he felt the same.

"Don't give me garbage, Shax. Why?"

"Because," he said, his liquid honey voice doing obscene things to her insides. "I thought I'd never see you again. And in all my life, the only thing I would ever regret was not kissing you."

How in the nine spheres of Heaven had he given her the exact right answer? Desire washed over her, and she closed the last few inches between them. Kheone sealed her lips to his, dipping her tongue into his mouth. She tasted him in long, languorous strokes. Salty and spicy. Shax melted into her, his heat mingling with her own until every inch of her was on fire with wanting him. She tore the jacket off him and slid her hands under his shirt.

His skin was smooth and silken over hard, lean muscle. She'd never felt something so exquisite. Shax moaned at the contact and pressed her back to the wall. Framing her face with his palms, he eased his tongue between her lips.

With her own moan, she wrapped a long leg around his. His hard cock pressed into the juncture between her thighs. She rubbed against him, wanting him, *needing* him.

"You're killing me, Blue," he said, letting her come up for air.

She smiled and pulled off his shirt, running her hands up and down his chest, teasing the line of skin at his waistband. A frustrated growl escaped his lips, and he yanked her shirt over her head. Shax trailed kisses down her neck, lingering a moment over the scar he'd given her. Had it only been a year ago?

He ran his tongue along the line of her bra as he undid the clasp in the back. Shax brushed the straps off her shoulders and fastened his lips around one of the hard buds he'd revealed. Kheone leaned her head against the wall behind her. He slid his hands around her, gently tracing the outline of her wings. Kheone bit back a cry of pure pleasure.

"Oh, God, Shax," she murmured against his mouth.

He arched into her. Kheone nearly lost her mind with need.

"Less clothes," he mumbled.

She dropped her leg and fumbled at the button of his jeans, kicking off her shoes. She pushed the thick denim down along with the silken boxers he wore, freeing the hard length of him. Kheone grazed him with her fingers and smiled as he shuddered in pleasure. Shax returned the favor, stripping her bare, then cupped her ass. He lifted her up, using the wall as leverage.

Kheone wrapped her arms around his neck, and he slid into her wet depths. She cried out in pleasure. Once again, he reached around her, his butterfly touches to her wings changing to firm pressure, the heat settling low in her belly, the tension unfurling. She shattered, clenching around him, while his kisses swallowed her cries.

Shax removed her hands from around his neck and held them against the wall above her head. He pinned her there as he increased his thrusts, the dull thud of their two bodies hitting the wall loud in the otherwise silent room. His rhythm became frantic, and with a long, low groan, he came.

He released her and leaned his head on her shoulder. She wrapped her arms around him until his breath slowed. Shax lifted his head, and Kheone forced herself to let him go. As impossible as it sounded, she could have stayed like that for hours. He kissed her again, softly, the last ember of their passion flaring between them.

"I'm—" he started.

"If you say you're sorry, I'm going to hit you," she said with a small smile. God knew she wasn't sorry. "I wanted it just as much as you."

He answered with a fierce grin and pulled up his jeans. They dressed quickly, and Shax looked around.

"Where the Hell did you say we were, again?" he asked.

Kheone pushed aside her emotions for the moment. Survival had to take priority over whatever had happened between them. She'd chosen the one safe place that came to mind as she regained consciousness and realized how totally screwed they were. But something was off. If she could wrap her head around what. She closed her eyes. The pain ebbed some more without the light.

She was exactly where she wanted to be. She'd glimpsed the storeroom crammed full of extra chairs once when attending a lecture in the basement. Except—

"What time is it?" she asked, her eyes flying open.

"Not sure, but it was near dawn when I found you."

"I don't think the museum is open yet, so where is the light coming from?"

Together, they looked up at the ceiling. They clearly saw the light fixture in the middle of the ceiling, a standard industrial fluorescent model which was definitely not on. A blue-gray light suffused the room, nonetheless. Shax's expression changed from confused to worried.

"What?" he whispered, echoing her own thoughts.

He took her hand in his, grasping for whatever comfort he could find. Sweet heat snuck up her arm, setting her body on fire again. Now was not the time for more wall banging. There were more important puzzles to figure out.

Looking for something to distract her from that idea, Kheone grabbed the dagger off the floor and idly twirled it.

"Be careful," Shax said, stepping away from her.

"Why?"

Kheone stopped fidgeting with the dagger and examined the black blade and bone handle, oddly cold in her hand.

"It's a weapon of oblivion," he said so matter-of-factly it took a moment to register.

She nearly dropped the damned thing, all thoughts of more sex driven from her mind.

"How do you know?"

"Let's just say that dagger and I go way back. Unfortunately, it's the least of our worries at the moment."

True, having a soul-eating dagger was a worry, but it could wait. One problem at a time. What number were they on? Fifteen?

She turned the knob and cracked the door open. Dead silence greeted her ears. No whir of ventilation, not a creak from the hinges. The same twilight filled the hall, coming from everywhere and nowhere all at once, but not from the industrial light fixtures lining the low basement ceiling. She stepped into the hall.

"Kheone—"

She held up a hand, and he snapped his mouth shut, letting her take the lead. Her sneakers made a soft squeak on the tiled floor as she slowly crept down the hall. It was the only sound until Shax's booted feet followed her out of the storeroom. Together, the sound of their brief journey echoed irregularly off the walls, ceiling, and floor, as though the air was thicker here.

Kheone glanced over her shoulder, unable to tell how far behind Shax was, but stopped mid-stride. The door to the storeroom was closed. There had been no noise to indicate it.

"Did you close the door?" she whispered.

Shax shook his head and looked back.

Kheone fought the urge to run in the opposite direction. No footsteps, no breathing, no evidence at all anyone else was here. She lifted the dagger and returned to the storeroom. Shax stood behind her with a hand on her shoulder, ready to pull her out of harm's way should they have both missed another person sneaking behind them. She turned the metal knob and pushed the door open. No one was there in the gray-lit room.

She took a step back and looked at Shax, who pointed. The door was shut again. They had been standing right here, no one else was there, and the door to the storeroom stood implacably shut as though they had never opened it. What the Hell was going on here?

"Now what?" Shax asked.

She shrugged. She was in the right place, but not, somehow.

"This is definitely the basement of the museum, but something is wrong."

"How safe are we here?"

"I kept my off-hours to myself. Serel was the only one who knew I liked to come here. If they can perform a tracking spell, they'll find us, eventually. But if I've somehow taken us back or forward in time, we'll be safe for a while."

"Is time travel even possible?"

"Is it possible for the Archangel Michael to betray God in order to free his accursed brother?"

"So, yes, maybe?" he said, a smirk twitching up one side of his lips at her sarcastic tone that felt raw and new.

Kheone huffed out a breath and turned on her heels, striding toward the stairs at the end of the hall.

"I can only think of one way to find out," she said.

"Can you open another rift?"

"I don't know, Shax. It really hurt to get here. I will try again if Michael and Aeshma show up, but for now, I'd really like to know what in the bloody blue blazes happened the last time."

"Fair enough." The clomp of his boots followed her down the hall and up the stairs to a gallery.

Kheone walked into the middle of the large room. One thing stood out. The colors were all wrong. In the utilitarian basement, painted an off-white, it hadn't been apparent. Here in the gallery, the gloriously colored paintings of her memory were muted, the colors muddied, laced with grays and browns. The clean lines of the painter's hand fuzzy and out of focus. Realization dawned on her.

"Oh, shit. Purgatory," she whispered.

She had seen it before, quick glimpses while escorting those sentenced to Purgatory to its Gate. Kheone had noticed the blue-gray eternal twilight and the muted colors, a shadowy copy of the Earth, as the souls had stepped through. Purgatory was a punishment, though a sentence of self-reflection rather than torment. The things which brought joy on Earth were subdued or missing to encourage introspection and reduce distraction. No hunger or thirst, but no cheer or song or comfort. None of the things that made life worth living.

"Seriously?" Shax asked, face pale.

"Yes."

"How the fuck did you do that?"

Kheone glared at him.

"Okay, okay," he said, holding his hands up in surrender. "Can you get us out of here?"

"Give me five more minutes, and I'll try."

She turned around and headed toward the stairs. Before she reached them, Shax gripped her elbow, halting her in her tracks.

"What is it?" she asked.

"We might be safer here. I mean, who would think to look for us in Purgatory?"

Kheone shuddered. "I don't like it here."

He tugged gently on her arm, and she turned to him. Shax reached up and hesitated, his hand hanging in the air before he lowered it back to his side. Kheone grasped his hand, holding onto it like she would a bit of flotsam in a great, wide ocean. An ember sparked in the depths of his golden eyes.

"I don't either, but until today, I thought the only way to Purgatory was through the Garden. How long until anyone thinks to look for us here? Is there any place on Earth where Michael couldn't find you?"

At the mention of Michael's name, Kheone lost the fragile thread of control she'd been clinging to. The tears started falling. The ones she'd been keeping in since she realized Michael was not who she had thought he was. He had betrayed her trust and wanted her dead. Shax tugged her into a tight embrace and held her as she cried. He made no demands, just held her until she stopped.

"I'm sorry," she said many minutes later, voice hoarse.

"Nothing to be sorry about, Kheone. You've had a crappy day."

She wheezed out a laugh. That was putting it mildly. Shax gave her a crooked grin. Master of the understatement.

"I'm tired and scared, Shax, and I don't want to be here. But you may be right. I'd like to open a rift to Earth, though. If anyone figures out we are here, we'll need an escape hatch. We don't have to step through."

"Okay."

She'd expected more of an argument, but he trusted her to make the plan.

"Okay," she said. "Let's go back to the storeroom. Maybe it'll be easier there since that's where the rift opened."

Kheone walked down the hall and pulled open the door without hesitation. Shax followed her into the cramped room. Taking a shaky breath, she reached through the mental goo. Lightning flickered through her mind and down her arms and legs, the pain excruciating, rivaled only by the rite she had just endured. The other side of the rift remained out of reach.

"Kheone, what's wrong?" Shax's voice came through like an old phonograph, tinny and faint.

She did not have the energy to reply. The stakes were high. Trapped in Purgatory forever if she couldn't open a rift. She had to do this, no matter the cost.

Kheone did not see the red light as the rift formed. She was too busy blacking out.

Chapter 35

Shax caught Kheone as she collapsed and swung her into his arms. The red line of the forming rift disappeared with a snap as she lost her battle with consciousness. His dagger dropped from her fingers and thudded to the ground with more weight and noise than he had expected. He left it.

Panic ripped through his heart. Shax examined Kheone as best he could. Her breathing was regular, if a little shallow, and apart from an ashen undertone to her warm, brown skin, she seemed fine.

"Kheone," he whispered.

Her lashes fluttered, but her eyes stayed closed. She needed to rest. Whatever the Rite of Revelation was, it had taken almost every ounce of her considerable strength to survive. And then she had still rescued them both. Jesus Christ, she was incredible. No wonder he loved her.

He should have realized it when he couldn't kill her a year ago.

Shax held her tight, feeling oddly comforted by her lithe body pressed against his. He had never thought it possible she might return his feelings, but that hadn't been mere fucking. It had been more than a few millennia since sex had felt that good, that right.

Stuck at the museum with an unconscious angel for the foreseeable future, Shax didn't know what else was around and if, or when, Michael might come after them. Some mess they had landed in, but at least they were still alive to appreciate it.

He needed to ensure her safety until she awoke, but the thought of leaving her on the cold floor of the storeroom was intolerable. It reminded him too much of the dank storeroom where he had found her. Shax carried Kheone through the echoey halls in the weird half-light permeating everywhere in this shadow world. The air was perfectly clean. No dust motes caught the light. No odors tickled their noses. The only sound was their breath and the scuff of his foot. Everything seemed magnified tenfold in the silence.

Once up the stairs and back to the gallery, he gently placed her on an upholstered bench in the middle of the room. He ran the entire way to retrieve the blanket and the dagger, loathe to leave her, even for a minute or two. Mostly, he wanted that blanket. It was cool in Purgatory, and it would come in handy.

He didn't give a shit about the blade, but it wouldn't do to having the thing lying around where anyone could pick it up, *if* anyone could pick it up besides the two of them. It was the only weapon they had against a gathering, a horde, a Duke of Hell, and the Archangel Michael.

The dagger still vibrated, the handle unnaturally warm, as though happy to return to its owner. Doomed to wield it once more, would it haunt him forever?

Shax didn't make it a habit to question Lucifer, but he had wondered why the Prince of Hell wanted Kheone dead. The Morning Star rarely concerned himself with underling angels. Although she was one of the most successful Guardian Angels he'd ever had the pleasure of fighting, Kheone was insignificant in the grand scheme of things. All of Shax's previous assignments had been too powerful Dukes or demons scheming against Lucifer. From time to time, the Prince had wanted to rid himself of a lover who strayed or someone who declined an invitation to share his bed. Kheone was the first angel on Shax's hit list.

Now that he knew about Michael, it made a sick sort of sense. Michael may have thought all would be forgiven by freeing his brother, but the Prince of Darkness did not let go of grudges, petty to the bone. Kheone was Michael's most trusted lieutenant, and perhaps Lucifer had some inkling of the other emotions lurking below their outward relationship. He had wanted Kheone dead to teach Michael a lesson.

Shax slipped the dagger under his belt and rushed upstairs. Kheone was almost exactly as he had left her. The only change was in her breathing, now even and relaxed as her chest rose and fell in restful sleep, and her color returned. So hard to tell in this eternal twilight. He tucked the blanket over her and stood against a wall, keeping watch. His job right now was to make sure she stayed safe while she recovered. They would figure out what to do once she felt better. Together.

That last thought filled him with a joy that seemed misplaced given their circumstances. An injured angel and a demon with only one superpower stuck in Purgatory, on the run from the two of the most powerful beings on Earth. Their chances of making it more than a few days were slim to none. But they were together. If Shax had learned anything, it was he and Kheone working together might pull a miracle out of their asses.

Shax was not sleepy, adrenaline still coursing through his system. After almost dying today, he didn't want to close his eyes and waste what precious little life was left to him. He sat down on the floor, leaning against the bench, and took stock of the situation. The mental gymnastics necessary to make sense of this place already lodged the nugget of a headache deep in his skull.

Something was missing, though. The thought scratched at him, then smacked him. The buzzing sensation he'd fought for the past year had disappeared. Not just in Kheone's presence, but since he'd realized he loved her. Lucifer's compulsion to kill her, always just a lapse of control away, gone.

Good. With angels and demons on their trail, it was one less thing he needed to worry about. Kheone was in no shape to help at the moment, and there was no telling if what she had done was common or just some massive screw-up due to fear, exhaustion, or even the Goddamn dagger. They needed a plan, and they needed it three hours ago. Instead, they had the clothes on their backs, his dagger, and a barrier between worlds to keep their enemies at bay. It would have to do for now.

Movement from the bench drew his attention. Kheone thrashed in the middle of a dream, dislodging the blanket. He tucked it in around her again. She stirred.

"Shax?" Her voice was heavy with fatigue.

"I'm here." He gently stroked her cheek. The simple gesture reignited the inferno of his hunger for her.

Kheone reached up and covered his hand with hers, stilling his movement.

"I forgot to thank you," she said.

"For what?"

Her silver irises shone, and the corner of her lips twitched up.

"You came back for me. You could have run away, but you saved me. Thank you."

Of course, he had saved her. He loved her. The whole truth would have to wait, but he could tell her *a* truth.

"You showed me kindness when no one else would. You trusted me when no one else would. You are my friend, my *only* friend. And I think there may be something more. I wasn't going to let anything happen to you."

She smiled at him, a sleepy, beatific thing which made his heart beat faster.

"No more secrets, Shax."

"Agreed," he said. "But I have ten thousand years of secrets. It will take time to tell them all, and then there are the secrets I have forgotten, intentionally or otherwise."

"We'll get to them. I'm so tired."

She shook beneath his hand.

"Sleep, Kheone. I'm not going anywhere."

He stroked her hair, but the shivering worsened. As bad as things were for him, he had not trusted the wrong person. Of course, how was she to know the Archangel Michael was the wrong person to trust?

"So c, c, cold."

Shax changed, and a small, black shadow leaped onto the bench and nosed under the blanket. Kheone dug her fingers into his warm, soft fur, and he purred. Her shivers subsided, his presence lulling her to sleep.

She had forgiven him, and she trusted him. A strange feeling filled up his chest. Hope? Maybe, just maybe, they would pull this off. Escape Michael and Aeshma, find a way to bring them down, find a way back to Earth.

Whatever happened next, they could decide when she awoke. For now, his only concern was for Kheone. Love had led him to Hell once upon a time. Maybe this time, it could save them both.

Acknowledgments

If you liked this book, please rate and review wherever you bought it. Even a sentence or two telling others what you liked can help share my work with others.

Thanks to Mirka Andolfo (@mirkand) for sharing a panel from her *Sweet Paprika* comic on Twitter. I wanted Kheone and Shax to bang but couldn't figure it out until I saw her characters yelling at each other while stripping down. It was perfect.

Thanks also to my beta readers: Ciara, Lauren, Christine, and Pam. Their feedback helped make this story better. I'd be remiss in not thanking the wonderful people of Saguaro Romance Writers, who encouraged me to keep going.

For those interested, my playlist for this book featured music by Klergy and drew heavily from the soundtrack of the *Lucifer* TV show.

This book started life as my 2019 NaNoWriMo project. If you have ever thought about writing a novel, join me some November and write one during National Novel Writing Month. I revised and edited it during the COVID-19 Pandemic in 2020 and early 2021. Many thanks to the healthcare workers, delivery drivers, US Postal Service Workers, and the Click List staff at Fry's Food and Drug for keeping us safe and fed.

And, as always, I couldn't do this without the support of my husband and kids. My undying gratitude for their patience when dinner is late, listening to me problem solve, and just being wonderful humans. Ushering a book baby out into the world is only slightly less nerve-racking than doing so for an adult human being. That happened for my first-born this year. I hope they both soar.

Excerpt from Devil's Claw & Moonstone

Rhys Carter snapped out of his deep, dreamless sleep when the kitchen door banged open but relaxed in the next second as he recognized his brother, Owen, grumbling to himself downstairs. The scent of oranges surrounded him, and a smile formed on his lips. For once in his life, he was content. While the sex had been amazing, he was actually looking forward to waking up next to someone he gave a damn about.

Annie, the incredible Gifted witch who had invaded his life two months ago, had somehow managed to get under his skin. What had started out as mere attraction grew to respect as she pulled his ass out of the fire more than once. Her dedication to her mission and her courage only added to her allure, and when he finally discovered that her feelings mirrored his own, Rhys counted himself one lucky son of a bitch. But now she was going to leave him for a chance to complete her mission: destroying the demon who had killed her mother and her husband. She'd been up front about it before their encounter, her tenacity making any other choice impossible. He wished it wasn't so.

The clock on his nightstand read noon. Rhys turned over to caress Annie's soft skin and bury his face in her red-gold hair, ready to tease her about being discovered. His hand met cool sheets instead. Frantic, he rose from the bed and pulled on his worn-out jeans. He barreled down the stairs, hoping he could still catch her before she left. He wanted, needed, one last goodbye.

"Did you see Annie?" he nearly shouted at his brother.

"No, and her truck's gone," Owen replied. "Why? What's happened?"

Annie had left while he slept. All Rhys wanted was to rewind the clock, just a little bit, so he could ask her to stay. Before the betrayal could sink in, Rhys ran back up the stairs. He grabbed the first shirt he could find, pulling the ratty t-shirt over his head. It clung to his muscular chest like a second skin, the only reason he kept the damn thing. His boots were next, standard Doc Martens, good for ass-kicking, monster-hunting, and motorcycle-riding. He threw his wallet into his small go-bag, a backpack containing a change of underwear, socks, and a toothbrush. After thundering down the stairs, he snatched his motorcycle jacket from the coat rack by the front door before racing out of the kitchen door, straight for the garage. He sent Annie a text.

"Where r u?"

Owen followed him. "Wait, what's happened, man? Where's Annie?"

"She's gone, Owen," Rhys answered over his shoulder. "She got a call, and she had to go. Some witchy thing."

"Shit, Rhys, I'm sorry. She thought this would take at least a few days."

"You *knew*?" He stopped in the middle of opening the door to the garage and looked up at his brother. Rhys was tall, just over six feet, but Owen had a few inches on him. He clenched his empty hand at his side. "You knew, and you didn't tell me?"

Owen paled. "She wanted to tell you herself," he said, quietly. "Dude, it was less than a day!"

The hurt in Owen's amber-flecked brown eyes quelled his anger. It wasn't his brother's fault. She'd said things had happened fast, but it didn't matter. What did matter was catching up to her and telling her to stay. In a place in his mind he would never admit to, he had thought that maybe, just maybe, what they'd shared would change her mind. *Stubborn witch!* He was left with tracking her down and telling her how he actually felt. Which meant he had no more than two hours to figure that shit out.

"Doesn't matter. I gotta find her," he said.

"Did she say where she was going?" Owen asked.

"Near Dallas."

"How long has she been gone?"

"I dunno, maybe an hour."

A tiny spark of hope burned in the deep recesses of his mind. Tyler was a two-hour drive from Dallas, but on his motorcycle, he could cut off at least twenty minutes. He might be able to catch her.

But she left you. The cold, rational part of his mind, the part that always needed to be in control, tried to douse the spark with bitter reality. *And what, you're going to drive around Dallas looking for one truck?*

"Are you really going to drive around Dallas looking for her, Rhys?" His brother echoed his own thoughts.

"Yeah, I am. You gonna try to stop me?"

"No, man. But you gotta know it's nearly impossible, right? There's over six million people in the Dallas area."

"Never tell me the odds," Rhys said with a smile as he donned his helmet over his dark-brown, unruly hair and started up the Kawasaki he'd bought two years ago as a treat for his birthday. "She left a note for you in her room."

He steered around the more robust Harley that belonged to Owen and opened the throttle down the driveway. Rhys looked back once at the turn in the drive that would put the house out of sight. Owen stood next to the garage, his hand raised in farewell.

As he sped toward Dallas, Rhys maneuvered on auto-pilot. He lost himself in his thoughts of Annie. Annie running through the woods, looking like a victim on their first meeting. Now that he knew her, victim would be the last word he would use to describe her. Strong, funny, and sexy suited her much better. He would miss the feel of her on the sparring mat. Or watching her sneak up on his brother during their training and laughing when she pelted him with a barrage of paint balls. And he would miss the quiet moments. The intense set of her face as she made her way through a book on magic, how peaceful she looked when she fell asleep on the couch, the animation in her face and sparkle in her gray eyes when she talked with her family. Despite himself, his thoughts drifted to Annie in the last minutes they had spent together. She was glorious naked, better than his imagination, calling his name and moaning in pleasure. He forced his attention back to the road.

He still couldn't find the words for how he felt about her. If he found her — *when* he found her — he was going to tell her what, exactly? *Don't go. I really liked fucking you?* What could he say that would change her mind? And if he said it, did he mean it?

Just over an hour later, and no closer to an answer, he drove through downtown Dallas. He pulled off the interstate and cruised the main streets, stopping occasionally to text her. After an hour of this, he pulled over for gas and to rethink his situation. He had known this would be difficult but had given in to the hope of a miracle. While fueling up, he reviewed their last real conversation. *What exactly had Annie said?* The other side of Dallas.

Fuck. He needed to be looking in Fort Worth.

Rhys got back on his motorcycle and rocketed the thirty-plus miles between the two cities. Looking for her truck in the glut of trucks in a large Texas city really was looking for a needle in a needle stack. Nevertheless, he continued to patrol up and down the streets of Fort Worth.

ANNIKA TURNER DROVE her truck around the block again, glancing at the antiques store that she was circling like a restless shark. The sun was bright in the mid-afternoon sky, and a wet haze rose from the Texas soil. Her route took her past the Fort Worth Stockyards, and her trusty GPS kept declaring that she had reached her destination. She knew more than that damned app. This was the beginning of her journey, not the end. All she had to do was park her truck and walk into that store. She'd been trying to persuade herself to do just that for the last half-hour.

Annie knew there were days that changed your life in ways you could never predict. The day she'd introduced her step-mom to her dad was one. The day she'd married Finn Price was another. So was the day he'd died protecting her from the demon she now hunted. The thought still struck sharp grief through her heart. The day she stopped Rhys Carter from shooting his brother had changed her life in ways she was just now figuring out.

And this one.

This day would change her life. She felt it in her bones and knew it in her heart. But she wasn't quite ready.

Three hours ago, she had walked out on a warm bed and a sleeping, sexy man, whose green eyes seared her soul. She'd spent the drive assuring herself that this was her only good move. She had a shitload of bad options to choose from, and she chose the one with the most risk and the most reward. She hoped, prayed, that it was the right one.

At long last, Annie forced herself to park her truck. As she exited and locked the vehicle, she absently looked at her phone to check her text messages one last time but turned it off instead before she could read any of them. It didn't matter.

She dragged herself to the shop and, taking a deep breath, reached for the door handle only to hesitate at the last second. Doorways signaled event boundaries, causing people to forget why they went into a different room. If she went through this door, she'd leave behind any hope of a normal life. She would be committing to this path.

Annie looked over her shoulder. It took a minute for her to realize what she was looking for — *who* she was looking for. Some part of her hoped Rhys would turn the corner, asking her not to go. She had to do this. To keep him safe, to keep everyone safe, she had to go through this doorway. With a shake of her head to dispel her thoughts, she pushed open the door.

An electronic bell chimed deep in the deserted store. Annie headed toward the sales counter at the back. Being so close to the Stockyards, cowboy and western memorabilia featured prominently, but there were touches of typical antiques store finds. In one corner was a lovely secretary desk, and in another, a well-worn, Mexican style dining table and chairs. Dust motes in the air caught the afternoon sun, lending an air of mystery to the entire store. The wall behind the cash register was lined with cubbies containing labeled apothecary jars that gleamed. They were full of various herbs that Annie knew well. She was definitely in the right place.

"I'm coming, I'm coming," called a gruff male voice from the back.

"I'm patient," Annie responded, wanting to put off this meeting as long as possible.

"Well, I'm not," said the voice as its owner turned the corner. Tall and rangy, he was at least sixty years old. His hair was white, his skin brown, and glasses were perched neatly on his nose. "You're lucky, miss. I was just about to close up. What can I do for you?"

"I'm, uh, supposed to wait for someone here?" She'd only received the address on her phone, not the name of the store, nor how she was supposed to get to the Homestead.

"Ah, you must be Annika Bauer," the man said with a knowing wink. "Let me lock the door, and we'll get you where you need to be."

"It's Turner," Annie corrected him automatically.

"What is?" the man replied as he turned off the neon "Open" sign and threw the bolt in the door.

"My last name. It's Turner."

"Good luck with that, young lady. The Assembly is slow to change and loves its traditions. Calling a daughter of a Founding Family anything other than her mama's name isn't gonna happen. Oh, where are my manners? I'm Sam Gordon, your transit specialist."

He stuck out his hand and Annie took it, giving it a firm shake.

"It's nice to meet you, Mr. Gordon. Are we waiting for anyone else?"

"Call me Sam. Only the Assembly is formal enough for titles. The rest of the Community is more relaxed. That your truck parked out front?" At her nod, he held out his hand. "I'll take the keys and your cell phone. Is the registration in the glove box?"

"Yes, sir," Annie replied, reluctantly handing over her keys and her lifeline to the common world.

Sam seemed to sense her hesitation as he tucked her possessions away.

"Annika, I'll take good care of your truck. I've got a place just outside of town, and it'll live in the garage. I'll take it out once a week and make sure everything runs. If anything breaks, I'll contact you at the Homestead, and we'll figure it out. Your phone isn't gonna work there, anyway. Witchy technology jamming. I'll keep it in my safe here at the store."

Annie sighed in resignation but nodded anyway. "Thank you, Sam."

"You ready, missy?" he asked, gesturing with his arms to the back of the store.

"No, but I don't really have a choice, do I?" she said as she stepped that way.

"There are always choices, Annika. I don't know your entire story, but everyone is talking about the lost child of the Bauer Family who didn't even know she was a witch."

"The Oblivious Witch," Annie muttered, but Sam heard her.

"I like that," Sam chuckled. "Not many get to nickname themselves, Annika, but if you're not careful, that just might stick. No one will stop you from leaving right now. I'm guessin', though, that you're here for a reason. I think the Homestead can help you with whatever that reason is. Give it a chance and you may end up with choices you like better."

Annie considered his words for a minute and nodded, recognizing the wisdom in them. They reached an open door, leading into a messy office. The only surface that wasn't covered with books, knick-knacks, and other assorted relics was the floor. That was consumed by a painted white circle about four feet across, quartered by straight white lines in the middle that jutted outside of the circle's perimeter. Arches inside the circle joined the points where the lines crossed, forming a diamond-like shape in the middle. Indigo candles were placed at the four points, still unlit. Annie had never seen anything like it. Her confusion must have shown in her face.

"I'm a Carrier," Sam said. At her blank look he continued. "I create Gateways, holes in space and time that join two places, temporarily. There are several of us in the US and many more throughout the world. We help witches get from point A to point B a bit quicker and without all the immigration fuss that the Commoners have to put up with."

"Yeah, now I remember. I've been so focused on my own Gift, I've forgotten most of what Dora told me," Annie said. "Now I'm afraid my brain won't be able to keep up."

"You'll be just fine. Are you ready yet, Annika Bauer?"

"Yes, Sam, I believe I am," she responded.

"Good. I knew your mama, once upon a time. She was a few classes behind me, but Ruth Bauer was pretty, kind, and powerful. I'm glad she had some happiness in her life. Good luck to you."

Sam indicated that Annie should step inside the circle. Once she did, he approached her with a small crock of ointment. He applied a dab on her forehead and each hand before he moved to a position at the north cardinal point of the circle.

"It's a mixture of devil's claw root and juniper berries," he explained while lighting the candle at his feet. He proceeded to light the others, going clockwise around the circle.

Those were both plants used in protection charms. Annie thought it ironic that a plant named after the devil would actually offer protection. The scent of cut cucumber filled the air, fresh and clean, and Annie took deep breaths of the relaxing scent of comfrey, for safe travels. Sam returned to the north point of the circle, faced her, and held up his hands, palms pointed at Annie.

"*Apertio*," he chanted.

A blue mist began rising from the candles and swirled gently around her ankles. Pressure built inside her head, then vanished an instant later. She looked up to ask Sam what had happened, but he wasn't there.

Instead of a messy office, Annie now stood in a small, stark room. The walls were white, the floor pine. The same circle was painted on the ground, the same candles lit, the same fragrance in the air. Where Sam had stood was another man. He was shorter than Sam, his longish hair white, with a close-cropped white beard and a lined face. If she had to describe him to someone else, she'd go with "athletic Santa Claus". She moved to leave the circle.

"Wait," the man ordered brusquely, holding up his hand. "I've got her, Sam."

The mist vanished, and the candles extinguished themselves.

"Annika Bauer, welcome to the Homestead," he pronounced and gestured for her to leave the circle.

Annie tried to take a step, but dizziness overwhelmed her, and she fell to her knees.

"Oh, for crap's sake," he bellowed. "Robin, get in here."

The door opened, and a middle-aged woman with gray-streaked auburn hair stepped into the room. She took one look at Annie and rushed to her.

"What happened?" she asked.

"I'm dizzy," Annie explained, not allowing the Santa look-alike to answer for her.

"Dad, you know that usually happens the first time," Robin scolded. "Deep breaths. In through the nose, out through the mouth."

"I *know*," Annie snapped. She continued to breathe until the dizziness lessened. Rising, she stepped out of the circle and into her new life.

Also by Emily Michel

A Memory of Wings
A Memory of Wings

Magic & Monsters
Witch Hazel & Wolfsbane
Devil's Claw & Moonstone
Brimstone & Silver

Watch for more at https://www.emilymichelauthor.com.

About the Author

Emily Michel spent most of her life as a military family member. She has called many places home, including Germany, Belgium, and Kansas. After nearly twenty years traipsing around Europe and the US, she settled back in her home state of Arizona a few years ago with her husband and kids.

When not writing, Emily reads, walks, hikes, and pets her feline overlords. She also volunteers for the PTA, but do not accuse her of being a PTA Mom. She's cooler than that. Maybe.

In 2019, she self-published her Magic & Monsters trilogy, a steamy witchy romance, making *A Memory of Wings* her fourth published book. Please buy them. Her two teenage boys eat a lot of food.

Read more at https://www.emilymichelauthor.com.

Made in the USA
Monee, IL
08 September 2021